standalone novels with devilish twists on genre conventions… A fizzy whodunit with pace, panache, and surprises galore."

—*Kirkus Reviews*

"Gentill's latest slowly unravels as a traditional mystery but then evolves into a self-aware, Grisham-esque thriller. Readers will root for Theo, then for Gus, to find the answers they need to find closure. With likable side characters (including a dog named Horse) and a truly unexpected third act, *The Mystery Writer* is sure to please literary crime fans."

—*Booklist*

"Impossible to put down… A good mystery has multiple twists and turns, leading the reader through a maze of clues and red herrings and foreshadowing until the truth is uncovered. To say that Sulari Gentill follows this path would be an understatement of huge proportions. Just when the reader thinks they know who the real murderer is, Gentill throws in a sharp turn, and we start all over again. And don't be surprised if January 6, 2021, doesn't make a brief appearance! Gentill fans will find this read beyond entertaining and will anxiously await her next story."

—*New York Journal of Books*

"A mischievous twist on mystery novels and the people who write them."

—Benjamin Stevenson, author
of *Everyone in My Family Has Killed
Someone* and *Trust Me When I Lie*

"Some mysteries need a crime writer to solve. Clever, twisty, and surprisingly unexpected."

—Michael Robotham, two-time winner
of the CWA Gold Dagger Award

The Woman in the Library

"A sharply drawn fictional hall of mirrors sure to tantalize."

—*Kirkus Reviews*

"A page-turner from beginning to end. A riddle, wrapped in a mystery, inside an enigma. As Gentill's characters grow, the desire to know more about each ensnares us, and the only way out is to read to the end."

—*New York Journal of Books*

"A wonderfully nimble play on the relationships between writer and reader, and writer and muse...tackling complex literary issues with both wit and panache."

—*Criminal Element*

★"A smart, engaging novel that blurs genre lines. It's an inventive and unique approach, elevated by Gentill's masterful plotting, that will delight suspense fans looking for something bold and new."

—*BookPage*, Starred Review

"Investigations are launched, fingers are pointed, potentially dangerous liaisons unfold, and I was turning those pages like there was cake at the finish line."

—*Seattle Times*, Must-Read
Books for Summer 2022

★"A complex, riveting story within a story. An innovative literary mystery."

—*Library Journal*, Starred Review

After She Wrote Him

(A standalone previously published as *Crossing the Lines*)
2018 Winner of the Ned Kelly Award, Best Crime Fiction

"A pure delight, a swift yet psychologically complex read, cleverly conceived and brilliantly executed."

—Dean Koontz, *New York Times* bestselling author

"A tour de force! A brilliant blend of mystery, gut-wrenching psychological suspense, and literary storytelling. The novel stands as a shining (and refreshing) example of metafiction at its best—witty and wry, stylish, and a joy to read."

—Jeffery Deaver, *New York Times* bestselling author

"A delightful, cerebral novel featuring a crime writer who grows dangerously enamored with her main character. As the interplay between creator and created reaches Russian-nesting-doll complexity, it forces us to question the nature of fiction itself."

—Gregg Hurwitz, *New York Times* bestselling author

"This is an elegant exploration of the creative process, as well as a strong defense of the crime-fiction genre, as Gentill illustrates the crossing of lines between imagination and reality."

—*Booklist*

"In this intriguing and unusual tale, a stunning departure from Gentill's period mysteries, the question is not whodunit but who's real and who's a figment of someone's vivid imagination."

—*Kirkus Reviews*

"Fans of postmodern fiction will enjoy this departure from Gentill's 1930s series. It's an exploration, as one character puts it, of 'an author's relationship with her protagonist, an examination of the tenuous line between belief and reality, imagination and self, and what happens when that line is crossed.'"

—*Publishers Weekly*

"Literary or pop fiction lovers will enjoy."

—*Library Journal*

Where There's a Will
The Tenth Rowland Sinclair WWII Mystery

"Rowland's leisurely tenth case colorfully recreates the flavor of serial mysteries of Hollywood's golden age."

—*Kirkus Reviews*

★"Witty, rip-roaring. This is historical mystery fiction at its finest."
—*Publishers Weekly*,
Starred Review

Shanghai Secrets
The Ninth Rowland Sinclair WWII Mystery

"A frothy retro cocktail with a whodunit chaser."

—*Kirkus Reviews*

"Eccentric but authentic characters bolster a cracking good plot. Gentill captures in telling detail a political, moral, and cultural milieu."

—*Publishers Weekly*

A Dangerous Language
The Eighth Rowland Sinclair WWII Mystery

"A thrilling eighth mystery."

—Publishers Weekly

"Fans of historical fiction and murder mysteries will consider her treasure trove of novels to be a rich discovery."

—Bookreporter

Give the Devil His Due
The Seventh Rowland Sinclair WWII Mystery

"This is a great addition to a fun Australian mystery series...a fast-paced and captivating novel set during a turbulent period in Australia's history. Containing an intriguing mystery, a unique sense of humour, and a range of historical characters, this is a highly recommended read for lovers of Australian fiction."

—Sydney Morning Herald

"Devil of a good read."

—Herald Sun

"This 1930s Sydney is vibrant and authentic, and the inclusion of a relevant newspaper cutting at the beginning of each chapter is a neat touch... In order to get the best value out of this highly original series with its quirky characters...seek out the earlier titles and follow them in sequence."

—Historical Novel Society

A Murder Unmentioned

The Sixth Rowland Sinclair WWII Mystery
Short-listed for the Davitt Award for Best Adult Novel 2015
Short-listed for the Ned Kelly Award for Best Crime Novel 2015

"Each chapter begins with a brief excerpt from an Australian publication, such as the *Camperdown Chronicle*, that offers insights into the popular culture of the times. Fans of historical mysteries will find a lot to savor."

—*Publishers Weekly*

"A charmingly complex hero whose adventures continue to highlight many worldly problems between the great wars."

—*Kirkus Reviews*

"This sixth entry in the Rowland Sinclair series, which blends historical figures seamlessly with fictional ones, clarifies and advances the family dynamics of its appealing protagonist, which should delight fans and win new readers."

—*Booklist*

"Investigating the past has never been more fun."

—*Sydney Morning Herald*

Gentlemen Formerly Dressed

The Fifth Rowland Sinclair WWII Mystery

"This book has it all: intrigue among the British aristocracy, the Nazi threat, and a dashing Australian hero. I didn't want it to end!"

—Rhys Bowen, *New York Times* bestselling author

"Rowland's determined attempts to open British eyes to the gathering storm combine mystery, rousing adventure, and chance meetings with eminent figures from Churchill to Evelyn Waugh."

—Kirkus Reviews

"The pleasure of this novel lies…in observing Rowland at dinner with Evelyn Waugh, trading insights with H. G. Wells, and setting Winston Churchill straight on the evils of nationalism. Fans of upper-class sleuths will be in their element."

—Publishers Weekly

"Fascinating history, entertaining characters, and a hint of romance make *Gentlemen Formerly Dressed* irresistible."

—Shelf Awareness

Paving the New Road

The Fourth Rowland Sinclair WWII Mystery

Short-listed for the Davitt Award for Best Adult Crime Fiction 2013

"The combination of famous historical figures, detailed descriptions of a troubling time, and plenty of action makes for a tale as rousing as it is relevant."

—Kirkus Reviews

"This installment takes the aristocratic Sinclair into a much darker place than did the previous three entries in the series but does so without losing the stylish prose and the easy way with character that have given the novels their appeal."

—Booklist

"Stylish, well-paced murder mystery…cheeky plotline… This tale is told with such flair and feeling for those extraordinary times… Verdict: thrilling."

—Herald Sun

Miles Off Course
The Third Rowland Sinclair WWII Mystery

"Gentill's third reads like a superior Western, alternating high adventure with social and political observations about prewar Australia."

—*Kirkus Reviews*

"Set in Australia in 1933, Gentill's entertaining third mystery featuring portrait artist Rowland Sinclair will appeal to fans of Greenwood's Phryne Fisher… Gentill matches Greenwood's skill at blending suspense with a light touch."

—*Publishers Weekly*

"Rowland is an especially interesting character: at first he comes off as a bit of a layabout, a guy who feels he's entitled to a cushy life by virtue of his aristocratic roots, but, as the story moves along, we realize he has a strong moral center and a compulsion to finish a job once he's started it. A great addition to a strong series."

—*Booklist*

A Decline in Prophets
The Second Rowland Sinclair WWII Mystery
Winner of the Davitt Award for Best Adult Crime Fiction for 2012

"I thoroughly enjoyed the glamour of the ocean voyage, the warmth and wit among the friends, and yet all the time, simmering beneath the surface, was the real and savage violence, waiting to erupt. The 1930s are a marvelous period. We know what lies ahead! This is beautifully drawn, with all its fragile hope and looming tragedy. I am delighted this is a series. I want them all."

—Anne Perry, *New York Times* bestselling author

"Set in late 1932, Gentill's lively second mystery featuring dashing Australian millionaire Rowland 'Rowly' Sinclair takes place initially aboard the luxury cruise ship *Aquitania*, as it steams along toward Sydney… The witty and insightful glimpses of the Australian bourgeoisie of this period keep this mystery afloat."

—*Publishers Weekly*

"A delightful period piece."

—*Kirkus Reviews*

"Rowland Sinclair is a gentleman artist who comes from a privileged background but whose sympathies are with bohemians, lefties, and ratbags. It's a rich political and cultural era to explore, and Gentill has a lot of fun with a hero who is always getting paint on his immaculate tailoring."

—*Sydney Morning Herald*

A House Divided (formerly *A Few Right Thinking Men*)
The First Rowland Sinclair WWII Mystery
Short-listed for Best First Book, Commonwealth Writers' Prize 2011

★"As series-launching novels go, this one is especially successful: the plot effectively plays Sinclair's aristocratic bearing and involvement in the arts against the Depression setting, fraught with radical politics, both of which he becomes involves in as he turns sleuth. And Sinclair himself is a delight: winning us over completely and making us feel as though he's an old friend."

—*Booklist*, Starred Review

★"While the vintage Down Under settings might make this debut… comparable to Kerry Fisher's Melbourne-based Phryne Fisher 1920s mysteries, Gentill works in historical events that add verisimilitude to her story. VERDICT: Thanks to Poisoned Pen Press for bringing another award-winning Australian crime writer to U.S. shores. Her witty hero will delight traditional mystery buffs."

—*Library Journal*, Starred Review

FIVE
FOUND
DEAD

FIVE
FOUND
DEAD

SULARI GENTILL

Poisoned Pen
PRESS

For Jacob,
whose journey was not as long as any of us would have liked.
You are remembered, my friend.

Published by Poisoned Pen Press, an imprint of Sourcebooks
P.O. Box 4410, Naperville, Illinois 60567-4410
(630) 961-3900
sourcebooks.com

Cataloging-in-Publication Data is on file with the Library of Congress.

Printed and bound in Canada.
MBP 10 9 8 7 6 5 4 3 2 1

Chapter 1

I t is nine p.m. at Gare de l'Est. The evening is that sharp kind of cold that makes you gasp and then immediately regret the intake as frigid air cuts into your chest. The travelers waiting on the platform wear long coats over evening gowns and dinner suits. Larger bags are carried away by young men who are unremarkable on the streets of the city. Smaller cases, valises, are taken from their owners by white-gloved stewards wearing the conspicuous blue-and-gold uniform of the Orient Express, unchanged in style for a century.

Most people remove their face masks so they can take photographs of themselves with the midnight-blue carriages in the background. The face mask recommendation has been in force only for a couple of days in response to a spike in infections of the latest COVID variant, but, of course, it does not apply inside the train…or for a quick photo.

An official party greets excited passengers as they are checked in at the polished wood lectern set up for the purpose and shown to the length of red carpet that leads to the appropriate coach door. They pose for more photos in front of the train, bright-eyed and smiling. Most are in couples or larger groups, but there is one man who appears alone. He walks with a stick, though he seems too young and unstooped to have been crippled by any of the usual complaints of old age. His hair is dark and parted precisely on the left. In quiet French, he thanks the steward who finds his name on the passenger list and takes his luggage.

Behind him, a man and a woman. The man is publishing's latest blue-eyed boy, a literary sensation. Joe Penvale's first book was a runaway hit and has transformed him from an obscure Australian with a story about murder on a sheep station to an international hot property. It is the kind of phenomenal success that normally invites resentment, but Penvale has a gift for easy-going boyish banter that endears him to readers and publishers alike. Though he is wearing a dinner suit, there is still a country ruggedness and ease about Joe that high-end tailoring cannot eradicate or even disguise.

The woman is me, Meredith, his twin sister, first editor, partner in crime, the wall against whom he bounces his ideas. I'm his cheer squad, his reality check—I tell him that he can do it and that he should get over himself. Not always in that order.

Joe has been telling me stories for years… It was a game, occasionally a bribe, or a cheap birthday present when he was skint, which, for the years he was working on farms and orchards, was often. I was the first person he told when his manuscript was picked up by an agent, and then by a publisher. It became crazy after that—publicists, film agents, journalists, awards. And polite inquiries about how the second book was going. I was happy for him, proud of him, perhaps a tiny bit jealous. I am still happy and proud.

However, it seems there is a cruel balancing in all things, and the hand of fate pressed hard on the other side of the scale. Joe was diagnosed about eighteen months ago. The initial shock was followed by a roundabout of tests, of surgery and chemo and radiation. My mad, funny, strong brother became so thin, lost his dark hair and, for a while, his sense of humor. All sorts of numbers and readings crushed hope time and again. And Joe stopped writing, and that, more than anything, frightened me.

So, the Orient Express had been my idea, initially something for him to look forward to during the months of treatment. Now a celebration of survival and the fact that his hair had grown back! And a way of shaking loose his muse by walking into the world's most famous mystery. And so here we are. A little battered, but standing, and taking in every sight and sound and smell for preservation in memory.

"Is it your first time on the Orient Express?" One of the blue-uniformed stewards beams at us. Of course, the inquiry is perfunctory. He knows.

"It is," I reply.

"Ah, lucky you." He takes charge of our carry-on luggage as he speaks. His accent is European, but my ear is not trained enough to discern more specifically than that. "There is nothing like your first time. So many of our guests tell me, I wish I could have my first time again. I wish I could board with no idea and be so surprised and delighted again." He gathers the overnight cases we've put down on the platform beside us. "*Bonsoir, madame*. My name is Maxim—I will be your steward."

"*Bonsoir*, Maxim. I am Meredith Penvale." I extend my hand and then let it drop as I realize that the gesture is physically problematic. "I'd shake your hand, but your hands are full!" I say instead. "This is my brother, Joe."

"Let me help you with that, mate." Joe tries to relieve Maxim of at least one bag, but the steward will have none of it.

"No, please, take your photographs. I will carry the bags to your cabin. It is no trouble."

"Come on, Joe." I lean into him and angle my phone to capture the carriage and Maxim in the background. The steward grins obligingly and the image is made.

Joe laughs. "The Penvales on the Orient Express—clearly standards are slipping."

I slide my phone into the pocket of my overcoat and wave at the two young men stepping onto the red carpet for the carriage two down from ours. Felix Shannon and Benjamin Herder, otherwise known as Flex and Herds. The gentlemen, well, they're barely more than teenagers really—are podcasters, though Joe has been known to introduce them as his stalkers. When Joe's book was first released, they interviewed him on their mystery podcast—*Death of the Reader*, which at the time was recorded at a university studio. Joe was relatively unknown then and happy to talk about his work to anybody who was interested. Felix and Ben were students with a passion for the mystery genre and a podcast too obscure to attract more established authors. As Joe's book surged, that interview became something of a coup. Their star as podcasters rose with his as a writer.

Joe told them about our tickets for the Orient Express and, when they expressed enthusiasm for the idea, added, "You should come too." Which is very Joe. He's invited at least two dozen people to join us. Flex and Herds accepted, seeing it as an opportunity to record a show from the mystery world's most famous train. In fact, I believe *Death of the Reader* received an Australian Arts grant to do so.

I grab Joe's sleeve as he begins to charge up the steps, telling him quietly to wait until the gentleman with the walking stick has climbed the stairs before following. The Frenchman turns, and I am embarrassed that he's overheard. But he nods and smiles warmly.

"*Bonsoir, monsieur*," I return, eager to use my few words of French, hastily learned. And then more haltingly, "*C'est excitant, pas vrai?*"

His smile broadens. I am not sure if my awkward French has amused him or if it is simply a gesture of kindness. "*Oui, madame*. It is very exciting."

Joe extends his hand. "Joe Penvale—pleased to meet you. This is my sister, Meredith."

"*Bonsoir, bonsoir*," he says, shaking Joe's hand and then, more gently, mine. "Napoleon Duplantier, at your service."

I notice the slight flare of Joe's nostrils. The name entertains him. Napoleon is not a name we have heard since high school history, but it is probably not so unusual for a Frenchman.

Napoleon chuckles, slips one hand into the front of his coat, and assumes a Bonaparte-esque pose. "You have heard of me, no?"

Joe laughs. "Are you traveling alone, mate? Or is Josephine somewhere about the place?"

"No, no, *monsieur*." Napoleon sighs, though he does not seem unhappy. "I make the journey alone."

Maxim escorts us all into the carriage—the doors to the individual cabins are to our left, windows to our right all set in panels of polished wood, detailed with veneers of contrasting colors and grain. Joe glances at me.

"What do you think, Meri?" he asks.

"I can't believe we're really here." I breathe in deeply as if I can somehow inhale this feeling and hold it within me. "I keep expecting Hercule Poirot to peer out from behind one of these doors."

Joe puts an arm around my shoulders. "Maybe he will, Meri. Maybe he will."

Maxim opens the door to 16F. "Your cabin, *madame, monsieur.*"

We walk into the day sitter, delighting in every detail. I feel a ridiculous impulse to applaud, but thankfully I am able to resist. There's no point giving Joe more ammunition with which to mock me than he already gathers in our day-to-day interactions. A plush upholstered seat takes up one wall. On the opposite wall are curved doors that open to reveal a washbasin, complete with complimentary toiletries. The Art Nouveau veneer in the cabin is a pattern of flowers and swagging at picture-rail height. On the table under the window, a lamp, a platter of hors d'oeuvres, and a silver bucket containing a bottle of champagne chilling in ice.

Maxim lifts our overnight bags onto the chrome luggage racks. He takes charge of our passports, as we will be crossing the border into Italy in the night, assuring us that they will be returned at the end of our journey. "I will be back while you are at dinner to convert your cabin for sleeping," he says. "Would you prefer to be seated by yourselves or with other guests in the dining car?"

"Definitely with other guests," Joe replies. "What's more, if there's a Belgian detective about, my sister will be particularly pleased to share his table."

"It is not an unusual request, *monsieur*," Maxim says, shrugging. "Sadly, in the current economic times, there is a shortage of Belgian detectives. We can only provide them to the Grand Suites…" He grins. "Now, if you will excuse me, I shall check that Monsieur Duplantier is settled in."

As he leaves, another steward comes in to open the bottle and pour the champagne. Joe declines the flute she offers him. "I'm sorry—I can't."

"It's dealcoholized, *monsieur*," she says.

"Oh." Joe is surprised. "In that case…"

She leaves us to it.

"Did you tell them?" Joe asks me. He's a little prickly about people knowing about his illness, even now.

"I told them you were a recovering alcoholic," I reply, drinking. I look at my glass. "This isn't bad."

We take off our coats and hang them on the hooks by the door before thoroughly exploring the cabin while sampling hors d'oeuvres. We exclaim at the compact perfection of the room, the attention to detail, the bits we recognize from the various cinematic versions of *Murder on the Orient Express*, and we speculate as to how it might be transformed into a sleeping chamber. Joe takes his laptop out of his bag while I touch up my makeup.

"Are you going to write?" I ask, trying hard to keep the excitement out of my voice. I don't want him to hear it as expectation. It isn't. Just hope.

"Not right now…but maybe later." He runs his hand

wistfully over the aluminum casing. "I've been playing with an idea."

"Tell me."

He shakes his head. "Tomorrow. Let's not spook the muse by getting overexcited."

"Look at where we are, Joe." I twirl. "How could we not be excited? This is the coolest thing we've ever done. It's inspirational."

Joe places his laptop on the table beside the champagne bucket. He looks at me, smiling. "Stop worrying, Meri. I am happy, and inspired, and think this is beyond cool. But I'm starving. We should go find this dining car."

Half past ten is an odd time to sit down to dinner, but the late seating is designed for guests who board in Paris. Joe and I have resisted snacking through the early evening, determined to be hungry enough to enjoy a five-course formal dinner in the celebrated dining car.

"We should call Mum while we're still at the station." I pull up the video chat app we usually use to keep in touch with our parents. "Coverage will probably be patchy once we get going."

"We have stationery and postcards." Joe points out the Orient Express–emblazoned compendium.

"That'll take ages to get home, and we rang Dad this morning."

Joe's face clouds. The conversation with our father had consisted of a lecture on Dad's latest stock investments—a topic as dull as it sounds—and complaints about our mother, whom he has not actually seen in fifteen years. Dad and I had ended up arguing about something that had happened too long ago for either of us to remember it accurately, until Joe had made static noises and conveniently cut the connection.

Dad and Joe had never been particularly close, and Joe's illness had only driven them further apart. Dad has rarely spoken of the cancer, expressing his concern only through the purchase of pharmaceutical stocks—most of which crashed at some point or another.

Regardless, I hold up the phone so the two of us and the cabin will be in frame. "Just a quick call…to be fair…and to tell her what we're doing. She'll be worried."

Mum picks up on the third ring and her face fills the screen. "Hi, Mum, we're—"

"Darling, I'm sick," she says. "I was not feeling well these past few days, but somehow, I managed…and then I thought I really must see a doctor because there's so much going around, don't you know. And, of course, he was appalled that I wasn't in hospital… I need around-the-clock care, he said. He thinks I may have colic, or maybe diabetes. I don't know, darling… I suspect I'm in the departure lounge… I may not be around when you return. Anyway, I'm very tired. The doctor has asked me to rest." Her face is replaced on the screen with a call termination icon.

Joe starts to laugh. "Well, there's nothing wrong with her lungs at least—she barely drew breath!" He pulls a face. "Good thing we called her from the Orient Express… Mum's clearly been dying to hear all about it."

"Yes, okay," I mutter. I don't know what I was thinking. Mum has always been thus. Even when Joe was most ill. In fact, she became worse when he was, a kind of competitive infirmity.

Joe claims our mother's imagined maladies always cheered him up. Every time the news was bad, he'd distract himself by trying to work out what disease, disorder, or disability Mum would conjure to trump it.

I can't quite laugh about it the way Joe does. At least not as heartily.

He pushes me playfully. "Come on, Meri. Don't let the old girl get under your skin."

I exhale. "I don't know how you do it, Joe. She—both of them make me want to explode sometimes."

"I'm writing them into this next novel…parts of them, anyway. Nobody would believe either of them as a whole. It's hard to resent good material."

I smile, glad I am not an only child.

Chapter 2

We take a couple of selfies in our compartment and step out into the narrow corridor. I can see out the windows that the train is still at the platform. Of course it is. We haven't felt the train move, after all. But I feel so transported within it that I would not have been surprised to find that we were no longer at Gare de l'Est.

A couple of old ladies are walking down the red carpet farther up the train, their heads close in conversation, but the other passengers have boarded now, and the lectern is being dismantled. The station is all but deserted. There's an eerie, expectant beauty to it all.

A bearded gentleman struts briskly toward us and opens the door to 16G. Joe moves to introduce himself to our neighbor, but the man cuts him off with a curt nod and closes the door of his cabin—resoundingly, in fact, and so quickly that Joe is forced to draw his extended hand back to save it from being caught.

Joe looks at me. "What's his problem?"

I shrug, determined not to let a grumpy neighbor spoil even a moment. "Let's just go to dinner."

We make our way through our carriage and then several more, until we come to the first dining car. A gentleman in a navy suit lavishly adorned with gold trim and epaulets introduces himself as Verner Fleischmann, the manager of the train, who has apparently done his research on the passengers.

"You, I believe, are the writer!" he exclaims as he shakes Joe's hand. "Wunderbar! Perhaps we can inspire you."

Joe laughs. "No perhaps about it. I know it's been done, but there are other stories here."

Fleischmann nods enthusiastically. "Wonderful, wonderful! If you have any questions…"

He ushers us smoothly to the second dining car, Étoile du Nord, which features exquisite marquetry, lavish wood paneling, and green tones. As in the one before it, all the tables are positioned against the curtained windows so that each set of diners is afforded a view, or would be afforded a view if it were daylight. On one side of the car, the tables are for four, and on the other, two. Each table is lit by a shaded lamp and set with a full silver service, gleaming in the soft light. We are seated at one of the larger tables on the left side of the car. Joe and I slide in opposite each other, grinning absurdly at everything. I take out my phone as subtly as possible and take photos of the table, the car, the menu.

Joe makes a face. "What are you doing?"

"I'm afraid I won't remember. I want to remember everything."

"I thought I saw a sign that requested passengers not use their phones in the dining car…"

"I'm not using it as a phone. I'm using it as a camera," I reply. "It's fine."

Joe rolls his eyes. "You're such a lawyer…not to mention a tourist."

I ignore him. He'll be glad I took photos when he needs to check some detail for the new manuscript.

Étoile du Nord is beginning to fill up. Our fellow passengers are also dressed formally; a few have gone that extra mile, donning bowlers or headpieces that evoke the 1920s of Poirot. I smile at the two old ladies I saw scurrying on board a few minutes earlier as they are seated behind Joe. They smile and wave as if we are old friends. They, too, are watching everything, no doubt as amazed and delighted as Joe and I are with every detail.

"What?" I ask as Joe's eyes narrow and his gaze becomes fixed on the distance behind me. I begin to turn.

"It's nothing," Joe says. "I thought I saw someone, but I was wrong."

"Who did you think you saw?"

"That actor."

"What actor?"

"Peter Ustinov."

"He's dead."

"Definitely couldn't have been him, then."

Napoleon Duplantier is directed to our table. "I am told you wish to dine with a Belgian detective," he says, handing his walking stick to the steward as he sits down beside me. "I hope that a retired French policeman will suffice. We are not as famous, but much more handsome."

"Well, I suppose we can make do," Joe sighs. He squints at Duplantier. "I knew the French retired young but…"

"Ah… *Merci, monsieur*," the Frenchman replies. "My retirement was a necessity, I am afraid. An injury in the line of duty."

"Oh, I'm so sorry," I exclaim. "Will you never be able to return to policing?" Unless Duplantier is some kind of Dorian Gray, he is surely too young to stop working entirely.

"I am engaged in private practice now," he says. "I will not return to the gendarmerie. And perhaps I will grow the mustaches."

"Are you here on a case, then?" Joe whips his gaze over his shoulder as if we might have missed that there was a body on a table behind us.

Duplantier laughs. "I am here on holiday. The Stamboul train has always held a certain enticement, and so when I leave the gendarmerie, I say to myself, why not?"

Joe raises his glass. "Why not, indeed!"

A plump middle-aged woman wearing a beaded flapper dress and a feathered headpiece over braided hair walks down the carriage toward us, pausing to say "Evening" to every person she passes on the way. She makes up our four. Napoleon and Joe stand until she is seated.

"Good evening," she says brightly, her smile shining from her face. "Don't you all look nice?" She proffers her hand. "Abigay Williams. Very pleased to meet you."

We introduce ourselves to responses of "How nice" and "How do you do." The arrival of Abigay is a signal to the waiters, who are soon pouring wine and taking our orders. My vegetarianism is easily dealt with, and Giovanni, our waiter, is discreet in offering both Joe and me dealcoholized beverages. Abigay is apparently lactose intolerant, and Giovanni is also very accommodating with dairy-free options for the various courses, even as she slathers her bread roll with half an inch of butter.

Flex and Herds stop to say hello as they make their way to their own table, and we introduce them as Felix Shannon and Benjamin Herder—the renowned podcasters—to our dinner companions.

"I wonder which cabin was Poirot's," Flex ruminates as we praise our accommodations.

Joe raises a brow. "You do know that Poirot wasn't real, don't you, mate?"

"Hold your blasphemous tongue, sir!" Herds gasps, clutching at his heart in staged horror. "Monsieur Poirot walks among us!"

"Though we are headed in the wrong direction," Flex notes. "Poirot caught the Orient Express from Istanbul to London. He was racing back to deal with a case." He shakes his head. "We're doing this backward."

"Felix and Ben are experts on all things crime fiction," I explain to Napoleon and Abigay. Then in a loud and pointed whisper, "They sometimes forget the fiction part."

Napoleon laughs. "We French love our *romans policiers*. Surely, here, we can indulge in believing, at least until we reach Venice."

"Aye, that's right, pet," Abigay declares. "Mr. Poirot won't be troubling me. Let him go about his business in the corridors."

Gratified, the podcasters wish us "*bon aperitif*," pronouncing the *f* in a way that makes Napoleon visibly flinch.

They remind Joe that they'd like to record an interview the next day and make their way to their own table. And the first course—a glorious green soup of fresh peas, cucumber radish, and avocado—is placed before us, and our glasses refilled.

I ask Abigay if this is her first trip on the Orient Express.

"Aye, it is that," she replies. "I've always fancied taking a rail holiday, and I have some leave owing."

"And what do you do when you're not catching trains to Istanbul, Ms. Williams?" Joe inquires.

"That's Detective Inspector Williams, Mr. Penvale."

"Really?" I meet Joe's eyes, delighted. Maxim apparently took our request for a Belgian detective seriously enough to scour the passenger list for guests who might serve as worthy substitutes.

"Yes, Mr. Penvale. Twenty-three years with the force." Abigay adjusts her feathered headpiece.

We spend that course exchanging stories of ourselves and the paths that led us to the Orient Express.

Jamaican-born Detective Inspector Abigay Williams is now a Novocastrian. She's lived there long enough to speak with a wonderfully hybridized inflection. "Married to the job," she'd felt she was overdue for a honeymoon and decided that a few days in Paris and a berth on the Orient Express were the least she was owed after twenty-three years of devotion.

Duplantier shakes his head. "My dear Madame Williams, surely there is someone more…more…*séduisant* than 'the job' you might take to Paris…"

Abigay waves him away. "Pfft! I'm too old to have my head

turned now," she says. "The job and I rub along very nicely, thank you, Monsieur Duplantier."

I sit back and leave Joe to speak to what brought us here. I've learned that it's better to let him decide how much of his illness he wishes to reveal. Tonight, he's quite open. He tells them that he's a writer, that he's been ill, and this trip is to celebrate his recovery and to begin to write again. He clinks his glass against mine. "We're also celebrating that Meredith can finally return to the law after taking an extended sabbatical to look after her malingering brother."

I side-eye him. "I hardly looked after you... I just kept you company."

He grins wickedly. "Nothing like taking a lawyer into consultations to keep the doctors on their toes."

"We're celebrating that Joe is well," I say firmly. "I'm not sure I'll return to the law just yet."

Joe sighs. "Whatever happened to my ruthless corporate sister?"

"She got a bit of perspective." I sound flippant, but I'm not. When I'd first put my life on hold to support Joe, I'd done so with a sense of virtue and sacrifice, a ridiculous belief in my own nobility. But that changed. I changed, thankfully. I saw a side of Joe I'd never known, and discovered a side of myself that had been lost in some pursuit of what I'd thought was success. I wish that Joe had never been sick, of course I do, but I don't look at the last year and a half as time we've lost.

"Good for you, girl!" Abigay says. She fixes Joe with her gaze and speaks softly. Her voice, to me, seems touched with some past loss. "And good health to you, young man. May your troubles be behind you."

Joe changes the subject, asking our companions about their work and their lives. And so we all tell stories about who we are and what we do. Abigay shares her life with five cats and a chicken who thinks it's a cat. Apparently, the fowl is the best mouser of the lot. Duplantier lives with two old dogs, both of which he found at crime scenes, the confused, terrified pets of victims. I am, to be honest, moved by the kindness of the detective who would take them in rather than allow them to be impounded and, ultimately, destroyed. I feel myself becoming teary at the image of the dogs trying to rouse their murdered masters, and I try desperately to fight the onslaught of emotion that hounds have always elicited in me. It's ridiculous, not to mention embarrassing.

Joe notices and runs interference with funny stories about life on the land in rural Australia. "And Wheelbarrow tried to—"

"Wheelbarrow?" Duplantier asks.

"Just a nickname, mate; his real name was Jake, I think."

"Why do you call him Wheelbarrow?"

"He needed to be pushed to work."

And so, my brother holds our companions entranced with stories of the mildly abusive nicknames Australian men are willing to answer to, while I try to stop thinking about Duplantier's dogs. Abigay and Napoleon are fascinated, and Joe has an excellent selection of monikers to share.

"Brake Pad was so called because he wore out easily and then started to squeal, and London Fog—he wasn't really English, just never lifted."

"And what did they call you?" Abigay inquires archly.

Joe laughs. "Blister."

"Why?"

"Because I'd appear when the hard work was done."

"And you were not offended?" Duplantier is clearly bemused.

"No. You can't get offended. You wouldn't last long if you did." He tries to explain. "A nickname says as much about you being a good sport as anything else…the worse the name, the easier the bloke."

"What of *les femmes*?" Duplantier looks at me. "Do they also insult each other in this way?"

"Not so much," I reply.

Abigay tries to understand the motives at play. "Aussies value hard work, then," she ventures. "The nicknames seem to be about people not working hard enough."

Joe considers it. "I guess. But we also have a kind of grudging respect for those who manage to avoid working too hard. It's an Australian paradox." He grins. "Not all nicknames are about work ethic. There was a bloke everyone called Bus Shelter. He had a big nose."

I can't tell if our fellow travelers are quietly appalled, but they laugh. "And what would you call me?" Duplantier asks.

"Oh, mate," Joe says. "You have to earn a nickname. I need to know you're a strong enough bloke to take an insult and a good enough bloke to deserve it. That takes time."

The train starts to move, and for a moment we are captivated by the fact that we are finally under way. We can't see much out of the window aside from the reflection of ourselves at dinner, but we can sense the movement, feel the rhythm of the Orient Express. It becomes a kind of background score to our conversation, which is lively and exhilarated. Duplantier is an elegant man, embodying all the style for which Parisians are famous. His humor is dry, and his manners beautifully Old World, despite the fact that he could not be more than thirty-five. Napoleon Duplantier tells us that he was married once, when he was too young and ambitious to know how not to give all of himself to his work. She left him for a pâtissier. And so now he has dogs. The Frenchman has an understated way about him, and there is something quite mesmerizing about his slow, careful movements.

Abigay is the opposite. Down to earth and solid in all things, she exhibits a practicality in the manner in which she uses the silverware, an efficiency in her enjoyment of the meal. Her conversation is peppered with wry observations about the human condition, and her questions are direct and leading. To me, she seems very much a policewoman on holiday.

She glances at the table behind me and tsks. I turn around. Flex and Herds are seated with a couple to whom we've not been introduced. They're all taking photographs of their meals.

"It's a pity people don't snap murderers the way they do the soup," she says. "It'd sure make our job a darn sight easier."

"Murderers? On the Orient Express?" Joe regards her with mock alarm. "Whoever heard of such a thing?"

I laugh, looking around Étoile du Nord, full of diners in their formal finery. "It certainly looks like the set of a Christie mystery." I lower my voice to a whisper. "Green plaid dinner suit at the table by the door must be guilty of some sort of crime."

Abigay twists to look at the gentleman in question—a middle-aged man whose gym-sculpted body bulges against the seams of the emerald-green checks of his probably haute couture attire. "Against fashion, if nothing else," she agrees. "I'll keep a watch on him."

Duplantier shakes his head. "No, no… *L'habit ne fait pas le moine*. Murderers are rarely so visible…the perpetrator will be one you have barely noticed. He will sit at dinner being perfectly ordinary…or he will take his refreshment in his cabin."

"May I direct your attention, then, to the two old ladies behind Abigay and Joe?" I lean forward and make my case. "They arrived at the very last moment, slipped on board after everyone else had already done so, and they look like quintessential grandmothers. What's more, I'll wager that they knit. Surely that's suspicious?"

"Old ladies are poisoners," Joe says sagely. "Who's at their table? I don't want to alert them we're onto them by turning around."

"A couple. Two men." I cock my head to pick up the conversation and the accents. "They're American, I think. Identical tuxedos, with white silk scarves and…"

"Victims," Joe concludes. "Definitely victims!"

Abigay elbows him. "Go on with you, cheeky monkey!"

And so, our first meal on the Orient Express is accompanied by a conversation of absurd speculation in which we cast our fellow travelers as players in a mystery. The murder itself is nebulous—poisoning grandmothers, green plaid suit in the dining car with a candlestick, the embittered writer with a knife in the restrooms, obsessed podcasters after the ultimate true crime podcast. It is both wonderfully fitting and gloriously inappropriate, and by dessert we are laughing hard and thoroughly acquainted. Or so we believe.

Not just one scene, but several, have been set.

Chapter 3

The Midnight Bar on the Orient Express is an extensively stocked cocktail bar with a grand piano on one end of the long carriage. The curved ceiling is highlighted with lacquered wood trim and Lalique crystal light shades. The lighting is muted, the seating varied, in intimate fours or longer couches facing into the center of the carriage, near low side tables on which one might place a cocktail, or a tray of coffee, delivered by unbelievably agile and surefooted waiters. The train's resident pianist is playing—a jazz number that only sinks us deeper into the bygone era this journey evokes. "Green plaid suit" stands beside the piano clapping his hands and dancing, occasionally whooping.

"I've changed my mind," I say to Joe. "He's definitely a victim."

Joe winces as the flamboyantly dressed gentleman begins to drum on the top of the grand piano with his palms. "In that case, the pianist has to be a suspect."

"Among others," I say as the man starts to trill to the music. "He might be less annoying if we had cocktails."

"Well said, Meredith," Duplantier agrees, summoning a waiter.

Joe orders a mocktail made with fresh pineapple, jalapeños, and pink peppercorns. He encourages me to have a real drink, but I am determined not to break our solidarity and order a strawberry ginger lemonade. Duplantier requests a Mata Hari. Abigay has retired already, and so we are just three, for a few minutes at least.

Flex and Herds spot us and shuffle and weave over with the couple who'd been their dinner companions and who introduce themselves as Noel and Siobhan Ferguson. The moment they speak, we hear that they are Irish.

"We've heard so much about you from Felix and Ben," Siobhan says, shaking Joe's hand.

"I apologize," Joe says. "I hope it wasn't too desperately boring."

"Truly terrible!" Noel's smile is broad, his brogue stronger than his wife's. "We tried to get off, but wouldn't you know this bloody train doesn't stop till tomorrow…"

"I reviewed your wonderful book on my blog," Siobhan effuses. "I can't believe we're talking to you, here of all places."

Joe poses with her for a picture and then introduces me and Duplantier. We crowd onto a set of facing couches to enjoy the music and snatch bits of conversation over the noise. Siobhan, it turns out, is a travel writer with a considerable following on social media. She shows me her feed, already full of photographs of the beautiful details of this train: the fringes on the velvet curtains, the reflections in the windows, the chrome luggage racks high in the cabins, and, of course, the food. Siobhan's husband, Noel, is in some kind of finance, and he is socially aware enough to know that that's about all people really need or want to know about what he does. When Siobhan takes a photo, he sighs and tries to avoid being in the frame, but with undisguised pride he tells me about Siobhan's upcoming book and the publishers who came to her.

"So, is this trip for the book?" I ask.

"No, I'm afraid the book has already gone to print," Siobhan replies regretfully. "The Orient Express was Noel's idea. He's a bit of a train nut."

"I think you'll find the word is *enthusiast*," Noel corrects blithely.

The train lurches slightly, and a passing redhead spills her drink on Joe. "Oh, hello!" She speaks with a distinct, if slightly slurred, Scottish enunciation. It is the only thing that doesn't fit entirely with the impression that she might have stumbled out of a glamourous Hollywood film set from the forties. "Elle Baird, Duchess of Kinross. I'm afraid your shirt has soaked up my wee martini." She looks sadly at her now-empty glass.

Joe laughs and blots at his shirt with the silk handkerchief that had poked out of the breast pocket of his dinner jacket. "Joe Penvale," he says, smiling. "I apologize for my shirt. It's always been a bit greedy. Allow me to buy you another drink, Your…" He struggles for the correct form of address.

"Grace," she informs him, laughing, "however inappropriate that might be, considering I've just tripped over my own feet and dumped my martini on you." She gives him a gentle shove. "Gaun yerself! Just haste ye back!"

Joe blinks and then decides she means she does want another

drink. He steps away to find a waiter and request a martini for the duchess.

While they wait for the drink to arrive, Joe introduces the Scottish noblewoman to everyone in proximity. She is welcomed into a crowd of new acquaintances and virtual strangers, who are not a little intrigued by her title. Elle Baird, the Duchess of Kinross, is traveling alone, the duke having passed away some years ago. But it's not her first time on the Orient Express. This is a journey she takes every year to a yoga retreat in Venice.

I watch Joe watching her while she holds court. According to her own account, Elle Baird married the duke in the late 1990s, when Joe and I were toddlers, so she must be at least fifteen years our senior, but I wonder if my brother is smitten nevertheless. He might well be. Or perhaps he is simply researching. Through the evening, he and Elle fall often into conversation that includes no one else.

Felix and Ben try to interview waiters and bar staff, even the pianist, but, while they are all unerringly helpful, I suspect they are also too busy doing their jobs to afford much time or attention to answering the questions of a couple of Australian podcasters. Nevertheless, *Death of the Reader* perseveres.

I find myself talking with Napoleon Duplantier about the cuisines of our respective nations. He seems to believe that Australians live almost exclusively on a diet of avocado, toast, and beer.

"Nonsense!" I defend my national palate. "Australians will eat just about anything…with the possible exception of snails."

"Escargot? Why would you not eat escargot? He is delicious!"

The exchange descends into teasing and laughter and a level

of comfort that belies the fact that we met only a few hours before. Napoleon Duplantier seems to me to be a part of the experience that is the Orient Express, reflecting our surroundings in elegance and style, though I know he is as much a passenger as Joe and I, that he has a life in the real world with work and bills and dogs. But not for now. Perhaps it's my imagination that is imbuing the Orient Express into my fellow travelers. Perhaps I will see them all differently when we step off the train. But right now, this all seems a world apart from everything.

"Who are you, Meredith Penvale," Duplantier asks, "apart from your brother's champion? Who are you apart from him?"

I am both startled and seduced by the question. Who am I apart from Joe? "I'm not sure, yet," I say in the end. "I was a lawyer. I loved the work—I thought the law was important and I was good at it, but…"

"You no longer think the law is important?"

"It's not that." I try to answer honestly, which is more difficult than it sounds because I'm not sure if I know precisely what's changed. "Now that the crisis with Joe's health is over, I'm not sure I can go back to my old life. I'm restless." I laugh. "I think the answer is that I'm not sure who I am, but I'm trying my best to find out."

"It is a worthy quest," he says, looking at me intently.

"I do like dogs," I say suddenly. Don't ask me why. I sometimes say ridiculous things when I get nervous. And Napoleon Duplantier does make me a little nervous.

He smiles. "And that is who you are?"

"As much as anything else."

He tells me more about his dogs, then, Savarin and Madame

La Chienne. "I did not name them," he is careful to point out. Savarin is a Doberman, and Madame La Chienne a standard poodle, and according to Duplantier, they are the best dogs that ever were. If I had not grown up with a Labradoodle that owned that title, I might have believed him.

Joe and I eventually call it a night, or a morning, at about two a.m. He seems suddenly quite anxious to leave the Midnight Bar. Somewhat hastily then, we bid good night to our new friends, who with the benefit of actual alcohol are still dancing and mingling. We walk through the dining cars, empty but for the chef, who sits at a table doing what looks like paperwork. Chess and backgammon sets have been placed on the tables. I might be tempted, but I don't want Joe to overdo it. The cancer is gone, but the memory of how desperately ill he'd been is still too vivid to allow me to relax completely. I tell myself not to be silly, but still, I don't suggest we pause for a game.

Although he is initially a little quiet, by the time we reach the sleeping carriages, Joe's high spirits return, and he gloats that he's been collecting characters all evening, that the train is writing his next novel for him.

"The duchess is brilliant, is she not? She's..." He searches for the perfect word. "She's swashbuckling!" I shush him as we approach 16G, lest we disturb our taciturn neighbor.

Our cabin has been transformed into a sleeper in our absence, and so there is more excitement when we open the door. The seating has become two beds, a lower and upper bunk, each made up with sheets and blankets and pillows. There are robes and slippers set out. I shoo Joe into the corridor for a moment, so I can take a photo of the room while it is still immaculate.

He waits, leaning impudently against the door of 16G. When I finally let him in, he claims the lower bunk on the grounds that he's forty-six minutes older than me. I don't fight him—I've always preferred the upper bunk. When we were kids, he did too, and he used his firstborn status to demand it. I could do nothing but hope he'd fall off in the night. And so, deprived of the opportunity as a child, I find the elevation a novelty.

Joe lies on his bed facing the wall and flips open his laptop while I use the little basin to have a cat wash and change into my pajamas. The Orient Express is a historic train, and so only the Grand Suites have showers. For that reason, we'll stop in Venice tomorrow and disembark to spend a night in a hotel before we resume the journey to Istanbul.

I don't chat to him as I normally would, happy to hear the click of the keys, to know he is writing. I brush my teeth, moisturize my face and hands, and grab one of the robes and a pair of the slippers to visit the restroom.

"Watch out for murderers," Joe murmurs without looking up as I step out of our cabin.

The carriage is quiet, and the corridor deserted, initially. It's not until I'm making my way back from the restrooms that I see Duplantier at the door of the cabin beside ours.

"Napoleon—hello."

He looks up at me and releases the handle. "Meredith, *bonsoir*." He glances at the number on the door and shakes his head in disgust. "I am at the wrong door—it is no wonder my key would not operate."

I laugh. "It's rather fortunate the gentleman in 16G seems to be a sound sleeper. You're calling it a night, then?"

"*À contrecoeur*, Meredith." He moves over one door to the correct cabin. "But, clearly, it is well past the time."

I smile. "They've made the compartments up delightfully. I am sure you'll sleep well."

"I shall see you at breakfast then, Meredith. *Bonne nuit.*"

I wish Duplantier a good night and return to 16F. Joe is still typing. I climb the ladder and settle myself onto the top bunk. "So, are you going to tell me what you're writing about?" I ask drowsily.

"I would have thought it obvious," he replies. "A murder on a train…"

"It's been done," I murmur. "And rather well, if I recall."

"I agree," Joe says, still typing, "but I wondered if it was time for a new take."

I roll over onto my stomach. "Keep talking."

"Sometimes the stories we know become part of the setting," he says.

"Like *Murder on the Orient Express*?"

"Exactly… It's everywhere here; it's in the furniture and the staff, every flourish, every detail. It's the reason most of us are on board… It's the story we've come to be part of. Poirot and Christie's suspects linger here as well as in her pages, as do Highsmith's and White's, not to mention Hitchcock's depictions of the same, and sometimes we catch a glimpse of them in the periphery of our vision."

"So how does that—"

"Well, it's interesting. It's like the old story is a character in the new one."

"And you're writing a new story with the old story in the shadows?"

"Nicely put! Yes. I'm trying to see how the old story will change how the new story unfolds. If I can still do this."

"If you can…what do mean by that?"

For a moment there's silence and then, finally, Joe explains. "When I wrote the last book, Meri, I was dying. I didn't know it, of course, but I was dying. I remember how clear everything seemed, how easy it was…I don't know if…I sometimes wonder if it was supposed to have been my last work as well as my first. I'm not dying anymore…maybe—What? Are you laughing?"

I am. Hard. "What a load of pretentious garbage!" I say when I'm finally able to talk. "Your talent was not some super-power granted by the proximity of mortality." I turn over and rest my head on my elbow. "Look, Joe, you're just nervous because the first book was so big. I get it."

"Yeah, but—"

"Come on, Joey. You're writing a murder mystery, not the American Constitution! You'll write it just fine without the help of impending death."

"Yeah, okay. I feel a bit stupid now."

"You are stupid."

"And you're a shrew. This conversation never happened —agreed?"

"Like hell…"

Joe's words are starting to swim a little. It's too late to be contemplating the finer points of meta literature, or anything else, really. "I'm glad you're…" Vaguely, I'm aware I haven't finished the sentence, but I can't seem to make my mouth form words. The soft, almost non-sound of Joe's fingers on the keyboard is the last thing of which I'm conscious until Maxim knocks gently on the door of our compartment.

"*Signore* and *Signorina* Penvale, breakfast will be served in the dining car in thirty minutes."

Maxim has changed languages, or at least titles—we must have crossed the border into Italy. I'm silently thrilled by the linguistic detail.

I hang my head down from the top bunk. "Good morning."

Joe squints at me. "Did you sleep well?"

"Actually, yes… Did you sleep at all?" The laptop is still open on the covers.

"I'm not sure," he says. "If I did, I dreamt I wrote something brilliant."

I laugh. "Would you like me to bring you back something from the dining car so you can catch a few minutes' kip now?"

He sighs. "No. I'm more hungry than sleepy…and desperate for coffee."

I swing myself onto the ladder and climb down as Joe emerges from the bottom bunk. We collide and then jostle for space in front of the vanity as we brush our teeth. Like we did when we were kids. I look closely at my face in the mirror and grimace.

Joe grabs a robe and heads for the restroom, warning me that I have till he gets back to dress in privacy. He begins whistling as opens the door.

"Joe!" I scowl at him. "You'll wake everyone."

"Just in time for breakfast," he says. "It's part of the service. Perhaps our neighbor will be more agreeable this morning."

I dress quickly. Very quickly. It's my superpower. I can

change clothes, put on makeup, and make my hair look something like respectable in under five minutes. It's the other side of the fact that I'm always running late. Not out of carelessness or indifference… I just seem to be one of those people the universe conspires to delay. Things go missing, or spill, unexpected people suddenly call by or taxis don't turn up.

So, by the time Joe returns, I'm ready to head to the dining car. He sends me out of the compartment while he gets dressed—not out of any false or real modesty but because there is not enough room in the cabin to make the movement required to don clothes if there is another adult taking up valuable space. I spend the time gazing out of the carriage windows. A mountain vista looms and recedes with the passage of the train. We are climbing into the Italian Alps. It is already a snowscape—soft and brilliant white. This journey is the last of the year. Soon it will be too dangerous to traverse the Alps, but for now it is merely breathtaking. Soaring peaks and cobalt lakes, alpine forests on the lower slopes through which the train winds. There are occasional houses and even towns by the tracks, but the Express will not stop again until we reach Venice this evening.

Waiters bearing covered silver trays tap on the doors of those who have elected to take breakfast in their cabins. I catch glimpses of bed-ragged passengers in the blue deco robes of the Orient Express as they open the door to admit the bearers of coffee and pastries. I have a moment of regret for the idea of sipping coffee in the privacy of the cabin while watching the glory of the Alps pass. But it's only a moment. I can hear thumps and the occasional crash from behind our cabin door, and I'm reminded that the sleeper cabin is somewhat short on space. And there will be other mornings on the way to Istanbul.

Napoleon Duplantier emerges from 16H in a dove-gray suit, crisp and sharp as if he'd somehow had it pressed in the night. Perhaps he did—it's probably a service the Express provides.

"Meredith! *Bonjour!*"

"*Bonjour,* Napoleon. Are you ready for breakfast?"

"*Bien sûr.* Is your brother not joining us?"

"He's just getting dressed." Another thump. Duplantier looks a little concerned. I tap on the door. "Joe, what on earth are you doing in there?"

He comes out and shuts the door quickly, if sheepishly, behind him.

"What have you done?" I demand.

"I may have accidentally collapsed the top bunk."

"What—how?"

Joe rakes a hand through his hair. "I was trying to figure out how the mechanism worked…"

"For God's sake, Joe!" He has ever been a compulsive button pusher. When we were small, things always seemed to be crashing around him. Not without reason.

"It's a lot harder to put back up than to take down."

"I suppose I should be glad you waited until I was out of the bunk before you started poking about."

Duplantier smiles. "I am sure the excellent Maxim will restore order by the time we are finished with breakfast."

We make our way back to the dining cars. This morning, we are seated not with Abigay and Napoleon but the two elderly ladies who boarded in Paris. It turns out they are sisters: Clarice and Penelope Mayfield from someplace called Lower Slaughter in Gloucestershire. They are wholly picturesque— pearls and lace edging, soft-powdered cheeks, snow-white hair, and a kind of smallness about their postures, but their eyes are shrewd and lively, and they move confidently, if a little slowly. Clarice has a walking stick upon which she leans occasionally, silver-handled polished wood. We're assigned a table in Dining Car 4141.

Fleischmann appears again to wish us good morning and point out the ornate glass panels designed for the carriage by René Lalique, which are mounted in mahogany between each set of windows. The bacchanalian maidens are exquisite in frosted glass, and for a time I am mesmerized by the manner in which the muted light within the car seems to make them glow. I wonder about the craftsmen who somehow managed to capture that light in molten glass and cast it into forms that seem to breathe.

"They are most fine, don't you think, dear?" Clarice says as we take our seats. "Quite naked, of course, but that's very European."

Penelope rolls her eyes. "Clarice likes her decor to be dressed."

"I can't help it," Clarice declares. "I'm English."

"Is this your first time on the Orient Express?" I ask, as coffee and pastries are placed before us. The question, it seems, is the traditional opening between fellow travelers on the midnight-blue train.

"Why, yes, dear." Penelope takes a chocolate croissant

from the basket of pastries. "I suppose some people do this sort of thing all the time, but it's a rare treat for Clarice and me. Impossible but for the generosity of the Lower Slaughter Civic Society."

"They sent you on the Orient Express?" Joe does not hide his curiosity.

"The society engaged us to find someone. It is just our luck that the man in question was taking the Orient Express, and so here we are."

Chapter 4

Joe's eyes meet mine. Octogenarian bounty hunters. Odd but intriguing.

"Why does the Lower Slaughter Civic Society want you to find him?" Joe asks carefully.

"He has rather a lot of money that belongs to the society. They would like it back."

"And they sent you to…?"

"Demand the return of their funds," Clarice says.

"With whatever menaces necessary," Penelope adds.

A beat of silence as Joe and I try to work out whether they're serious.

"Jeffrey Kynaston would have wanted to go, I expect—volunteers for everything, that man, thinks he's James Bond," Clarice says waspishly. "But Sarah, his wife, poor woman, dragged him off to see her mother in Scotland last year, and they seem to have settled in the Highlands somewhere."

Penelope chuckles mischievously. "Poor Sarah might have finally poisoned him—she was always trying new recipes, you know—and run off with that nosy Michael Blenkins… No one's seen him for a while either."

"Now, Penny, that's just gossip," Clarice says reprovingly. "We're better than that."

"What's his name?" Joe asks. "The bloke you're looking for. Perhaps we've met him."

"Lower Slaughter knew him as Gregory Harrington, but he could be calling himself anything. They have multiple identities, these people." Clarice frowns. "A truly despicable man—he made off with all the funds raised to build a nursing home in Lower Slaughter."

"And do you do this sort of work—finding people—often?" Joe inquires. I note the gleam in his eye. He's collecting characters again.

"Good heavens, no!" says Clarice. "We're old ladies. We take a keen interest in the goings on of Lower Slaughter, of course, but finding thieves, goodness me…"

"So, what's different about Mr. Harrington?" I ask, spreading butter on a croissant after being momentarily distracted by the fact that the butter pat is beautifully embossed with the crest of the Orient Express.

"He lodged with us—in the spare room—you see," Penelope explains as she pours coffee. "So, we feel…well…not exactly responsible but obliged."

"Could you not have called the police?" Joe appears preoccupied with a bagel, but I know the ladies have his complete attention.

"Oh, yes, well the police." Clarice rolls her eyes. "I'm afraid the constabulary is not what it once was… The boy in charge…" She shakes her head. "Penny and I were compelled to take things in hand."

"And you discovered that Mr. Harrington was taking the Orient Express."

"Oh, yes. He talked often of this train when he lived with us. When his ship came in, he said."

Penelope nods. "He's always loved trains…even as a child, it was Thomas the Tank Engine, and those battery-operated sets—"

"That's what he told us anyway," Clarice interrupts her sister. "The point is that the Orient Express has been for Gregory Harrington what you young people call a bucket item."

"Bucket-list item, Clarice," Penelope corrects, huffing.

"But how do you know he'll be traveling on this day?" Joe goes immediately to the flaw in the narrative.

Clarice's and Penelope's chins rise, and their lips press into self-satisfied smiles. "We have our sources, young man," Clarice says.

"And we protect them," Penelope adds sternly.

"Naturally." Joe retreats. Briefly. "So, have you confronted him yet, or are you waiting till after breakfast?"

"My, you are an inquisitive fellow!" Penelope snaps. "Impertinent, even."

"Professional habit, I'm afraid." Joe smiles. "I'm a writer."

"A journalist?" Penelope's tone is suspicious now.

"No, a novelist. Mysteries mainly." He tries to look contrite and very nearly manages it. "I can be unsocially curious about actual crimes."

"A novelist!" Clarice softens. "How splendid! Penelope used to write poetry. She's been published often in the *Lower Slaughter Bugle*. We moved with a very creative set back then."

"And what do you do, my dear?" Penelope directs this at me.

"I'm a lawyer by trade but—"

"A lawyer!" Clarice turns back to Joe. "You married well, young man!"

Joe pulls a face. "Good grief, I wouldn't marry her!"

"I'd never be desperate enough to accept the likes of him," I return flatly. "A girl's got to have some standards."

Clarice and Penelope glance at each other and then back at us, clearly unsure how to respond. Joe finally puts them straight. "Meredith is my sister."

Their smiles are relieved. They have not been seated with warring lovers.

"How very nice to meet siblings who get along so well!" Penelope declares. "Clarice and I have never had a cross word, but that is so rare."

Joe laughs, but he doesn't contradict her. We fight like any other siblings, but life of late has given us perspective about the importance, or lack thereof, of who received preferential treatment from one or the other of our parents. Though, for the record, Joe always got away with much more than I did— which is why he spent years larking about cattle stations playing cowboy, while I became a lawyer. Of course, he'll tell you it was because our parents always considered me the clever one, while he was only good for carrying stuff.

"So back to Mr. Harrington," Joe says, picking up the bone once again. "I presume he'll be traveling under an alias?"

"I believe we've already established that," Clarice says gravely.

"So, what does he look like? Perhaps we could help you find him."

The Mayfield sisters are shaking their heads before Joe finishes. "Don't be absurd, young man. This is not a task for amateurs. Harrington is a dangerous man, and slippery."

With Joe put back in his place, for a moment at least, we receive the next course—truffled eggs on brioche with caviar on the side. A number of waiters walk past with covered trays.

"Did you hear?" Clarice offers gossip in appeasement. "They've quarantined the last two carriages. The guests are being confined to their cabins!"

"Why?" Joe asks.

"The new strain," Penelope whispers. She inhales deeply and begins. "A couple boarded in Paris—they're in the last carriage. Luckily, they are newlyweds so they didn't actually go to dinner, or we might all have already been exposed. Anyway, they took ill in the night and have apparently tested positive. The conductor quarantined their carriage and the one that adjoins it for good measure—I suppose it's the only way they can stop the whole train being infected. They say this Paris strain is resistant to antivirals and so very dangerous indeed." She pauses, a little breathless now.

"What? But—" I turn to Joe in alarm.

"Don't panic, old mate," he says quietly. "My cells are all in order."

I breathe. Joe's right. His cell-counts, in fact all his blood readings, have been normal for months. There is no reason to believe that he is any more vulnerable to infection than anyone else on the train.

"They're just going to lock these people up until we get to Venice?" Joe's uneasiness is for the passengers in the quarantined carriages.

Clarice nods. "I expect they'll detach the last two carriages and disembark the passengers into ambulances. The fact that we've crossed the border is probably going to cause a bit of bother. This new strain—what letter of the Greek alphabet are they up to now?—is making people a bit hysterical."

Penelope snorts. "You'd think people would have calmed down by now, but panic appears to be the latest fashion."

"Oh…" It seems to me that this news is much more alarming than the reactions of our breakfast companions suggest. "So, what are we going to do?"

"Do?" Clarice purses her lips. "We're going to carry on, my dear. What else is there to do?"

"Well…we could stop and get those poor people off the train and into hospital… Locking them in seems barbaric."

"This is the Orient Express, dear girl. Not being able to take your meals in the dining cars may be a nuisance, but if you must be quarantined for a day with the sniffles, a berth on the Orient Express is surely one of the better addresses. I'm sure they will be compensated financially for inconvenience."

"There's no way of knowing if the newlyweds actually have the Paris strain," Penelope says more softly. "I'm sure they're not in any immediate danger, dear, and we will be in Venice this evening. I expect continuing is the quickest way to get them to a hospital."

"What if your Mr. Harrington is in one of those carriages?" Joe is making mischief now. "You won't be able to get to him."

Clarice waves away the notion. "You are in carriage 16, are you not?"

"How did you…" I begin.

Clarice smiles and glances at the keys to our cabin, which Joe had placed on the table alongside his phone and a paperback. Joe, for some reason, feels the need to empty his pockets when he sits down to eat. The key ring clearly marked 16F, declares the location of our cabin.

"You'll find Mr. Harrington is your neighbor," Penelope confides.

"That guy?" Joe says. "I never liked him."

"You met him for about ten seconds," I point out.

"He made a lousy first impression."

"Only because he chose not to charm you," Clarice assures us. "If you had something he wanted, you would be his best friend by now, and your sister would be in love."

Joe snorts. I choose to believe it's at the idea I would be so easily taken in.

"Perhaps you should make your citizens' arrest soon," Joe suggests. "There's a chance they might disembark us all in Venice…and then you will have lost your opportunity."

"Or you could speak to Mr. Fleischmann." I'm a little concerned that Joe is goading two old ladies into confronting a criminal, or at least not dissuading them. "I'm sure he could have the police waiting at the station in Venice."

"Oh, no, that wouldn't do!" Clarice places her knife and fork together. "Penny, dear, I think we should be going."

Penelope stands, and Joe does likewise. "It's been lovely to meet you both," she says. "But we must be off."

"We might head back to our cabin too," Joe says cheerfully.

The Mayfields glare at Joe. "Touché, young man," Clarice adds, smiling now. "Come on then; you might as well lead the way."

We proceed in single file back toward our own carriage.

I pull Joe down and whisper into his ear. "What the hell are you up to?"

He looks at me innocently. "I thought I'd write for a bit."

"Joe…"

"Don't tell me you're not curious."

I stop suddenly as Napoleon Duplantier's cabin door opens. The Mayfields all but crash into me.

"Oh, hello, Napoleon. I thought you'd still be at breakfast."

"I was…I am…I returned to my cabin for this." He holds up the embossed box of stationery that is in every cabin. "I will write some letters to pass the time."

"What a lovely idea," Penelope says over my shoulder. "We won't keep you then."

Napoleon's right brow arches, but he does not argue. "*À bientôt, mesdames…*Joe."

As he walks away, Maxim makes his way down the carriage from the opposite direction with a tray balanced on one open hand. If he wonders why we are all gathered outside 16G, he does not ask. He beams at us, maneuvers expertly past the Mayfields and me, and knocks on the door.

"*Buongiorno*, Signore Blackwell, I have your breakfast!"

There's no answer.

"He's probably got earplugs in." Joe isn't even pretending to be returning to our cabin.

Maxim knocks again. "Signore Blackwell, I can open the door if you are still in bed."

Still no answer.

"Perhaps he's in the restroom," I venture.

"I'll just leave his tray," Maxim replies, pulling a key from his pocket with his free hand.

I pretend to be waiting politely for him to enter 16G so I can pass. The Mayfields are fussing with their handbags, and my brother just stands back, waiting to see what will happen.

Maxim unlocks the door, but it resists. It seems the latch has been secured from within. "Signore Blackwell." The steward is clearly worried now.

"Here, allow me." Joe pulls a pen from his breast pocket and slips it into the slight gap created by unlocking the door. He jiggles the pen against the internal latch and somehow knocks it loose. The Mayfields applaud. I roll my eyes.

Maxim pushes the door in and uses his hip to hold it open as he steps into the room. The tray crashes to the floor, and croissants and assorted pastries scatter at our feet. Maxim is cursing in a number of languages now, pressing the attendant button within the cabin like he's trying to tap SOS in Morse code. And as he does so, I can see into 16G.

Chapter 5

What I register immediately is blood: blood on the walls and the curtains, the lower bunk is soaked, and the linen is shredded. I step back, unable to speak.

The Mayfield sisters push in front of me and peer in. Maxim directs them to step back as he continues to frantically press the button for help. Clarice staggers, clutching her chest and gasping. In doing so she enters the room. Joe now goes in to help her, and I can see their eyes darting about the cabin, observing, memorizing, as he supports her to stand. There's a duffel bag on the luggage rack. The blankets have been pulled off the lower bunk, and the sheets and mattress are crimson. The carpet is dark with blood, and the walls splattered with the same. Maxim continues to press the service button, but with a ferocity that must surely convey that something is terribly wrong. There's no sign of Harrington or Blackwell or whoever our neighbor was.

"What the hell happened here?" Joe says more to himself than anyone else.

"Please," says Maxim, "you should all step outside."

I'm a little surprised when Clarice and Joe comply without protest. They come out into the corridor, Clarice still clutching Joe as if she might otherwise collapse.

I am almost convinced.

Fleischmann marches down the corridor toward us with an entourage of stewards behind him.

Joe opens the door to our cabin and motions me to follow him in. We slip in just in time, before Fleischmann suggests to the Mayfield sisters that they might be more comfortable in the Bar Car. Joe leaves our door slightly open and positions himself in the best place to eavesdrop on any conversation in the corridor. He hands me a glass and gestures that I should place it against the wall we share with Harrington's cabin.

"You've lost your tiny little mind!" I mutter, but I do it.

I can hear Fleischmann, his voice muffled but still comprehensible.

He asks Maxim when he last saw Signore Blackwell.

"Not since dinner. He was at the first sitting and did not go to the Bar Car afterward."

Fleischmann says something about calling ahead to the carabinieri in Venice. He instructs Maxim to touch nothing and lock up the room.

"Should I have a man stationed at the door, sir?"

Fleischmann considers it and then seems to decide that doing so would be prudent despite the alarm it might cause passengers. "Yes, make sure there is a man guarding the door at all times. We'll call for instructions."

Joe and I sit quietly as we listen to them lock the room and leave. And then we both speak at once.

"What did you hear?"

"Are you crazy…you're not a detective!"

"What did you hear?"

I shake my head, but I tell him. "His name is Blackwell, not Harrington."

"That's what Maxim called him, and I suppose he wouldn't be traveling under his actual name." He smiles. "The Mayfield sisters made that very clear."

"Maxim hasn't seen him since the first sitting of dinner."

"We saw him after that…when he went into his compartment."

"Only for a moment."

Joe scowls. "The door was securely latched from the inside."

"Could he have somehow done that himself when he left?"

"Not from the outside. Anyway, did you see the amount of blood in that room, Meri? I doubt he could have walked out, and if he did, there would have been a blood trail or bloody shoe prints at the very least."

He's right. "Where is he, then? He wasn't in the cabin."

Joe shrugs. "Beats me. Maybe whoever killed him tossed him out of the window." Joe gets up to test the window in our compartment. It does open, filling the cabin with frigid mountain air, but the opening is small. You'd be hard-pressed to throw a cat out, let alone a grown man. He shrugs. "Perhaps the killer took him out in some kind of box or suit bag."

I'm skeptical, but I leave it for now. "I wonder if he really was Clarice and Penny's Mr. Harrington."

"I'm inclined to believe he was. Those two old birds seem pretty sharp to me. I can't imagine them getting on this train if they weren't sure he was on it."

"In that case, if he is all that Penny and Clarice claimed, he may have had other enemies who followed him on board."

Joe agrees. He turns to me then as if something has just occurred to him. "Do you want to ask them to move us... you know, away from the scene of the crime? They may even upgrade us."

I smile. I can hear the reluctance in his voice, and I'm touched that he asked anyway. Being in the cabin next door is probably a mystery writer's dream. "No...lightning doesn't strike twice in the same place. We're conceivably safer here than anywhere else on the train."

He can't keep the relief from his face. "If you're sure?"

"I am."

"I wonder how our murderer managed to leave with a body and lock the door behind him from the outside?"

"A puzzle, to be sure." I remove my shoes and sit cross-legged on the padded seating that runs along one wall of our compartment. I glance at Joe's laptop sitting on the little table. "Are you going to let me read what you're working on?"

Joe shrugs. "I have to do an interview with Flex and Herds. You can read while I'm gone, if you like. You know my passwords."

"What are they interviewing you about?" I stretch to retrieve the laptop.

"Ghosts."

"What?"

"Flex has this notion that the Orient Express is haunted by its place in literature, the inequities it romanticizes." Joe shakes his head. "He thinks that passengers can't help but be possessed by the novel, that by traveling they absorb the social sensibilities of that era—"

"The social sensibilities?"

"Wealth, class, privilege, propriety, and so forth—Ben and Felix are political science majors, Meri. And idealists. Riding the Orient Express was never going to be about a train ride for them. It's completely bloody daft, but Flex wants to explore his cockeyed theory by interviewing Joe Penvale about whether he can feel the presence of Agatha Christie and whether she's still trying to blame the butler for the deeds of the capitalist classes or some such thing."

I laugh. "Don't be such a spoilsport, Joe. They're really just talking about inspiration and the relevance of old stories in a new world. And that *is* why we're here."

Joe sighs. "The problem is I can feel something. It seems I'm doomed to be their proof."

"Go, and let me read."

"You're not worried being here on your own?" Joe glances pointedly at the wall we share, or shared, with Harrington.

"I'll lock the door behind you."

"It seems like Harrington did too."

"There's a steward standing outside Harrington's door," I say. "I'll be fine."

Joe grins. "Well, since you'll be here anyway, keep your ears open. I want to know what Fleischmann plans to do about a murderer on the train."

"You think he's still here?"

"Unless he jumped from the train."

I open his laptop and pull up his manuscript. "Go if you're going, Joe; I'm reading."

He grabs a glass from the table and hands it to me. "Place it against the back wall if you hear Fleischmann."

He steps out and then, a second or two later, back in, slamming the door.

"What?" I demand.

"There's someone coming down the corridor. I'll just let them pass."

"Why?" The corridors are narrow, but it is perfectly possible to maneuver past people if necessary.

"Good manners," Joe says. He opens the door a crack, peers through, and then waits another minute before finally leaving with the instruction: "Lock the door, Meri."

I mutter to myself as I put down the laptop, and lock and latch the door to our compartment. Joe is behaving a little oddly, but given the circumstances, I don't wonder too much about it. Perhaps I should be more afraid, or at least horrified. A man was murdered in the next compartment after all. But I'm not really. I'm staggered, and alarmed, and sad, but I'm not really scared for myself. Maybe it is shock—I'm told people process trauma in different ways. Though I don't feel traumatized. Possibly, it is the lack of a body to make it real.

Or perhaps I'm not capable of being really scared anymore. When Joe was first diagnosed, he was given two years, and we'd sat with that prognosis for what seemed lifetimes before the news started to get better. I've learned that about cancer, the worst news comes first—tears you apart and leaves you tossed in recurring waves of fear and despair and disbelief. After that, any tiny sliver of hope is a lifeline to the shore that was once your life. And from there the news gets better. Well, it did for Joe, anyway.

Reading Joe's manuscript is a familiar salve. Joe's writing remains as lyrical and witty as it was in his first book. This story opens with a man boarding the Orient Express. An echo of Poirot catching the train at Istanbul. The man's name is Joe Penvale. I'm surprised, a little intrigued. Joe's never named a character after anyone he knows, let alone himself. He's always laughed about writers who couldn't draw the line between fiction and reality, what he called the "High Art Brigade" and their self-obsession.

The Joe Penvale in Joe's manuscript is not just Joe by name but in entirety. It's him. An Australian writer from the High Country working on a new book. I spend a few minutes staring out the window, contemplating why. The snowcapped peaks and ridges drift past lazily, and for a moment I wonder if it would have been possible to dispose of a body by throwing it off the train. The windows don't open far enough, but might there have been some other way that a corpse could be disembarked?

I shake myself away from the temptation to go deeper into the mystery of our missing neighbor and return to Joe's manuscript. The train in Joe's story is inhabited by ghosts of a sort. The manifestations of literature…Poirot and Miss Marple, Holmes and Watson, Rowland Sinclair, James Bond, and Inspector Singh. They haunt the manuscript's hero with their own theories of everything. I smile. Joe has always been able to see what no one else can. He has brought all the history and literary romance of the Orient Express to bear on the beginnings of a contemporary novel that grapples with several of the ideological difficulties with which he claims Flex and Herds are obsessed.

Many times in the past year and a half, Joe had voiced the fear that he could no longer write, that the treatment had poisoned his creativity. "I don't dream anymore, Meri. How am I supposed to write without dreams?"

"They'll come back," I'd assured him with no real idea that they would. My job had been to keep his spirits up, to reframe every negative outcome and thought until we were through. When his spirits failed, it was my job to carry us both with an outward determination that did not allow for failure. But privately I lived those months in abject, unmitigated terror.

Reading his manuscript now, I still have no idea if his dreams had returned, but if they haven't, he doesn't need them.

I close the laptop reluctantly, and then, almost as an afterthought, I listen for any sound above the rhythm of the train. There are people talking in the next cabin. Some part of me wants to ignore them, to not be drawn into Joe's understandable but probably unhealthy interest in the bloody disappearance of Harrington. But perhaps it's not just him. In the end, I place the glass he gave me against the shared wall and press my ear to its base. The resultant acoustic coupling allows me to hear the voices quite clearly. Unfortunately, they are speaking French and Italian. I pick up the words *Venezia Santa Lucia*—the train station in Venice. I also hear *COVID*. That alarms me more than the bloodletting in the next carriage. Joe is well, but it's too soon to test how strong his immune system is. Fleischmann is talking, in English now, about the quarantined carriages—at least I hope they're still quarantined. It sounds like "They can't refuse us with sick people aboard." The reply is from a voice I don't recognize. "That's exactly why they will refuse us." I hear mention of Innsbruck, but they have lapsed into French and Italian again.

I decide to join Joe and the podcasters in the Bar Car. There's no point in eavesdropping if I can't understand the language. I shut down the laptop. I place it on the table, but I think again. The compartment next door was the scene of a murder...or something very like a murder. What if someone broke in here? I start the laptop up again. Joe has, as I suspected, only saved his manuscript to the laptop's hard drive. I sigh. He won't learn until he loses an entire novel. I try to save the document online, but it appears that we don't have coverage at the moment. The train is probably passing through a dead zone. I attach the file to an email and send it Joe, knowing it will be sent automatically as soon as we are in range again. That completed, I am able to leave knowing that I have done all I can to ensure that the beginning of Joe's return to the life he had will not be lost, not on my watch at least.

I see Napoleon Duplantier as I open the door. He smiles and places a finger to his lips, not even attempting to hide that he's listening at the door of 16G. No one has yet been posted outside 16G, or perhaps the guard is currently inside the cabin, talking to Fleischmann. I step out, close the door to 16F, and spend a couple of minutes trying to jiggle the latch into place from outside. I only manage to make a lot of noise. Napoleon watches me curiously—I sense he knows what I'm doing and is interested only in the result. As far as I can tell, setting the latch from outside is impossible. I lock the door with my key, and Duplantier and I soft-foot it past 16G.

"What were you doing?" I demand as we reach the next car.

"Paying attention," he says quietly.

"Why?" I ask. As far as I know, he doesn't know anything about the state in which Harrington's compartment was found. It turns out my knowledge is limited.

"I wondered if they knew whose blood was coating the walls."

"Do you know?" I reply.

"I may be able to suggest," he says.

"Harrington?"

"He is known by that name and others."

"How do you know him, Napoleon?"

"I am the policeman, Meredith. He is the *criminal*. We play in the same circles."

"Did you know he was on board?"

"Of course." He glances at his watch. "I have another appointment, but shall we meet in the Bar Car in an hour? I will explain."

I am going to the Bar Car to find Joe anyway, so I agree. And with that we part ways.

I pick up speed as I enter the next car and maintain that slightly sea-legged pace until I reach the Bar Car. Joe is seated with Flex and Herds, and they are recording. There are a couple of other people in the bar, hanging off every word of the conversation among the three, laughing quietly at the repartee. I join the impromptu audience, ordering a virgin cocktail as a disguise.

"You sure you don't want me to add a little something to this?" A New Zealander accent. The barman hands me a tall, frosted glass of a frothy green blend of something that hopefully includes apple and not spinach.

"You can add anything but alcohol," I reply.

He laughs and holds up his finger. I watch him rummage behind the bar, spinning theatrically as reaches for jars and bowls. He drops a jar of little pickled onions and grins sheepishly at me as he cleans up the mess. Like Maxim and the stewards, he is immaculately attired in a pristine uniform. His eyes are deep brown, his follicles nearly black, though I can only tell that by the color of his goatee and elaborately waxed mustache. His head, in contrast, is clean-shaven. Not even a shadow of new growth.

Eventually he drops an umbrella, chunks of fruit, and a long toothpick skewering three maraschino cherries into my drink. "Ta-da!"

"Thank you, Mr.—?"

"Frank," he says, offering me his hand. "Just Frank."

As I take his hand to shake it, I notice his fingernails are polished—a tasteful neutral color, as one would expect on someone in the uniform of the Orient Express. "Meredith Penvale. Thank you for all the…garnishes, Frank."

"All part of the service, Senora Penvale." He winks at me as he turns his attention to another customer, and I am able to return mine to my brother and the podcasters.

I'm not sure if they are recording at this stage. Felix seems to be ranting about the anachronism of the sheer luxury we are enjoying on the Orient Express.

"That is part of the experience, mate," Joe says. "What makes it feel like we're going back in time."

"Yes, back to a time of strict class boundaries. A time when one doesn't notice the men and women scurrying about the place to cater to our every need." Felix shakes his head in disgust, at what, I don't think anybody is sure.

"I'm not entirely certain what you mean, mate," Joe says carefully. "The stewards do an amazing—"

Ben chimes in now. "Exactly! But do we notice their labors as we gorge ourselves on fine food and look for our next drink? Do we recognize one from the other, do we wonder what their experience of the *world's most famous train* is?"

"We could ask them, I suppose." Joe is clearly bemused. "It'd be an interesting angle for your show about the Orient Express. Just don't get anyone fired with a well-meaning exposé."

"Well, that's the rub," Felix replies. "The stewards are professionals. They are probably bound by a public relations policy that requires them to say that all the passengers are kind and considerate and this is an egalitarian train. One would need to be a fly on the wall to really find out how the worker is treated, what they eat, whether they are appreciated by those they serve or simply ignored as long as the drinks keep coming."

Joe regards the young podcasters thoughtfully. "I understand, comrades. But, as a personal favor, would you mind holding off on the revolution until we get to Venice?"

Frank, who has apparently been listening, laughs out loud. For a moment I'm afraid Felix and Ben will drag the poor barman into the conversation, but instead they check their sociopolitical critique and couch it in terms of the place of the servant in Golden Age mysteries.

For a while the conversation is about books. It refines to Agatha Christie's *Murder on the Orient Express*, and I am lulled until Joe mentions the blood-soaked compartment beside our own. I choke on my virgin cocktail; the other passengers start to murmur; and Ben Herder and Felix Shannon stop talking for a few beats. And then "What? Real blood? Are you sure?"

"Yeah, I'm sure. Tomato sauce smells like tomato sauce."

"Joe!" I move to the seat beside my brother to try to shut him up.

"Why haven't we stopped?" Felix demands. "There's a killer on board!"

Joe glances outside at the snow-covered wilderness. "What would be the point of stopping here?"

"The original Orient Express did…"

"They stopped for an avalanche, not a murder." Joe flaps his hand dismissively.

"For pity's sake," I add, "that was a story. Joe, we probably shouldn't be talking about this."

"Do you think it might be a part of the show?" Ben asks.

"What show?"

"You know…all this." Ben gestures widely. "The Orient Express experience."

"You think they kill someone on every journey?" I am undeniably skeptical.

"No, but they might stage a murder, just to get everyone in the mood—"

"In the mood for what?" Joe scoffs at the notion.

"I wish that was what it is," I say, "but I don't think so, Ben. It seems like the kind of thing any half-decent lawyer would warn against, if not forbid outright."

Felix pipes up in support of his podcast partner. "Maybe the lawyer thought the publicity was worth the risk, or perhaps he wasn't very good—not all lawyers know their prima facie from their mens rea."

I'm pretty sure that Felix also has no idea what either term means, but I let it pass. Instead, I tell them about the few words I overheard.

"Venezia Santa Lucia is our destination in Venice," Joe says, frowning. "It sounds like the Italians might not let us disembark."

"So we just sit on the train?"

"They may send us back to Paris."

"But there's a murderer on board," Ben protests.

"I thought you'd decided it was a publicity stunt," Joe says, casting his eyes about the bar. I follow his gaze. Several members of the impromptu audience are gone. I wonder again if we should have been more circumspect about sharing what we'd seen and overheard.

Joe glances at me. Apparently, I'm wearing my concern on my face. "Don't worry, Meri. The Mayfields have already told half the passengers. These guys are only staging shock for the podcast. I reckon our barflies just got bored and headed back to Clarice and Penelope."

"Have you finished your recording?" I ask carefully. I don't want to accidentally become part of it.

Joe looks at Felix and Ben. "Whaddaya reckon, fellas—are we done?"

"I think we've got enough…but you will tell us if you find the body?"

"Believe me, if I find the body *everyone* will know."

I grab Joe's arm. "I need to talk to you," I whisper.

Joe motions me to a set of upholstered chairs facing each other. Felix and Ben already have headphones on, probably listening to the interview they just recorded. Joe goes to the bar and orders coffee for both of us before he sits down. We wait for them to arrive.

Joe takes a sip and pulls a face.

"Still tastes weird?" I ask sympathetically. One of the side effects of chemotherapy was that Joe lost his sense of taste. For a long time he couldn't taste anything, or worse, everything tasted, in his words, "slimy." Joe's ability to taste particular foods returned randomly after the therapy ended, but coffee has not yet. Every time Joe orders coffee, it is with the hope that this time he will be able to taste his beloved brew.

"No. Tastes like a mouth full of wax. Hopefully the caffeine still works."

I sip my coffee guiltily, enjoying the spread of caffeine into my extremities nonetheless.

"So, what's up, Meri?"

"I think we're going to be on this train for longer than we expected."

"It'll give us a little longer to solve this, I guess."

I look to see if he's joking. He grins at me, but I'm not convinced he's speaking in jest.

"Joe, you're not a detective. Leave this to the police."

"Sure, when they turn up." He leans toward me and lowers his voice. "Come on, Meri, it's bloody fantastic material."

"Damn it, Joe, can't you just use your imagination?"

"I could. But you said yourself we'll be on this train for a while, and so will whoever killed Harrington. For all we know, he may be planning to work his way along our carriage. We can't do nothing."

I groan, exasperated. Joe could always make the ridiculous sound like the most sensible course of action. And I can't say I'm not partially persuaded. I stop resisting and offer up my information.

"Napoleon Duplantier was lurking outside 16G, listening to what Maxim and Fleischmann and the others were saying."

Joe is interested but not alarmed. "It'd be a bit hypocritical of us to condemn the man for eavesdropping…"

"But he may have understood what they were saying," I point out.

"Could be helpful." Joe nods. "So you're thinking that Duplantier might do as a sidekick…"

"Don't be idiotic… You're my goofy sidekick… Napoleon is an informant at best."

Joe smiles. "All right—I'll be in that. We should talk to Duplantier."

"I've already taken care of it," I reply with what I hope is an enigmatic smile. "He should be here in a few minutes."

Chapter 6

We talk about Joe's manuscript while we wait for Napoleon Duplantier. I ask him why he's written himself into this story.

He shrugs.

"You've never done it before."

"I've only written one book, Meri; maybe I just didn't think of it before."

"You've only written one book that was published," I correct. "I've read all your others…even the poetry…"

Joe grimaces. "I thought we'd agreed to never speak of my poetry period."

"The point is that you've never put yourself into the narrative before."

"Do you think it's lame?" He is uncertain now.

"No, I think it's brilliant, but I wonder what you're going to do with the character."

"The me-character? I don't know really. Perhaps, after everything that's happened, I want to make Joe Penvale immortal, somehow." He shakes his head, and kind of half-laughs. "I'm sitting on the Orient Express writing a mystery set on the Orient Express—it makes sense, gives me a direct connection to the narrative. And I can always do a global find-and-replace to change his name and remove myself back to obscurity."

"Don't. I think it's part of the magic of this book." I pause, but I've got to ask. "Why am I not there?"

Joe laughs fully now. "Because, at some point, even if it's just fictionally, I've got to walk alone."

"Why?"

"Because you have a life, Meri." He leans forward to look me in the eye. "We're fraternal, not conjoined. And I'm okay now. I want you to do what you want…meet someone, have a wild, mad affair, or go back to work, or travel, or find something else that gives you new purpose. We've both been living in limbo since the diagnosis. I'm the one who got cancer; it shouldn't take your life."

I shake my head. "Great speech, dude, but I'm way ahead of you."

"What do you mean?"

I reach into my pocket and show him the letter I've been carrying with me for weeks, reading it over from time to time when I needed to remind myself that I was doing this. Joe looks down at the typewritten document, scanning quickly.

"You're going to art school?"

"Yes."

"Can you even draw?"

"Actually, I intend to specialize in sculpture, but yes, I can draw. I used to illustrate your stories, remember?"

"We were children… What about the law…your job?"

"Joe, I was seventeen when I decided to become a lawyer. And even then, it was more because I wanted people to think I was clever. I don't mind being a lawyer, but it's more an arranged marriage than a passion. This"—I tap the page in his hand—"is my wild, mad affair."

He looks at the letter again and sits back. "Cool." A crease forms between his eyes as he thinks. "You used to make those insane sandcastles at the beach. They were amazing—I should have guessed."

I smile. "We all made sandcastles."

"Not like you. Yours were architectural feats." He bites his lower lip. "That blond kid smashed one, just threw himself onto it screaming 'cowabunga' or something… What was his name?"

"Dale Keneally," I say immediately.

Joe grins. "I knew you'd remember—even after all this time. You punched him in the face. His mother threatened to call the police. I was so proud of you." He raises his coffee. "Let's drink to you doing the same to Rodin."

"You want me to punch Rodin in the face?"

"Metaphorically. I'm not a philistine. I know he's dead."

I'd applied before Joe was given the all-clear, and then I'd worried that I'd jinxed him by thinking of life after cancer. That the disease would remind me that it was in charge, by taking away the hope at the heart of my hubris. I was sure of it. It seems absurd now, but cancer makes you stupidly superstitious. Lucky socks for chemo, pancakes on the morning of oncologist's appointments, no purple foods… Perhaps it was a futile attempt to take back some sort of control, an unspoken offering to seal a bargain with any god willing to intervene. Anyway, there's no need for that now, and I can step away without the sky falling in on Joe.

"Did I hear you mention Rodin?" Napoleon is suddenly beside us. "The Rodin Gallery in Paris is magnificent. Have you been?"

"Not yet," Joe replies, relocating us to the longer seat so that Napoleon may have the one opposite. "We have a few days in Paris before we fly out, so we shall remedy that." He signals the waiter. "What's your poison, Duplantier?"

"At this time of the morning, it is tea—orange pekoe with a dash of lemon."

"Did you pick up anything this morning?" I ask impatiently.

"I'm afraid not, Meredith. Did you drop something?"

"No, I mean when you were listening outside 16G?"

"Oh, *je vois.*" He winks at me. "I was not so much listening as overhearing."

"What's the difference?"

"The first is very rude, the second can't be helped."

"Well, then what did you overhear?" I ask.

"There are some sick and highly contagious people in the last two carriages. Fortunately, we have three heroic doctors on board who have agreed to treat the sick and quarantine themselves."

"That is noble," I agree. "Are we still going all the way to Venice? Surely there's somewhere we can stop to get them help."

"They will attempt to stop at Venice; there are the hospitals and the doctors."

"Attempt?"

"Apparently the borders are being closed to the Orient Express."

"Because of the sick passengers? But we're already in Italy."

"*Oui.*" He shrugs. "I tell you only what I overhear. We may return to Gare de l'Est."

"Is that possible though?" Joe asks. "Surely the train will need to refuel and restock with water and food."

Duplantier considers. "They can refuel and give us food and water without allowing us to disembark."

"What about the murderer?"

"They probably won't let him disembark either." I see a faint smile on Duplantier's lips.

I exhale impatiently. "I mean, will they not send authorities to find him, to arrest him, and protect the rest of the passengers?"

"There is no reason to believe he intends harm to anyone other than the resident of 16G." Duplantier speaks slowly, a policeman again. "It will probably be decided that it is not worth risking the lives of the carabinieri to apprehend him, and the lives of the Italians, should the carabinieri carry the disease out of the train with them."

"Surely it should be relatively easy for Fleischmann and his stewards to find him," Joe argues.

Duplantier shakes his head. "Even if they confined us all to our compartments, it is difficult to search a train this size with so many places to hide…restrooms, empty compartments, the bar, the dining rooms, the compartments of other passengers… There are not enough stewards to be everywhere at once."

"So, it's everyone for themselves?"

Duplantier raises his brow, but he does not reply.

"It seems to me," Joe says quietly, "that the only way to ensure that we, or our fellow passengers, don't meet the same fate as Mr. Harrington is to find out who killed him."

"I would advise against an unofficial investigation, Monsieur Penvale," Duplantier warns. "The killer of Monsieur Harrington, or Mr. Blackwell, as he is listed on the passenger manifest, could well be a professional. He will not hesitate to dispatch amateurs from Australia."

Joe nods. "Of course, you're right," he says with the dubious sincerity of a contrite politician. "We'll just mind our own business."

Duplantier looks at Joe, then me. There is nothing in his manner that indicates he believes Joe. He sighs. "Meredith, I ask you to be *des voix prônant la prudence* in the ear of your brother."

I do not need a translation. "I have always been thus, Napoleon."

Joe laughs. "In my ear, in my neck, in my—"

I ignore Joe's mistranslation and general buffoonery. I contemplate Napoleon Duplantier's plea. I'll do as he asks, but prudence is subjective. In this case the more prudent course may be to find a killer.

"You said earlier that you would explain how you know Mr. Harrington and how you knew he was aboard," I remind the Frenchman with more than a note of challenge in my voice.

"What now?" Joe begins looking from me to Duplantier. "You knew him? Are you on board because you were following him—"

Duplantier takes a breath and nods. "I have come across

Mr. Harrington, Mr. Blackwell, or as I knew of him, Monsieur Cheval, in a professional capacity."

"He was wanted in France?"

"I believe he is still sought in France."

"What did he do?"

"Many things. There is quite a list of criminal behavior attached to Monsieur Cheval."

"Was he the one that got away, then?" Joe leans forward as if he is taking notes, which I guess he is. "Are you trying to tie up loose ends, so to speak?"

Duplantier looks a little confused, and so I try to clean up Joe's metaphor hash. "Joe means, are you here, did you come on board, to arrest him?"

"I am retired, Meredith. I cannot arrest anyone anymore."

I fold my arms. "You know what I mean—what we mean."

Duplantier smiles. "Yes, I know. When I purchased my ticket, I knew he would be on board."

"How did you know?"

"An informant."

I glance at Joe. That seems an easy out, and as vague and noncommittal as the Mayfields' explanation for how they knew Harrington would be on board, but we've both heard of informants and their use by the police.

"Did you speak to him?" Joe asks.

Duplantier shakes his head. "He was dead before I had the chance."

I look directly into Duplantier's eyes. As far as I can tell, there's no deception in them...but really, how would I know? "Okay," I say. "Thank you."

"I am sorry I did not confront him the moment we came on board. All this might have been avoided." Napoleon Duplantier kisses my hand as he takes his leave. Joe grimaces. I laugh. Duplantier graciously ignores both reactions. "Remember what I said, Meredith." He regards Joe pointedly. "You must be careful."

"Of course." My reply is light. "You must not worry. Where are you off to now anyway?"

"I have discovered that there is an old colleague of mine on the train. He has invited me to join him for a drink."

"We shall see you later then."

Duplantier nods farewell and makes his way out of the Bar Car.

"Do you think he's really going to drink sherry with an old colleague?" Joe whispers.

I shake my head.

Joe stands. "Come on, old mate—before we lose him."

Chapter 7

It is actually quite tricky to follow someone on a train without being seen, or so we found. Duplantier's friend might have been in any of the compartments. We lost him fairly promptly. With no idea where he is, Joe and I decide to return to our own compartment where we can speak unheard. And so it is that we hear something from within 16G as we pass. Joe presses his ear against the door and listens. "There's someone in there," he whispers.

"We should inform—"

Joe shoves the door to 16G with his shoulder, and I note a fleeting look of surprise on his face when the door flings open.

"Napoleon!" I find myself looking at the Frenchman, who sidesteps hastily to avoid being bowled over by Joe. "What are you—?"

Duplantier places as finger on his lips. A couple of awkward seconds follow wherein we just stare at each other. Finally, the Frenchman speaks. "This isn't… I assure you… Allow me to…" He struggles for some explanation and then, apparently finding nothing even vaguely plausible, shakes his head. He motions me in.

I step into the cabin, plunging my hands into my pockets to avoid touching anything.

"How did you get in?" I demand.

Duplantier shrugs. "The lock was not difficult."

"You broke in?"

"No, no…nothing is broken. I just opened the door."

He's being coy. A policeman would know full well what breaking and entering entails. I notice now that he's wearing latex gloves. He pulls a pair out of his pocket and hands them to Joe. "Forgive me, Meredith. I do not have a pair for you."

"What are you doing?" I keep my voice low.

"I had a thought about Monsieur Harrington's body… I wished to verify."

"You know where the body is?"

"I know where it might be."

"In here?" Joe looks around the compartment dubiously. The blood has dried brown on the sheets and blankets of the lower bunk. On the walls it breaks the patterns in the marquetry, and the carpet still squelches underfoot.

"Touch nothing," Duplantier warns me. "We must not contaminate the crime scene."

"Then perhaps we shouldn't be in here—"

"Close the door, Meredith. Joe, if you'd give me some assistance with the bed."

I flatten myself against the wall without actually touching it. There is very little room to be poking about with three people involved. Napoleon beckons Joe over and directs him to stand at the foot of the bunks near the window. The Frenchman grabs the base of the bottom bunk while Joe follows suit at the other end. Together they lift and push the lower bunk up toward the wall, revealing the cavity beneath it, presumably designed to store the mattresses. We all look in, expectations high and taut. I am aware of the beating of my heart, and then the release of tension that accompanies disappointment. The space beneath the lower bunk is large enough to accommodate a body, but it is empty.

"Could someone have discovered and removed the body?" Joe ponders aloud.

Duplantier shakes his head. "There is no blood." He sighs. "There was no body here…even temporarily." He looks back into the cavity. "If there had been a body here, there would be blood."

"Unless the body was wrapped in plastic or something…" I offer.

Duplantier frowns thoughtfully. "It is possible. But it seems odd that a murderer would allow the room to be painted in blood and then wrap the body to keep the space under the bed clean."

Why hadn't I thought of that?

"Whatever happened to our missing body, it wasn't hidden here," Joe agrees.

Duplantier replaces the lower bunk. "I regret I have led you on the wild goose chase."

"It was a good idea," Joe says. "Worth a try at least."

"What happened to the guard Fleischmann was going to have stationed outside?" I ask suddenly.

"Je ne sais pas." Duplantier shakes his head. "There was no one when I came to the door."

"What did you mean when you said the lock was not difficult? Did you force it?"

He fishes what looks like a bunch of blades and picks from his pocket.

"Lockpicks?" Joe says curiously. "You take lockpicks on holiday with you? On which side of the law did you say you worked?"

Duplantier smiles. "We should go." He peels off his gloves and shoves them into his pocket. Joe does likewise, and we leave 16G pretty much as we found it. Duplantier uses his picks to lock the door behind us.

"Well, aren't you three as thick as thieves!"

"My liege!" Joe greets Elle Baird blithely as she saunters toward us. It's hard to tell how much she might have seen.

"What are you up to, Colonial?" she says in return.

"Monsieur Duplantier was just joining Meredith and me for a drink in our compartment. You must come too, though it might be a bit cozy." Joe opens the door to 16F.

The Duchess of Kinross peers in. "I see what you mean. It's just a wee space. How 'bout we all go to my quarters instead? They're larger."

Joe glances at me. We need to debrief, but what can we say? I signal my consent and Joe accepts. "Fair enough, Your Majesty. Lead the way."

The Duchess slips her arm through his, laughing, and speaks to our companion. "Monsieur Duplantier, will you come too?"

"Bien sûr, Your Grace." Duplantier casually slips his lockpicks into his pocket.

We proceed to the front of the train, where the most expensive berths are located.

The Duchess of Kinross occupies one of the six Grand Suites on the Orient Express, each of which is named and decorated in the style of a great European city. Hers is inspired by Istanbul and invokes all the opulence of the Grand Bazaar. The door to the suite opens into living quarters—a plush couch placed against a paneled wall hung with magnificent woven and embroidered rugs. On the opposite wall are a well-stocked bar and armchairs. A rolled-up yoga mat, tied with woven cord, leans against the bar, and a couple of bolsters are lined up beside it. There's a brass bowl and a kind of a wooden baton on the cabinet. The door to the bedroom is open, and through it I can see the double bed made with white linens and piled with fringed and tasseled cushions.

"Make yourself at home." Elle presses a button on the wall and within seconds a butler arrives. She orders coffee and tea as well as cakes, and Vegemite sandwiches for her Australian guests.

"Of course, Your Grace."

"You're dreaming if you reckon there's Vegemite on the Orient Express!" Joe laughs once the butler retreats.

"Stap yer haverin," Elle replies. "You and your sister are not the first Aussies on the Orient Express. I meet one every other year!"

We settle into the comfort of the Grand Suite, while Joe and Elle wager on whether the request for Vegemite sandwiches will be met. Joe loses. The butler returns with several silver trays, one of which bears a dozen crustless Vegemite finger sandwiches. I doubt Australia's national sandwich spread has ever been presented so elegantly. The Vegemite is, however, applied thickly like peanut butter, as it often is by the uninitiated. Joe grabs a butter knife and removes a good three-quarters of the spread from the surface of the bread before popping the narrow sandwich into his mouth. "That's worth losing a bet for," he announces contentedly.

Elle laughs. "So glad you think so."

The fluctuation in Elle's inflection, between broad Scots and what the English would call "posh," is fascinating. I can't tell which is the more natural. The change from one to the other occurs without pause, like two distinct people close enough to finish one another's sentences. I wonder whether it's conscious.

"Tell me, Your Grace,"—Duplantier pours coffee—"what brought you to the sixteenth carriage this morning?"

Elle looks surprised for a moment. "Ah dinnae ken, Monsieur Duplantier. I was just walking, in truth, hoping to run into someone interesting before I got too much exercise."

"Exercise?"

"Aye, I walk through the train and back a few times. It gets the blood circulating and allows me to align my inner self with the outside world. Of course, it's not so far now that the carriages on the end have been quarantined."

I pause my hand over the slice of Black Forest cake I intend to make mine. "How are they managing to maintain a quarantine? Presumably they haven't stopped feeding the people in those carriages."

"No, it's not that bad. The stewards responsible for looking after those carriages have been quarantined in with them." The duchess seems to be well informed on the matter. "Meals are left on trays in the bellows and distributed to the compartments.

There's a second kitchen on that end of the train, which makes it easy. Anything they need, aside from the freedom of the train, is delivered through the bellows."

Joe exhales. "I'm surprised there hasn't been more trouble."

"We haven't been on board twenty-four hours yet," I point out. "The trouble may be yet to come. Especially if they send us back to Paris."

Elle agrees. "It's a flamin' wonder they dinnae turn us back immediately, but I suppose we're closer to Venice than Paris."

Napoleon frowns thoughtfully. "We're not due in Venice until late this afternoon. I think Herr Fleischmann is hoping that there will be a diplomatic solution before we pull in."

We talk for a while about the missing passenger from 16G, the quarantined cars, the outbreak in Paris, whether the afflicted on board are dangerously ill, whether we should all be wearing masks, and how else the situation might be handled. Elle unrolls her yoga mat and demonstrates a couple of positions she promises will relieve the stress and tension of travel. Joe asks her about the brass bowl and, as he puts it, "the wooden cosh" on the cabinet. And this leads to the duchess demonstrating the Tibetan singing bowl, which she says surrounds the body with vibrations.

"Perhaps we could all have a sound bath later," Elle suggests brightly. "It might be interesting to see how the vibrations interact with the movement of the train."

"Sure…" Joe's eyes widen as he glances aside at me.

"I knew the moment we met that you were a fellow traveler, a spirit longing for a connection with nature." Elle clasps Joe's face in her hands. "Oh, bonnie lad, the darkness and light in me saw the darkness and light in you."

I choke on my coffee.

"Well, it is nice to be seen," Joe says finally. "But to be honest, I've never found sitting on the floor particularly comfortable and—"

Elle stops him. "You don't need to sit. We'll start you with Savasana—the corpse pose. I think it'll suit you."

"Hmmm…that sounds like a threat."

Napoleon and I drink many cups of coffee as we watch Elle teach Joe to lie down—I suspect we are all suffering the effects of a very late night. Suddenly Savasana seems very inviting, but I resist. Even if there hadn't been a murder in 16G, who would sleep more than absolutely necessary on the Orient Express? There is not a moment to be wasted in unconsciousness.

The butler steps into the room—from where, I'm not sure. He seems to simply materialize.

"Excuse me, Your Grace, Mr. Whitman requests an audience. He says it is a matter of some urgency."

Elle gets up effortlessly and gracefully. Joe puts his hands behind his head, apparently content to receive the duchess's visitor from the floor.

"Mr. Whitman and I might use the bedroom to talk," Elle decides.

The gentleman whom Antoine admits wears a pale-yellow trench coat over his suit and a matching fedora pulled low over his eyes—clearly one of those who've gone the extra mile in terms of attire for the journey. His hair is graying, at the temples at least, and his nose and eyes hawkish. He nods briefly at us all, steps into the bedroom with Elle, and pulls the partition closed.

Joe gets up instantly and hands me an empty glass.

"Don't be idiotic!" I whisper, refusing to take the glass. For some reason Joe seems to think we need to eavesdrop on everything.

"He looks like a private eye," Joe says quietly, as if that is some kind of justification.

"He's dressed like a private eye," I correct. "From the thirties. Clearly, some of our fellow passengers intend to cosplay the whole journey."

"A brilliant disguise. Who would guess the guy dressed like Dick Tracy is actually a private eye? He might know something about 16G."

"Joe, no!"

Duplantier watches us argue, clearly amused. "Monsieur Whitman is a detective in the American police."

"How do you know?" I ask, fully expecting Duplantier to share some minute and brilliant observation.

"We were introduced," he replies. "The excellent Maxim thought we might have much in common, perhaps."

"Is he here for work?" Joe asks.

Duplantier shrugs. "I assume Monsieur Whitman is traveling to Istanbul. He gives the impression of a man on the holiday."

At that moment the partition opens, and Elle and Whitman emerge. The duchess looks flustered, the American policeman, grim. He scrutinizes each of us openly.

"Duplantier," he says finally, nodding brusquely.

"Monsieur Whitman."

"Where are my manners?" Elle exclaims. "Allow me to introduce the renowned writer, Joe Penvale, and his wee sister, Meredith. Monsieur Duplantier, it seems you already know.

This is Bob Whitman, an old and dear pal, who as it happens is staying in the Venice Suite."

We exchange the usual "How d'you dos," and, in case there is any doubt he is a policeman, Whitman interrogates us on what we're doing on board the Orient Express and more particularly in the Istanbul Suite.

We answer honestly. There's no reason to be evasive, even if the questions are put somewhat curtly.

"What brings a member of the Chicago PD on the Orient Express?" Joe responds in kind. "In the Venice Suite, no less!"

Duplantier is clearly surprised. He knows he didn't mention the specifics of Whitman's Americanism. Whitman himself regards Joe suspiciously.

"Joe's publishers are based in Chicago," I say more for Napoleon's benefit than anything else. "It's the one American accent he can pick."

Whitman seems to soften a little. "If you're gonna take a fancy train, you may as well book a frunchroom."

Napoleon Duplantier's brow arches. I can feel his need to point out that Venice is not in France, held back by courtesy and perhaps pity for the American's apparently unfortunate understanding of geography. I've spent enough time with Joe in Chicago to know *frunchroom* is a term for a kind of parlor stocked with the best furniture and kept for the eyes of guests.

"The duchess tells me you are all staying in 16?" Whitman continues.

It takes me a moment to connect. "Oh, you mean the carriage. Yes, Monsieur Duplantier is nearly our neighbor."

"When did you last see the guy they had stationed outside 16G?"

We're all a little startled by the question. I wonder if we were seen entering Harrington's cabin. "I never actually saw anybody guarding the door," I volunteer in the end. "If there was anyone, they were gone when we last went back to Carriage 16 at about eleven."

"Why do you ask?" Joe presses.

"Because the body of a steward has just been found in the restroom in 16. Stabbed to death, apparently."

We all sit up, shocked and tense.

"Bloody hell!" Joe speaks first. "How do you know?"

"I just dropped by 16. Saw the commotion."

"My God. Do you know the steward's name?" I am gripped by a sudden horror that it is Maxim.

Bob Whitman shakes his head. "No idea. The management wants us all back in our own cabins… So that they can do a head count, I guess—in case anyone else has been done in. I just came by to check on Elle."

Joe glances at me. "Fair enough. I guess we should be going then." He turns to Elle. "Thank you for having us, Your Royal Grandness." My brother's made-up titles are getting progressively more stupid. "Are you going to be all right on your own here?" Joe asks more soberly.

Elle clasps his hands affectionately in hers. "Of course, dear cheeky man. Bob's just next door, after all." Elle gazes at him for a beat more than necessary before sending us on our way. "Away ye go, then. Be careful."

Chapter 8

The moment we leave the Istanbul Suite, we are met by a steward who requests we return to our respective cabins and await further instructions. "Lunch might be delayed today due to an emergency on board," he says. We don't question him, aware that he has just lost a colleague. Joe grabs my hand and squeezes it briefly.

Getting back to 16F from the head of the train where the Grand Suites are located takes a while. The passengers are frightened, excited, and outraged in equal numbers; some are all three. Several people have congregated in the dining cars through which we must pass, as though those communal carriages are de facto town halls. We are surrounded by a cacophony of conversation and protest about the murders, demands to know why the train is still running or why it isn't running as normal. At the no-man's-land between 15 and 16, we are collected by Maxim.

I do not let my relief and happiness show—a steward, even if he is not Maxim, has been murdered, after all. We are escorted to our cabins separately—those of us who have not demanded accommodations in other cabins, that is. As far as I can tell, that is only the two of us and Duplantier. Joe and I are guided past the now-sealed restroom and 16G.

"Please do not leave your cabin," Maxim says. He looks tight-lipped and pale. "If you require anything, just ring for a steward and someone will be with you as soon as possible." We wait while he checks that our cabin is empty.

"Thank you," Joe says.

"We're so sorry for the loss of your colleague, Maxim," I add earnestly.

The steward smiles sadly. "It is a terrible thing."

"He was your friend."

"We are all family here."

Maxim looks so forlorn, so heartbroken, that I embrace him before decorum can stop the impulse. I can feel him trembling, and so I do not pull away until it stops. "I wish there was something we could do, Maxim."

"You are very kind, Signorina Meredith." He smiles wanly. "I must proceed…find new cabins for the other passengers."

"Do you have that many spare cabins?"

Maxim frowns. "Not prepared for passengers. Perhaps we will squeeze some into staff quarters or ask them to share until we reach Venice." He straightens his shoulders. "We will make them comfortable somehow."

"We have no doubt," Joe says.

"I must go," he says, turning to leave. "We are not supposed to have favorites."

He closes the door behind him and locks us in. Of course,

we can unlock it from the inside, so the act is more a reiteration of the request that we stay put. I curl up on the seat beside the window. We're still in the mountains. The snow-covered landscape seems different now—stark and isolated.

"You okay?" Joe stretches out and opens his laptop. "You seem a bit freaked."

"Aren't you?"

He rubs the back of his head as he considers. "More startled than freaked."

"And the difference is…"

"It's a matter of degree, I suppose." He taps a few keys idly. "So, assuming the steward they found in the restroom was the poor guy stationed outside 16G, the question still remains, where did the murderer put Harrington's body?"

"We don't know for sure it was Harrington's blood we saw next door," I note.

Joe nods. "I suppose the head count they're conducting will help work that out. We'll see who's missing." He shrugs. "It could be that Harrington is the murderer, that he killed someone in his cabin and disposed of the body before going on the run."

"On the run? In a train?"

"As I said, we might know more after they finish this head count."

I smile despite myself, despite everything. "Joe, you don't really think they're going to share that information with us? You are a writer, not a *world-famous* detective."

Joe sighs and changes the subject. "Does it seem to you that there are an awful lot of people on this train who seem to be interested in what happened to Harrington?"

"There do seem to be a lot of police officers on board," I reply carefully. "I suppose one should expect them to be interested in a murder." I shrug. "We're not exactly indifferent either."

"No, I suppose not." He grimaces. "Lightning has now struck twice in the vicinity of 16G. Do you want to ask them to move us?"

I shake my head. "I might, if I were on my own," I admit, "but I'm not, and I don't really fancy sharing a space the size of this with another couple of people, even if it is for just a few more hours."

"There is that," Joe concurs, but he presses. "You're sure? You're not just ignoring your wiser self to keep me happy?"

"When have I ever done that, Joe?"

"More often than you think I know." He lets it lie and returns to his manuscript. I find my sketchbook and pass the time drawing. I work quickly, figuratively, trying to capture Joe at his laptop, his weight forward, his eyes fixed on the screen, details of the cabin around him. To me, he looks strong again, though he is still a little thinner than he used to be, his jawline sharper. There is something different about his eyes too—unchanged in color, but darker somehow. A shadow.

There is a popular myth that twins can read each other's minds. For Joe and me, not so. I've never found him easy to read, even now when I watch him more closely than I did before the diagnosis. To be honest, I'm never sure what he's thinking until he tells me.

"Did you notice, Meri," Joe says without looking up, "that the window above the booth in the Istanbul Suite opens?"

I hadn't really, although I do recall the window. It was a little over a meter wide, about half a meter tall, and set high in the wall. "If Mr. Harrington was anything but slim, you'd have a hard time squeezing his body through there—not to mention that you'd need to be pretty strong to lift him that high." I watch as he types. "Are you writing the window into your manuscript?" I ask.

"Sure."

"Why?"

"It's material." He sits back. "And it's life."

I roll my eyes. "Washing your socks is life. This is a bit more."

He smiles at me. "Washing socks would make a very dull book, Meri."

"This is not dull," I accept. "I just don't know how you can process it so fast into a story."

"You're assuming my work is processed," he replies, laughing. "I don't always know what it means when I write it, Meri. I don't always know where it's going." He looks at his screen and shakes his head. "This one's a bit like a chronological collage with pieces torn from life and memory and random thoughts. Hopefully it won't end up looking like a mess."

"I'm glad you're writing again." I return to my sketch. "It tells me you'll be all right."

His brow arches. "Does it?"

"Doesn't it?"

He says nothing for a breath. Then, "No, you're right. If I can write, everything important works."

A knock on the door interrupts. It's Maxim with a passenger

list, on which he ticks off our names. The Penvales at least are accounted for.

"Is anybody missing?" Joe asks.

"So far, only the gentleman in 16G, but there are many carriages to be checked." Maxim shakes his head balefully. "We have never lost a passenger before."

"What? Never?" Joe asks, clearly surprised. "Surely passengers have disembarked early or been accidentally left behind when they stepped out to take air on a platform?"

Maxim shrugs. "One does not deal so lightly with a berth on the Orient Express. It is not a ticket for the Tube. At the very least we are told where to forward luggage."

Joe leans past me to look out the window. "We're slowing down." He turns back to Maxim. "Are we stopping?"

"We can't be." I look out at the snow from track to peak. "We're in the middle of nowhere."

Maxim joins us at the window. The train is definitely slowing down. Maxim is very nearly successful in hiding his alarm. "I will find out what's happening," he promises. "Please remain here until I return."

Chapter 9

We don't watch the steward leave, our eyes glued to the window. We can see vehicles now—military trucks full of armed soldiers and smaller vehicles with mirror-tinted windows. The Express grinds to a stop at what might be a station but looks more like a shack beside the track. The platform, such as it is, is only about two carriages long and packed densely with soldiers, rifles to shoulders, in what look like gas masks.

"What the hell is going on?" Joe murmurs.

Fleischmann steps onto the platform, hand outstretched. The reaction is sharp and immediate. Half a dozen soldiers train their weapons on the manager of the Orient Express. Instructions in Italian are shouted through a megaphone. I hear myself gasp, and I instinctively pull back from the window. Without specifically being able to hear anyone, I am aware of alarm and confusion coursing through the carriages as we all watch from our cabins.

Fleischmann steps back onto the train, his hands up. Joe's

cheek is pressed against the glass. "Bugger… They're going to turn us around!"

"What? Are you sure?" I place my face on the window beside his. The line of soldiers now extends the entire length of the train, their weapons trained on doors of the carriages.

"Well, no, I can't be sure, but I reckon that's what they're up to." Joe taps the glass. "They're making sure we don't step off this train."

"Because of the infectious carriages?"

"Expect so." Joe shrugs. "We knew this was possible…didn't expect the guns, though."

Involuntarily, I shudder. This is getting frightening. As much as we'd discussed being unable to disembark, I never really expected that it would come to pass. The Orient Express had, after all, crossed the border into Italy sometime last night. That we would be turned back in the mountains before we came into Venice speaks of panic, of decisions being made in fear. Perhaps we have been distracted by murder and missing bodies, when the real danger had boarded with us in Paris.

"Take a breath, Meri."—Did I mention that though I can't read Joe's thoughts, he does, at times, seem to have an uncanny insight into mine?—"They acted pretty quickly to isolate the people who got sick, and we are completely up-to-date with vaccines."

"We all mingled freely on the platform at Gare de l'Est." I'm whispering, and I don't know why. Perhaps it is less real if I keep it between us. "Joe, you've lost half your liver and part of a lung. You can't get COVID."

Joe grabs my shoulders. "Meri. Look at me. I have still so

many antibiotics, steroids, and God-knows-what in my system that any intelligent virus is going to infect a more vulnerable host."

"Viruses are not intelligent, Joe; they don't choose dance partners." I'm still whispering, but stridently.

"Meri, you're losing it. Stop now."

"But—"

"I am no more vulnerable to infection than you, than anyone on this train or this planet, for that matter. This is not a good situation, but it's not me we should be worrying about."

I exhale. He's right. I get a grip. "I know. God, those poor people… It'll take us another day to get back to Paris."

Joe beckons me over to the window and directs my attention to containers being loaded onto the train by some kind of machine operated from the platform. A number were branded with logos we recognize as medical. "Antivirals or whatever the latest remedy is. The chefs are probably lacing the food with it, too. They're not exactly setting the train on fire and running us out of town."

"Not exactly."

A knock at the door, and Maxim is back. Napoleon Duplantier is with him. "Signorina Penvale, would you mind coming with me? Herr Fleischmann would like that you come to the dining car."

"For lunch?"

"He will explain."

"What about Joe?"

"Herr Fleischmann asked only for you."

I fold my arms across my chest. "People are being murdered. I'm not leaving Joe on his own."

Joe groans. "Meri, for God's sake—"

"Signor Penvale will be perfectly safe—"

I shrug. "Take it or leave it, Maxim. I don't know what Herr Fleischmann wants with me, but I'm not going without Joe."

Duplantier intervenes. "Perhaps Joe might accompany us for now. Certainly, it is natural for him to be concerned as to why his sister is required—"

"But she will be with us," Maxim protests. "No harm will come to her."

"Unless one of you is the murderer, of course," Joe mutters.

"Joe can always return to his cabin if Herr Fleischmann objects to his presence," Duplantier adds before Maxim can respond to the notion.

Maxim hesitates but eventually relents. "Very well. But we must hurry."

Joe grabs his laptop as we leave. It's easier to walk through the carriages with the train stationary and all the passengers locked in their cabins. And we can see that there are soldiers the entire length of the train on both sides with their guns still trained on the doors.

"Are they making us return to Paris?" I direct the question at Maxim.

Maxim nods. "The borders have been closed. We passed into Italy just before the barriers were put in place. So they send us back."

"Because of the Paris variant?" I press.

"It is a bad one, they say," Maxim replies. "And the world is vigilant for disaster. At least this kind."

"And so, they are just turning us around?" Joe's eyes scan the military line. "Can a train even do a U-turn?"

Maxim smiles. "There is another engine on the other end of the train. The last carriage will become the first and so forth, and we will travel back as we came. The quarantined carriages will have to be moved to a side track, then reattached, so that they will be on the tail of the train again, and we will be able to access the engine room without having to pass through them. The company is making sure we are restocked with food and water, and the Italian government is ensuring we have medicines. It is really just a minor inconvenience."

Duplantier laughs. "You are an admirable and loyal servant, Maxim. Your employer would be very happy, I am sure, with the perspective you paint for us. But you have forgotten about the murderer."

Maxim sighs. "I do not forget, Monsieur Duplantier. But what can you do? This is the Orient Express—where even murder is glamourous and cannot be allowed to interfere with the comfort of our passengers. We must carry on."

"Are you not scared, Maxim?" I ask gently, aware that carrying on has already proved fatal for one of the stewards.

"A little, I am scared," Maxim replies, "but more I am angry, and I am ready to defend my passengers."

"And we, you, mate," Joe says firmly.

"Do you know why Herr Fleischmann has summoned us?" I change the subject.

"He will explain." Maxim directs us into Étoile du Nord. The dining car has not yet been laid for lunch, though it is not empty. Indeed, there are fellow passengers seated at most of the tables. I recognize Abigay, who smiles and waves. Bob Whitman nods curtly as he sips coffee with Elle Baird, the Duchess of

Kinross. The Mayfield sisters share a table toward the back of the carriage. There are also people with whom we are not particularly acquainted, including the gentleman in the green plaid suit who put on something akin to a floor show in the bar the night before.

"If you'll take a seat, Herr Fleischmann will be here shortly to explain."

We slip in beside and opposite Abigay. "Do you know what's going on?" I whisper. "Why are we here?"

"I'm sure I don't know, pet." Abigay glances around the dining car. "It's gone three, so I'm assuming they've not decided to start serving lunch. Still, a few sandwiches wouldn't hurt."

I assume someone on the Express's staff must have overheard because plates of savory pastries and petite cakes are brought out with fresh pots of coffee. I am surprisingly hungry despite the multicourse breakfast with which we started the day. I help myself to a steaming parcel of spiced potato as I contemplate how much has changed since that morning, when Joe and I shared a table with two old ladies who'd boarded the Orient Express in pursuit of a swindler. The blood-soaked cabin beside ours, the missing passenger, the murdered steward, and now we are to return to Paris in a train sealed to contain an entirely different type of killer. Somehow, time on board has stretched to accommodate it all, but perhaps that's simply the nature of travel on something like the Orient Express. We embark determined to take in and savor every ordinary moment and detail, aware of the train's history, its place in literature, and so each passing minute seems to contain the conscious experience of sixty. And then the extraordinary is imposed on top of that, and it feels like we've been on board both forever and for just that instant.

"You're a million miles away, pet." Abigay's crooning voice brings me gently back.

"I was thinking about something Joe said about old stories being characters in new ones." I smile. "I wonder what they would say about this."

"The old stories?"

"The one that most easily comes to mind would probably wonder why we're not politely questioning the suspects," Joe says, grinning.

"What suspects?"

"The ones in this car, of course. I expect that's why we've been gathered."

"Us?" Abigay pulls back. "Murder suspects. Stuff and non-sense! I'm a detective on my honeymoon!"

"Well, perhaps you should conduct the interrogations," Joe suggests. "Napoleon here could be your Watson."

Duplantier sips his coffee thoughtfully. "Is that what you intended?" he asks Joe. "When you said the old stories are characters."

Joe stops fooling around. "Not quite. I just meant that we are influenced by the stories of trains that we have read or even viewed, in the past—they are imported into what happens now, they affect how we react and behave." He looks around at the other passengers in Étoile du Nord. "Has it occurred to you, for example, that everyone is dealing with this all in a manner that is very civilized? There is at least one murderer on board, and we are having high tea in the dining car. There is no panic, no attempts to flee the train. It's as if we are all waiting to be gathered for a grand reveal during which each of us is considered as a suspect before the murderer is finally exposed."

I laugh. "I've always wondered why the murderer accepts the invitation to the reveal. Surely it would be more sensible to decline and run like hell!"

"They're not always the sharpest, pet," Abigay confides.

"It is in the nature of a murderer to bury the body," Duplantier offers. There is just the hint of a smile on his lips. "Not necessarily beneath the ground, but under six feet of lies and misdirection." His smile broadens now. "Attending a meeting called by the presiding detective is the way he stands back and admires his handiwork."

Joe nods. "It's a final challenge of wits. By remaining, the murderer pits his ability to evade detection against the detective's investigative prowess… Of course, that's only in books. In real life, I imagine he'd run, or shoot the detective."

"Unless he can't," I point out. "Whoever killed Mr. Harrington and/or the poor steward hasn't had the opportunity to get off this train."

"Aye, love." Abigay agrees. "I don't envy Mr. Fleischmann dealing with this lot. I expect he'll have more than the usual number of complaints to deal with when this is all over."

I gaze out of the window at the soldiers and vehicles. Flashing lights cast colors onto the snow. The outside of the carriages is being sprayed with something—probably an industrial-strength disinfectant. It's all a little surreal. Like we are in a bubble removed from the world though we can see it from the glamourous mobile prison into which we have been incarcerated with a murderer and disease.

Chapter 10

Fleischmann enters Étoile du Nord. He looks grave. Immediately he is barraged with questions in English and French, Italian and German. I can only understand the first, but I suppose they are all demanding to know what is happening.

Fleischmann holds up his palms, calling with careful courtesy for calm. "Ladies and gentlemen, you will understand if I speak English for the benefit of our Australian friends."

I glance at Joe, vaguely embarrassed, but there's no point denying that we only speak English. Australia is an island— technically two islands. We share no borders and so are somewhat insular in terms of language. In Europe we must seem uneducated.

"As you may have already gathered," Fleischmann continues, "the Orient Express is being turned around and sent back to Paris. There is significant concern about a new variant of the coronavirus emanating from Paris, and borders across Europe have been closed to ensure it does not spread beyond France."

There is a murmur through the dining car, but I expect most of us have already worked this out.

"It will take us about twenty-four hours to return to Gare de l'Est. Arrangements are being made to ensure that you are all as comfortable as possible. However, as you probably know, there have been incidents that lead us to believe there is a murderer on board."

"Have you still not found him?" The gentleman behind the question sits alone. He wears a brown corduroy jacket with elbow patches and speaks with a strong Welsh accent.

"He has eluded us, as has the body of his victim," Fleischmann replies with a frankness that surprises me. "But there has been no opportunity to leave the train, so we know he remains on board."

Penelope Mayfield speaks up. "Can I ask why you have gathered us here, Conductor? This particular group of people, I mean." She looks around the dining car, smiling warmly. "Not that you aren't all charming."

A couple of voices support the question.

Fleischmann nods. "You are all either current or retired members of law enforcement, or have"—here he nods at the Mayfields—"a connection with the passenger who occupied 16G. We hoped that we might prevail upon you to assist."

"Assist how?"

"The passenger in 16G has gone missing; the cabin appears to be the scene of a violent crime, and it will be at least twenty-four hours before any authorities can take charge of the situation. For the safety of our passengers, we hoped that you might assist us, advise us on what can be done, what should be done."

"You are assuming that none of us is the murderer," Elle Baird points out archly.

"More hoping," Fleischmann admits.

Another murmur through the car.

I stand up. "Herr Fleischmann, why am I here?"

"You are a lawyer, Miss Penvale. We thought you might ensure that we do not compromise any evidence."

For a fleeting moment I consider confessing that I am a corporate lawyer. If they wanted advice on international swap agreements, I could help, but criminal evidence is not my area. But Joe nudges me with his foot. I meet his eye, and I see the barely perceptible shake of his head, so I say nothing.

"How do you propose to handle this, Conductor?" Penelope again.

"Well, I hope I might introduce you all to each other, and then perhaps those of you who wish will discuss what would be best, and so advise."

There is general agreement in the dining car—or at least no one leaves or protests.

We begin with a round of introductions, each of us standing to give an account of ourselves.

The Mayfields talk at length about their membership of the Lower Slaughter Civic Society and the lodger who stole the funds for the Lower Slaughter nursing home. "We know that Mr. Harrington, our erstwhile lodger, was the passenger in 16G, and so he is either your missing body or your missing murderer, Conductor," Penny finishes.

I notice that Fleischmann flinches just slightly every time she calls him "Conductor," though he maintains a polite silence.

Duplantier introduces himself as a recently retired member of the gendarmerie in which he served for twelve years, and Elle Baird explains that before her marriage to the Duke of Kinross she worked with a number of government agencies about which she cannot speak. Bob Whitman, in contrast, is frank about his thirty years with the Chicago PD and his recent work as a consultant for the FBI. Detective Inspector Abigay Williams declares that she is just that but concedes jurisdiction to Duplantier on the grounds that the first murder, at least, probably took place while the Orient Express was still in France.

A brief discussion about jurisdiction ensues until the gentleman who had worn the green plaid suit the night before takes the floor. Today he's wearing a striped blazer and a straw boater. He announces that he is Buster Sartori, a private investigator from Los Angeles. He cites membership of various associations that, aside from the Mystery Writers of America, I've never heard of before. Buster Sartori magnanimously volunteers to lead the investigation, pointing out his Italian heritage and the fact we are currently not far from Venice. Everyone seems to ignore the offer. Joe glances at me and mouths "idiot."

The gentleman with the Welsh accent who sits alone is Aled Rees. He declares a background in international and domestic terrorism. In contrast to Sartori, he is concise and to the point and claims no jurisdiction.

And finally, there is Ajeet Singh, a small, handsome man in a dark suit and traditional pagri. He speaks with an accent that is mostly English with an occasional hint of the subcontinent. He is evidently with Scotland Yard and discloses that the possible first victim is a person of interest in a number of ongoing fraud investigations.

I am so engrossed it is only when Fleischmann clears his throat that I realize I haven't introduced myself and what I have to offer. I stand nervously and decide to drag Joe into it. "I'm Meredith Penvale, and this is my brother, Joe. I'm a lawyer. We happen to be in 16F beside…16G."

Abigay nods emphatically. "The Penvale brother and sister, and Monsieur Duplantier are on either side of the crime scene. They may have noticed something…a noise, a smell…"

"Did you meet the man in 16G?" Ajeet Singh demands.

Joe answers. "Yes, when we first came on board. He was a bit of a prick."

"He was not very friendly," I correct, glaring at Joe. We're not at a pub in Wagga Wagga, for God's sake!

"What did he look like?" Aled Rees asks.

I think for a beat, trying to conjure an image of the man. "He was shorter than Joe, dark hair and a full beard. He was wearing a dinner suit when we saw him last."

"He was slightly pigeon-toed." Joe stands and turns his right foot in to demonstrate, in case the term is unfamiliar. "His shoes were scuffed, but his dinner suit seemed brand new. I think his eyes were blue."

"You spoke to him for some time, then?" Abigay is sharp though not hostile.

"Not at all. He didn't even say hello. As I say, a bit of a—" He glances at me. "He was unfriendly."

"You seem to have noticed quite a lot for a passing encounter," Singh says, frowning. "Did you have a particular interest in him?"

"Not really. The corridor is quite narrow so we had to wait for him to get out of the road before we could go to dinner. I had time to notice as he walked down the carriage. Of course, none of these details are any use in telling us what happened to his body."

Joe has apparently decided not to mention that it is his practice to make mental notes about people in order to turn them into characters—possibly because he intends to do the same with our current company. I'm concerned that it makes him seem vaguely suspicious, but I suppose I can alibi him.

"We went to dinner after that," I volunteer. "It was about two in the morning when we finally returned to our cabin. The door to 16G was shut. It was still shut when we went to breakfast."

"And Monsieur Duplantier?" Bob Whitman leans back in his chair and meets the Frenchman's eye.

"I regret I have nothing to add. I did not meet the gentleman at all, and I heard nothing."

I remember then, Napoleon Duplantier trying to open the door to 16G when I was returning from the restroom. I wonder if he's forgotten or if he's left out the detail intentionally. It might be important that Gregory Harrington did not wake or make a sound when someone was trying to open his door. But there's no way I can remind Napoleon here, in front of a car of detectives, without seeming like I was accusing him of an unreliable memory at least, so I say nothing.

Clarice and Penelope Mayfield stand.

"I think this is an appropriate time to share what we know about Mr. Harrington," Clarice says primly.

They take us through what they know about the gentleman, the fact that he was their lodger and his embezzlement of the Lower Slaughter Civic Society.

"I must say he did not have a beard when he lived with us," Penelope declares. "We wouldn't have taken in a man who wasn't at least clean-shaven."

"When did you last see him?" Joe asks.

"Oh, well, what do you think, Clarice? We spoke to him at the sod-turning ceremony for the nursing home…though I don't remember him at the tea afterward. That was about seven months ago. Yes, it was the end of April. That's if you don't count photographs. We have a photograph of him on the piano, and we see that every day at home. Oh, we did catch sight of him in London about two months ago, but he vanished before we could apprehend him or, rather, summon a constable to do so. And then, wouldn't you know it—"

"So, two months ago?" Joe tries to dig an answer out of the old lady's extended response. "He might have grown a beard in that time, I suppose. But can we be sure the man in 16G was Gregory Harrington?"

"Of course he was!" Clarice says affronted. "We've been looking for him since he left Lower Slaughter. We tracked him here."

"But you haven't actually laid eyes on him in two months."

"He has left very distinct footprints, on paper and online. Gregory Harrington bought a ticket on the Orient Express and was allocated 16G, as I'm sure the conductor will verify."

A couple of seconds pass before Fleischmann remembers that when she says "Conductor" she's talking about him. "A ticket was bought by a Mr. Gregory *Blackwell*, traveling alone. We did put him in 16G."

Penelope swats away the discrepancy. "One of his aliases."

"You are holding his passport, are you not, Herr Fleischmann?" Duplantier settles the argument or at least offers a way that it might be settled. "Perhaps we can use his passport photograph to check if Monsieur Blackwell is in fact Monsieur Harrington or anyone else?"

Of course! I'd forgotten that the Orient Express was holding all our passports.

Fleischmann stands and summons Maxim. He speaks to him in Italian, but I presume he is telling him to fetch the passports. The steward leaves the dining car briskly.

"We shall also need your passenger manifest," Duplantier says, "and a list of the stewards and chefs and other employees."

Maxim turns around and nods. "I shall bring them, Monsieur Duplantier."

Fleischmann's heavy brow furrows slightly, but he does not object. I expect he has the burden of balancing passenger privacy against security. Ever thoughtful of the comfort of his passengers, he suggests that now, while we wait, might be an opportunity to take a break, though he requests that we move about the train in pairs. The gathering breaks up to use restrooms, stretch legs, to try to get enough coverage to make phone calls. Joe opens his laptop, and I pour myself another coffee.

Aled Rees clears his throat as he approaches Fleischmann. "Herr Fleischmann, can I ask what you propose to do about the people in the quarantined carriages, not to mention the ordinary passengers confined to cabins?"

"I'm not sure I understand, Mr. Rees," Fleischmann replies uncertainly. "All our passengers have been very cooperative and understanding."

"They thought then that they would be confined until Venice. Now you're telling them they have another twenty-four hours on board. Confinement, however luxurious, is confinement. I would expect some agitation, perhaps even panic. They will become convinced that information is being kept from them, there will theories of conspiracy, and perhaps they will resist. It is best you be prepared."

I join the conversation. "How are the infected passengers, Herr Fleischmann? How bad is this delay for them?"

"We are taking care of them as best we can," Fleischmann replies, "and maintaining the quarantine to protect the rest of our passengers. Six passengers are suffering symptoms, but as far as I am aware, no one is in imminent danger."

"Not from the virus, in any case." Whitman walks back into Étoile du Nord in time to overhear. Most of the select group have now returned. "But we do have a killer on board. And it seems we can't even find the body, let alone the murderer."

Joe addresses Fleischmann now. "Are there any luggage or supply cars in which a body may have been stowed?"

Fleischmann shakes his head. "All your larger bags, those that cannot be accommodated in your cabin, are sent ahead by truck. The supply cars have already been searched."

"A body can't just disappear. Could it have been thrown from the train?"

Fleischmann exhales. "The windows in the cabins open, but one could not get an entire body through the opening."

Buster Sartori points at Fleischmann excitedly. "What if they cut it up? The body, I mean. What if the body was cut up and tossed out the window... There could be body parts all along the track."

"Cut it up?" Ajeet Singh too has returned to the dining carriage. "That's absurd, man."

"Perhaps not," Joe whispers.

Duplantier nods in agreement.

Penelope Mayfield calls out. "That would explain the state of his cabin!"

"What do you mean, his cabin?" Abigay looks sharply at Duplantier, Joe, and me. The dining car buzzes with conversation, as those who are unaware of the manner in which 16G was found are informed by those who are not.

Joe tells Abigay, "16G was splattered with blood."

"How much blood?"

Joe shrugs. "About a dismemberment's worth, I guess."

I shove him.

"What?"

"A little tact, Joe!"

He rolls his eyes.

"We've not got time for that." Abigay sides with Joe. "Was there blood 'round the window?"

Duplantier nods.

"And outside the window?"

"We did not open the window," Duplantier replies. "It would have compromised the scene."

Abigay stands. "Well, we had better be inspecting the scene now before too much time gets away."

Duplantier holds up a hand. *"Attendez un moment."* He looks around. "We are all here, I think, but we should still wait for the return of the steward with the passports."

Abigay pauses and then takes her seat again. "Where is that man? How long can it take to fetch a few passports?"

Joe checks his watch. "They're probably in a safe or something. Maybe I should go find him." He stands now. "I'll ask Fleischmann where he sent him and go check."

"Yes, Mr. Penvale, you check that everything is fine," Abigay says, waving him on approvingly.

"I'm sure Fleischmann could send another steward or I could—" I begin.

"Nah, I'm surplus to requirements anyway." Joe braces my shoulder. "You stay and chat to the professionals."

I let him go. Joe's right. It won't take two of us to fetch Maxim. I see Fleischmann nod when Joe speaks to him, so I expect he too has begun to wonder what's keeping his steward. Joe sidesteps Clarice Mayfield at the door and sets off.

Duplantier calls the various detectives and investigators to attention and suggests they discuss how they might approach the case at hand. He proposes that once they have used the passports to establish the identity of the passenger in 16G, they fingerprint the cabin to ensure that information is preserved. Abigay confirms that she has a fingerprint kit with her, and it is decided that she and Duplantier will dust the cabin for prints. Duplantier proposes that following that, they proceed by each inspecting the crime scene and then collating their impressions and observations. There is general consent, and a roster is drawn up. The dining car becomes a makeshift incident room, and polite arguments are conducted about the order in which individual inspections of the scene should be handled. I'm not really sure I want to look around the murder scene again, so I say little. It's Duplantier who suggests that I should be present throughout to ensure they all observe some form of legal protocol and so there will be a thread of consistency.

"Madame Meredith Penvale is an Australian, and so we will avoid any arguments about jurisdiction if she is willing to oversee the inspections of 16G."

I pull Duplantier aside and whisper, "Napoleon, I've never—"

"Just keep your eyes on them," he replies under his breath. "Just because these people are investigators doesn't mean they are not suspects."

"What about me? How do you know I'm not—"

He smiles. "I'll keep eyes on you. Don't kill anybody."

I groan. But we'll be back in Paris in a day. I can help out till then, I suppose. "Yes, okay," I say to the group in general. "Are we all agreed that we touch nothing unless I approve and it's recorded and tagged?" I add with my best impersonation of a forensic crime television cop. It seems to work.

A commotion in the adjoining car diverts and seizes our attention in the same moment. Shouting in Italian and then Joe's voice. "He's dead. I tried…but he's dead."

Chapter 11

Joe enters Étoile du Nord before I can make it past the press of people also trying to find out what is happening. He has blood on his hands.

I push past Sartori and Whitman to reach him. "Joe, are you—"

"I'm fine, Meri. This is Maxim's blood."

Fleischmann heads out, turning briefly to speak to Duplantier. "Monsieur Duplantier, will you manage things here until I get back?" He addresses the room. "Ladies and gentlemen, please remain in the dining car for the time being."

He leaves, taking a couple of stewards with him.

There is a shocked silence in his wake. Then Duplantier speaks. "Would you like to sit down, Joe?"

Joe nods.

Duplantier pulls out a chair for Joe. I take the one next to it. "What happened, Joe?"

Joe shakes his head like he's trying to dislodge an image from his mind's eye. "Herr Fleischmann told me that they keep the passports in a safe in the carriage that holds the second kitchen, so I figured I'd find Maxim there or on his way back." He clenches his hands on the table. The blood marks the crisp white napery. I put my hand on his arm. He smiles fleetingly at me, letting me know he's okay, and for a moment I'm taken back to that same smile before chemotherapy and surgeries. It tells me only that Joe doesn't want to scare me.

"And did you?" Abigay asks.

"Not in the corridors. I found Maxim in the kitchen carriage—there's a cabin in there. Not a sleeper. It has a couple of desks, a safe, and boxes. Maxim was covered in blood. I tried to get him breathing again but…I think he was dead. Another steward came in and started screaming in Italian… I think he thought I'd killed Maxim. So, I came back here because I thought it would be easier than trying to make him understand…"

They start with the questions now.

"How was the steward killed?" Whitman is blunt.

"How would I know?"

"Was there a gunshot wound, had his throat been cut?"

"There was a wound in his neck…more a stab than a cut. There may have been others, but I didn't examine him."

"What precisely did you do?" Buster Sartori's voice is raised.

"I tried to give him CPR," Joe replies.

"Did you call for help?" Elle Baird says more gently.

"I must have… I think so… I was just trying to get his heart beating."

"Do you remember, Joe, if the safe was open?" Napoleon Duplantier is specific.

"Yes."

"Did you see a murder weapon, or something that might have been a murder weapon?" Ajeet Singh, too, is interested in the crime scene, or what Joe might remember of it.

"No."

"What took so long, man? Why didn't you come back for help immediately?" Aled Rees brings the questions back to Joe's actions.

"I was trying to help him…to resuscitate him… I shouted while I was doing it, I think, but no one seems to have heard till the steward finally came in."

"Would you like a cup of tea? You look like you could use a cup of tea," Penelope Mayfield asks.

"You look like you could use something a good deal stronger." Elle slaps a flask down in front of him. It's silver and bears the crest of the Duchy of Kinross. Joe picks it up and studies the crest vaguely.

"Joe." I squeeze his arm. "Are you in shock?"

Whitman snorts. "You're asking him to diagnose himself!"

I don't respond. The last eighteen months with its thousands of blood pressure, heart rate, and temperature checks have left Joe very good at knowing what his body is doing. We'd relieve the boredom of long hospital stays by betting on his vital signs. "Joe?" I ask again.

"No, heart rate is normal, so's my breathing, and I'm not sweaty. I'm shocked but not in shock—it was a helluva thing. Poor Maxim."

"And you're sure he was dead when you found him?" Aled Rees presses.

"Well, I wasn't sure when I found him…hence the CPR… but I'm sure now that he was. There was no blood spurting, though I'm pretty sure at least one of his carotid arteries had been pierced."

"At least one of his carotid arteries," Singh repeats thoughtfully. "What exactly do you do, Mr. Penvale…or is it Dr. Penvale?"

Joe glances at me. Another time we might have laughed. In our parents' fondest and often articulated hopes, Joe would have gone to medical school, which if you really knew him—our parents apparently didn't—was an utterly stupid idea. Joe can't resist pressing red buttons, experimenting, fiddling just to see what would happen… He can't even follow a recipe. The very thing that serves him as a novelist would be distinctly problematic, even dangerous, in a doctor.

"I'm a writer, Mr. Singh," Joe explains in response to an unspoken question, perhaps suspicion. "I write crime fiction… I killed a character by cutting his throat in my last book. I researched the anatomy so I could write that scene. It's why I know there's more than one carotid—I'm assuming that's the knowledge you find unusual. It's easily googled."

Singh nods. "Is that the expertise you offer this group, Mr. Penvale? That of the mystery writer?"

"Not really, mate. I just tagged along with my sister."

Abigay is gazing out of the window on the other side. "I expect they are going to have to let us disembark now. The investigation will be in the hands of the Arma dei Carabinieri." She wiggles her head a little as she names the Italian police force.

"Do you think so?" I ask hopefully.

"Well, there's no question that this lad, Maxim, was murdered in Italy. While we were in this station, no less!"

I join her at the window. The soldiers are still there, guns pointed at the train. Perhaps they think Maxim's murderer might make a run for it. I expect Fleischmann is negotiating for an orderly disembarkation.

And so there is nothing to do but wait. I sit back down beside Joe. "Are you sure you're okay?" I whisper.

He nods. "I'm fine, Meri. It's just a bit weird… I've spent a year and a half fighting for my life, going through all sorts to be able to live. But you know, if I hadn't made it, I would at least have had enough time to get used to the idea, to put things in order. I got the chance to put up a fight. Maxim got none of that. He was fetching passports, for God's sake!"

I exhale. I know what he means. For Joe, being able to fight is important even if he ultimately loses. "For the record, I would never have gotten used to the idea—but how do you know Maxim didn't have a chance to put up a fight?"

Joe shrugs. "The cabin was quite cluttered, but it was neat. There weren't any signs of a struggle. If he'd put up a fight, or resisted in any way, there would be some small sign of disruption. But there was nothing."

"So he didn't see his killer coming or—"

"He knew him or her."

"But that doesn't help us," I moan. "Maxim probably knew half the people on the train."

"It's a start," Joe says. "Maxim can't have been looking after all the passengers. We can narrow it down to those he was."

"And everyone in this room," I add.

"What do you mean?"

"Well, Maxim wouldn't have been suspicious of anyone in this room…not after Fleischmann brought us together for a murder summit. He might have assumed they were bringing a message from Herr Fleischmann or something."

Joe begins to rub his brow but stops as he realizes he's spreading Maxim's blood onto his face. "I'll just step into the restroom and wash my hands."

I nod. It seems like a sensible idea. There is a restroom at the end of the dining car.

Joe stands, and immediately Robert Whitman, Aled Rees, Buster Sartori, and even Abigay rise from their seats and move toward him. It's only then I realize that my brother is a suspect. I mean really a suspect rather than vaguely a suspect, which we are all.

"Where are you going, love?" Abigay asks.

"Thought I'd wash my hands," Joe replies warily.

"Aye, I can see why you would." Abigay's eyes drop to his sullied hands.

Joe begins to move his hands, to hide them perhaps, but he stops. "So you have no objection if I use the restroom?"

"Perhaps it is too early to wash the blood from your hands," Rees says quietly.

"What the fuck do you mean by that?" Joe flares.

"Joe," I warn, "step carefully."

Joe takes a deep breath. "Look, everybody here has seen my hands." He holds them up. "I have not tried to hide them. I do not deny that the blood is Maxim's, and I have told you why it is there. I cannot see that making me walk about with bloody hands has any value, evidentiary or otherwise."

"He's right," I say into the silence that follows. "There is no reason, beyond some twisted sense of Shakespearean drama, to prevent him washing his hands."

They look from one to the other, wordlessly consulting. "Very well." Rees gives the final permission. "But if you wouldn't mind…" He takes out his phone and photographs Joe with his hands held out before him.

Joe nods curtly and walks calmly through the carriage to the restroom at the end. I glare at the detectives, seething on Joe's behalf.

Abigay offers me a resigned half-smile. "We have to be careful, pet. At least until we can talk to this steward who found Joe and Maxim."

Joe takes several minutes in the restroom. I can see that Sartori is becoming agitated. For a private detective, he has no poker face.

When Joe returns, his hands are red, not from the blood, but from scrubbing. His face is calm but his hair slightly wet. That's his tell. I may not be able to read my twin's mind, but I know the small manifestations of pain, or stress, or guilt, or simply not knowing what to do. Joe wets his hair to re-anchor himself. Has since he was a child. Says it cools his brain down. And usually, it works.

He sits back down beside me. "I wonder what's keeping Fleischmann?"

I shrug. "Perhaps he's negotiating with the Venetian authorities to have us disembark."

Joe leans across me and looks out the window. "I wouldn't hold out hope, Meri. The blokes with the guns are still there."

"Can you see Fleischmann?"

He shakes his head. "We can't see the leading carriages from here—he could be hanging out the window chatting, for all we know."

I lower my voice. "What do you think is going on, Joe?"

"Italy wants us to be someone else's problem. Letting us disembark could put the whole country at risk—"

"No, I mean the murders."

"I'm a little alarmed you think I'd know."

"You're a mystery writer, idiot—I thought you might have some vague insight."

Joe smiles. "I write fiction, Meri. I make things up."

"But it must be based on something real."

"Nope."

"What do you think, anyway?"

He sighs. "I think we'll know a lot more when we have located Blackwell's body."

I agree. "We don't even know for sure that Blackwell and Harrington are the same person." I turn back to him. "The passports! Did you see the passports?"

"No. But once I saw Maxim, I wasn't looking for or even thinking about them."

"Fair enough."

Joe rubs his face. "If it makes you feel any better, I'm pretty sure we're only dealing with one murderer, despite the number of bodies." He leans closer. "Whoever killed Blackwell had a motive to kill both the first steward and Maxim."

"The first steward was guarding 16G."

"Our killer would have needed to remove him in order to get out of the compartment."

"But the compartment had been searched," I remind him. "He wasn't in there."

"He might have been under the bed in the cavity Napoleon showed us." Joe scans the dining car.

"They're all listening, you know," I caution.

"Good. I won't have to repeat myself. He might have been hidden there the whole time. When we first walked into the cabin with Maxim, and later when Fleischmann was in there. "

"But he wasn't there when you and Napoleon looked under the bed," I point out. The circle of detectives around us is drawing closer. Napoleon himself is all but leaning on our table.

"Do you remember"—Joe doesn't bother to lower his voice anymore—"how clean that cavity was? It made it unlikely that there was ever a body in it, given the amount of blood in the rest of the compartment." He glances at Duplantier now, no longer speaking to just me. "But it might have hidden the killer."

"There was no steward outside the door when we entered the compartment," Duplantier says thoughtfully.

"But the steward wasn't killed until later that day," I protest.

"He wasn't *found* till later that day," Duplantier replies. Some of the others are taking notes now.

Elle chimes in. "The killer might have killed him earlier and stowed his body in the restroom."

Duplantier nods. "If you recall, Meredith, we commented on the absence of the guard when we entered. Indeed, it was only his absence that made entering possible."

The conglomerate of detectives begins speculating, offering

theories and arguing now. A couple cross-examine Duplantier on the unauthorized entry to which he's just admitted.

I look at my brother. "We're still missing at least one body," I say softly, "and, of course, a killer."

Chapter 12

The commotion begins with whistles. Not the train's, but police whistles. Shrill blasts are followed by shouting. And then sirens. The vehicles flanking the track begin to move. Everybody in the dining car is glued to the window. We shout what we can see to the passengers watching from the other side.

"That's a water truck."

"The medical supply vehicles just pulled back."

"Who's blowing that goddamn whistle?"

"Where the hell is Fleischmann?"

A gunshot, and then several, and we all fall silent. Instinctively, we pull away from the windows. All except Joe, who stands in full view of the lines of soldiers with their guns trained upon the midnight-blue carriages. The Orient Express begins to move, a lurch and then a gradual build of momentum as the rhythm of the wheels on the track compresses with the acceleration of the locomotive. We're heading back to Paris.

It is only then that Fleischmann returns to Étoile du Nord.

He looks pale. Again, there is silence as we wait for him to speak, to reassure us somehow.

"Ladies and gentlemen," he says finally, "the Italian government has decided that allowing us to disembark is too dangerous. We are returning to Paris." He takes a breath. "We have been generously provisioned for the return journey, and so we will endeavor to make this unforeseen extension and detour as comfortable as we can."

"Thank you, Mr. Fleischmann." Clarice Mayfield puts up her hand like we are in school. "It's very kind of you to consider our comfort, but what we all really want to know is, what happened to Maxim?"

Fleischmann clears his throat. "I regret to tell you that Maxim is gone. It appears he was stabbed in the throat with something like a letter opener. Despite Mr. Penvale's valiant attempts to save him, he…" Fleischmann trails off, shaking his head.

"We're so very sorry, Herr Fleischmann," I say. I feel like crying now. Helpful, cheerful Maxim murdered in cold blood. I wipe the sides of my eyes, desperate to cut emotion off at the pass.

Duplantier puts his arm around me. *"Oui, Mademoiselle Penvale parle pour nous tous. Sincères condoléances, Monsieur Fleischmann."*

The sentiment is echoed in several languages.

Fleischmann nods slowly and accepts the expressions of sympathy.

Aled Rees is the first to move on. "Can I ask, Herr Fleischmann, about the passports Maxim was fetching?"

"Gone." Fleischmann replies. "All gone. On behalf of the Orient Express, I apologize. Rest assured that I have apprised the offices of the Orient Express, and they will be contacting all your embassies to have your documents reissued."

I'm pretty sure the reissue of his documents was not what Aled was thinking about, but he thanks Fleischmann for the consideration. "And so," he continues, "we are to assume the killer of the steward took the passports."

"It seems most likely," Fleischmann replies gravely.

"But he wouldn't have known the combination to the safe," I venture. "So Maxim must have opened the safe before he was killed."

"Indeed!" Elle Baird gives me an encouraging smile. "Well deduced!"

"We'd all worked that out," Buster Sartori says petulantly.

"I didn't," Elle declares.

"Nor did I," Abigay adds, her hands on her hips. "I may have got to it in time, but it's better to have good thinking as soon as possible."

"Sure, of course." Buster scowls. "Good to see the *sisterhood* is still presenting a united front," he adds.

"Oh, grow up, mate!" Joe snaps.

Elle Baird stands. "Let's not start bickering amongst ourselves like children. May I suggest we all take a moment to center ourselves and just breathe... No, Herr Fleischmann, this won't take a moment, and I guarantee it will head tension off at the pass." The Duchess of Kinross raises both arms in the air, scrutinizing each of us until we follow suit. I am admittedly surprised that we all do. All except Sartori, that is, who folds his arms stubbornly. She ignores him and lowers her own arms slowly in a wide arc until she can press her palms together. "Breathe slowly now—gently does it. In through the nose and out through the mouth, releasing the tension and anger in your body with each exhale. Three…four…five…last one. Now don't we all feel better?"

Strangely, I do feel more relaxed, if a little ridiculous.

"Err…yes, *Dankeschön*, Your Grace." Fleischmann appears mildly embarrassed, but less pale. He addresses the rest of us now. "Ladies and gentlemen, I regret that this is necessary, but I must prevail on you to assist in keeping the peace on board and helping us ensure there is neither panic nor a repeat of this violence."

"My dear boy, I'm not sure any one of us is qualified to—" Penelope begins. It's her sister who cuts her off.

"Don't be so modest, dear; of course we're qualified!"

"*Bien sûr*," Duplantier says, nodding at Fleischmann. "We will do whatever we can to assist."

Aled Rees and Ajeet Singh agree hastily.

"Our talents, insight, and experience are at your service." Sartori will not be outdone.

I notice Elle Baird roll her eyes, but she too registers her willingness to assist, as do Abigay Williams and Bob Whitman. And so, we are twelve with Fleischmann. A jury of sorts, or a posse.

"Thank you," Fleischmann says. "But you should understand that we cannot simply keep people in their cabins. For one thing, they will not have it. The quarantined carriages are also agitating for release."

I glance at Rees for any indication of smugness. But he only looks concerned.

Duplantier takes charge. "May I suggest, Herr Fleischmann, that we make the Bar Car our incident room? That way the passengers not in quarantine may still dine. It will pass the time more easily, and people must in any case be fed. You will need to post men at both ends to make sure the car is not invaded."

Fleischmann nods. Sartori appears to want to say something but does not seem to know what, so the conversation moves on.

"Detective Inspector Abigay Williams and I will dust 16G for fingerprints now, and then Madame Penvale can escort two at a time to inspect the cabin," Duplantier continues. "Meanwhile, those who remain shall collaborate and consider what insights are gathered from the inspections."

"And then?" Elle Baird inquires archly.

"And then, perhaps the way forward will become clear."

Duplantier and Abigay depart to collect fingerprints, and the rest of us use the time to assist in moving the incident room to the Bar Car so that Étoile du Nord can again be used for dining, at least for those passengers whose cabins are on that side of the train. I wave at Frank, who seems quite alarmed when we all walk in. Fleischmann informs him that we will be taking over the Bar Car, and obligingly, he prepares to leave his post. It's Whitman who suggests that a barman would not be unnecessary in the circumstances, and probably a darn sight more useful than yoga.

Elle shoots him a withering look, but Fleischmann agrees to leave Frank at our service, for the time being at least. Frank soothes Elle's ruffled feelings with her favorite champagne cocktail and extravagant compliments about her attire.

The Bar Car becomes closed to all passengers aside from those on the manager's task force. The carriage necessarily remains a thoroughfare for stewards going about their business from one side of the train to the other. They take as direct and unobtrusive a route through as possible, and soon the blue-and-gold uniform seems to afford a kind of invisibility. Occasionally a steward delivers a tray of refreshments and we are almost startled, as if they have walked out of a background into our reality.

The forensics take well over an hour, and by the time Duplantier and Abigay return, the group is becoming concerned that they have met a fate similar to Maxim's. Frank has proved his worth by keeping us supplied with both stiff drinks and easing elixirs.

Duplantier shakes his head in response to the inevitable queries about what was found. "We could not find a single fingerprint within the cabin, aside from the door handle, which has of course been touched by Maxim and a number of others following the discovery of the scene."

"Could it be that you have just missed them?" I ask.

"We dusted the entire washroom, the windows and their surroundings, the light switches and call buttons, the luggage racks—there is nothing. Not one print in the blood. There are some smudges but not prints."

"So? The murderer wore gloves." Sartori seems unimpressed by the revelation. "You'd expect that."

"One would not expect, however, that both the murderer and the victim wore gloves," Duplantier replies.

"Or that the resident of 16G wore gloves the entire time he was in the cabin," Abigay adds.

"He wasn't wearing gloves last night," Joe says suddenly. "When he went into 16G after dinner. I would have noticed if he were."

"Do you mean to say that at some time between then and when he was killed, he wiped down the cabin and started wearing gloves?" Elle says incredulously.

Duplantier grimaces. "It is strange—an anomaly."

"With all due respect, Monsieur Duplantier"—Aled Rees presses his fingertips together and gazes into the distance as he speaks—"neither you nor D.I. Williams is a forensics specialist. It is possible that you have just missed the evidence?"

"We're talking about basic fingerprint-collection, not DNA analysis," Abigay bites back.

"Even so."

"Of course, it is possible, however unlikely." Duplantier remains unflappable. "We are simply reporting our findings or our lack of findings."

"So, what do we do now?" Sartori demands.

"We carry on," Abigay says. "And we make sure we do not disturb the scene in case, as Mr. Rees believes, there are fingerprints in the cabin that Monsieur Duplantier and I have missed."

"But we must have the opportunity to inspect the scene!" Sartori insists.

"Yes," Duplantier replies. "But it is more important than ever that we do not contaminate the scene—we must procure gloves and foot covers and maintain the utmost order in our inspections."

Chapter 13

stand. The issue of gloves and contamination-avoidance has, after several minutes of vigorous discussion, finally been settled. "Okay, who's first?"

Buster Sartori jumps to his feet. Abigay winks at me and raises her hand. "Presuming, of course, you don't mind being accompanied by the sisterhood, Mr. Sartori."

Buster pouts. "Haven't you just come from 16G?"

"Then, I was concentrating on fingerprints. Now I want to step back and consider the scene as a whole."

"Be careful," Joe whispers before I lead them out of the Bar Car toward Carriage 16.

"It's a terrible pity we don't have those passports," Abigay says. "Without knowing what Mr. Harrington looked like, we have no idea if it's him we are looking for."

"Or his body," Buster mutters.

"I beg your pardon, Mr. Sartori?"

"His body. We don't know if Harrington, if it *was* Harrington, was the perp or the victim."

I say nothing, choosing to let them forget I'm here, and listen.

"True," Abigay replies. "Though how he could hide a body on the Orient Express, I cannot tell you."

"The passengers would find it difficult," Buster agrees. "The staff may not. They'd know all the nooks and crannies, the storage places no one uses. They probably use them to stash what they pilfer from the punters."

"Keep your voice down, big man!" Abigay warns the American. There are two stewards outside the door to 16G. It's impossible to tell whether they overheard.

"Excuse me, gentlemen…" I explain why we're here. Fleischmann seems to have sent them a message to expect us, and they open the door and allow us in. I watch Buster and Abigay examine the room, making notes for evidentiary purposes of exactly what they do and the fact they are both wearing latex gloves and shower caps over their shoes. They both have phones, of course, so they take numerous photographs.

"Seems like someone put up one hell of a struggle, so we can assume our victim was not drugged or asleep," Abigay says.

"The window's too small to get a body out of here without some postmortem surgery." Buster opens and closes the window.

"Please don't do that." I suddenly remember my role as guardian of the crime scene. "Something might blow out or in, and the crime scene will be contaminated."

Buster puts up his hands. "Sorry, ma'am, my bad."

"It's just that…" I'm suddenly embarrassed by the authority

that has been foisted upon me. "Herr Fleischmann wants the crime scene undisturbed."

Buster smiles, a real smile rather than a sneer or some pretense. "You're right. I should know better."

Surprised, I smile back and thank him.

"Weapon?" Abigay calls for opinions.

"Knife. Could be a straight razor or a chainsaw, but a chainsaw would have been heard, right?" Buster Sartori is quick to fill the silence. "A cut-throat razor is possible, but a garden-variety knife is most likely."

Abigay seems to agree, and after checking the cavity beneath the lower bunk, they conclude their inspection. The cabin is locked behind us, and I escort them back toward the Bar Car. As we pass the restrooms, Abigay requests a quick stop, and I find myself waiting in the corridor outside it with Buster.

"What brings you onto the Orient Express?" I ask before the silence becomes awkward.

Buster's hand goes to his breast pocket for a second, the reflexive action of a smoker reaching for his cigarettes before remembering that he is not permitted to light up here. Perhaps that is why he is so generally abrasive. "A divorce," he replies. "I put the ticket on her credit card as a parting gift."

"Oh…"

He chuckles. "We met at Bouchercon…you know, the mystery convention. She owns a bookstore in LA called It's Simply Criminal. We hit it off, got married at the next convention."

"How…how long were you married?" I ask gently.

"Let's see.…Texas, San Francisco, New Orleans…there was Nashville in there somewhere…about five conferences.

We always talked of taking the Orient Express. She preferred cozy crime, you know. I was going to surprise her with tickets for our next significant anniversary. And then she met the guy who founded *Dead to Write*."

"*Dead to Write?*"

"It's one of those review magazines. Stupid huh? What does *Dead to Write* even mean? Anyway, I bought the ticket… I bought two, actually. Kinda hoped that once she saw what I'd done she might realize and come… But she didn't…so I have a cabin on my own." His smile is forced now as he pretends to be triumphant.

"Right…" I fumble for an adequate response.

Abigay emerges from the restroom and saves me. "Thank you for waiting. Now we'd best get back before they send a search party!"

We return to the Bar Car, which has become our new incident room and been accordingly transformed. Paper has been taped to the windows and is being used as whiteboards on which information is being recorded for the consideration of the entire group. Joe is sitting quietly in the corner, observing everything and typing into his laptop.

I take the Mayfields next, though they, of course, have seen the scene before. Nevertheless, they inspect again, with gloves and shower cap shoe covers this time.

Clarice looks up to the luggage shelf. "Where's his bag?" she asks. "He must have come aboard with something."

"If for no other reason than to steal the silverware." Penelope purses her lips.

"Was there a bag when we first looked inside? When

Maxim opened the door?" I stare at the luggage rack, trying to remember.

"I distinctly remember that there was." Clarice is certain. "It was one of those cylindrical bags that young men take to the gym."

"A duffel bag?"

"Yes, that's it…red. It was barely noticeable with all the blood."

I remember it now.

"But it's not here, is it?" Penelope's crinkled blue eyes dart the length of the luggage rack. "It's been removed."

"Perhaps Herr Fleischmann took it," I suggest uneasily. "He may have wanted to check its contents."

"Perhaps," Clarice sighs. "If not, we have another crime to contend with."

"The lamp has been knocked over and righted." Penelope bends to inspect a smudge of brownish red on the shade. She points to a disturbance in the blood splatter on the table and then the lamp's base. There's a barely perceptible clean line on the table along the base's edge. "They didn't quite line it up properly," she says.

Clarice looks at me over the tops of her bifocals. "I don't suppose that oaf from California knocked over the lamp while he was pretending to investigate?"

I smile as I shake my head. Clearly, Buster has made an impression. "No, he didn't."

"So, someone has disturbed the crime scene since it was discovered?"

"Several people have been in here," I offer as information

rather than excuse. "Herr Fleischmann and a number of his officers, yourselves, Joe and I, Monsieur Duplantier."

I return the Mayfields to the Bar Car and make my way back to 16G with Aled Rees and Ajeet Singh. Both men are mostly silent during their inspection. They seem to communicate with each other by way of glance and a slight movement of their heads. I can't really discern which of them suggests examining the bottom bunk. They move in unison to the bed and lift the mattress, studying the space underneath without saying anything out loud.

"Right then." Aled vocalizes finally. "I suppose that's it."

Ajeet nods, and they walk out. I follow, waving hastily at the stewards whose job it is to lock the door behind us and not be killed.

Bob Whitman and the Duchess of Kinross are next. Elle takes off her shoes outside the door to ensure that her stilettos don't pierce the shower caps we're using as foot covers. Whitman does not speak except to whisper to Elle every now and then. The duchess peruses the cabin like she's making an inspection of real estate. She opens the little washroom—it is clean, clear of even a drop of blood. She frowns. "The doors to the washroom must have been closed when all this"—she gestures around at the bloody compartment—"occurred."

Whitman grunts. "Obviously."

"Don't you think it's interesting?" Elle replies.

Whitman shrugs. "You can barely move in here as it is, my dear. Makes sense that they would keep it closed."

Elle sighs. "I don't know that closing the cupboards would be the first thing on my mind if I was attacking someone or indeed being attacked, but that's not why it's interesting." She waves her hand at the pristine washroom. "Our murderer did not even try to clean himself up, wash the blood from his hands. Considering that he was about to leave this room into a crowded and immaculate train, it does seem odd."

"Well, yes—that goes without saying…" Whitman grumbles.

I try my level best not to smile. It's not my place to take delight in Whitman being put in his.

Elle gives me a slow wink. "It's the breathing, Bob. In through the nose, out through the mouth. It clears the mind and balances the chakras—you really should try it."

"You had us all balancing chakras in the dining car, Your Grace."

"Now, Bob, you know I can tell the difference between conscious breathing and huffing and puffing to look the part. I'm a little hurt that you won't even try."

Bob Whitman shakes his head, muttering that he didn't need to be taught how to breathe; he'd been doing it for sixty-four years.

"I think we've seen enough," Elle says brightly. "We had better be getting back."

And so, we return to the bar. The papers taped to the windows are now scrawled with notes. Traversing stewards, trained in discretion or perhaps directed to do so, keep their gazes forward. Fleischmann's posse has broken into smaller groups, arguing about what each has seen in, and interpreted from, the crime scene.

All except Joe, who is seated at a table in the midst of it all, typing.

There is no one else who needs to be escorted to 16G, so I

quickly write an affidavit declaring whom I had accompanied to the crime scene and that they have, aside from Buster Sartori, who'd opened the window, touched nothing. I also make note of the missing duffel bag and the fact that it disappeared sometime after the crime scene was first discovered. Finally, I sign the document and have Fleischmann witness it before relinquishing it to his custody.

I check in with Joe then.

"Are you seriously working on your manuscript in the middle of all this?"

"Of course. It's like writing from within the story—couldn't pass that up."

"Are you okay?"

"Why wouldn't I be okay?"

"Maxim…"

Joe shakes his head. "Poor bastard…but I'm okay, Meri. This is all distracting, if nothing else."

"So what's going on?"

Joe nods toward a group that includes Whitman, Sartori, and Rees. "We have one faction in favor of interrogating all the passengers until the killer is found. Another"—he glances at Singh, Abigay, and the Mayfield sisters—"who believe our killer is a stowaway or a member of staff, and, finally, there's our mate Duplantier, who plays his cards very close to his chest."

"What do you think, Joe?"

"I don't know, Meri. They all have their points." He leans close. "I do wonder why there are so many bloody cops and spies on board."

I smile. "They are not all cops and spies, but surely it's not astounding that people in those lines of work would be drawn to the Orient Express."

"Yes, maybe. It just seems to be a coincidence that they are all on board when a murder, a real one rather than a fictional one, takes place."

I shrug. "Coincidences occur much more often in real life than they do in fiction."

"You're right, of course," he says without any conviction at all. "Have you noticed that with Fleischmann there are twelve of us…a jury?"

"You're starting to sound like a conspiracy theorist, bro," I say, though I had earlier made that observation myself. "Remember, you weren't actually invited, so there should have been only eleven of us."

Joe scowls, disgruntled by my logic as he often is. "Yeah, whatever."

"Can anyone here draw?" Elle Baird calls out to the room.

"Draw? Why?"

"Because Clarice and Penelope Mayfield have seen the man who they believe was occupying 16G. We need to improvise a police sketch."

"Meredith can draw," Joe announces with a confidence that belies the fact that he asked me if I could do so that very morning. He also seems to have forgotten that he's irritated with me.

"Good!" Elle Baird pulls out a chair opposite the Mayfields and invites me to take it. "Come on, Meredith. Let's all see what this chap Gregory Harrington looks like."

"I'll need something to…"

"Of course," Fleischmann says. He waylays a passing steward and directs her to fetch more paper and pencils.

And so, I sit down with a sheaf of Orient Express letterhead, a midnight-blue and gold lead pencil, and a packet of colored pencils kept to entertain the very occasional young passenger. I start with the eyes, question the old ladies about their shape and size and color.

"They were blue," Clarice replies. "An average size and round…quite bulgy, in fact."

"Did you think so?" Penelope is evidently surprised. She turns to me, tapping the paper. "They were more gray than blue, and shifty. Squinty, some would say."

"What nonsense!" Clarice is clearly annoyed. "They were cornflower blue and protruding…like a frog's."

"Clarice, my dear, the things you say!" Penelope exclaims.

"How about," I interrupt, afraid the process is going to be hijacked by the Mayfields' bickering, "I make two drawings." I place two sheets of letterhead beside each other on the table and initial the first CM and the second PM. I draw both, alternately defining eyes, nose, mouth, chin, face shape, hair. In the end we have sketches of two different men, though they might have been related…not brothers but maybe cousins. Even so, Penelope and Clarice each swear the relevant sketch is the spitting image of Gregory Harrington.

Chapter 14

The drawings, inconsistent as they are, are duly taped onto the windows, and our fellow travelers gather about them.

"I have seen him!" Aled Rees exclaims, pointing at the sketch described by Clarice.

"I know that man," Abigay says, frowning as she regards the sketch described by Penelope. "I've met him on this train."

Joe chokes back a laugh. I glare at him, but everybody else seems embroiled in the consideration of the sketches.

"Come on," he says, "let's get out of here."

"We can't—"

"Yes, we can." He meets my eyes. "We're just going back to our cabin to collect…my pills."

I sigh. "Okay, but quickly."

Joe puts his hand on his heart. "We'll be back before they stop bickering."

We tell the stewards at the door that we have to fetch medication from our cabin. They take our names and wave us through. Nobody in the Bar Car seems to notice our departure.

We walk through the dining carriages, which are being set up for the first dinner service. It seems strange under the circumstances, but the passengers will need to be fed somehow. "It's one way of keeping people calm, I suppose."

Joe nods. "Fleischmann is no fool, though I don't know what he's going to do about the quarantined carriages."

"Oh God, I wonder what those poor people are thinking."

"*How the fuck do we get out of here,* I expect."

"How long do you think before they figure that out?" I ask as we reach the ordinary carriages.

"How to get out of the quarantined carriages?" Joe shrugs. "Getting out of the cabins shouldn't be a problem—they have keys, after all, and even if they didn't, the doors are over a hundred years old. It wouldn't take much to break through. Once they get out, they outnumber the stewards looking after them, so my guess is that it's only reason and a sense of social duty that's keeping them in."

"But you don't think that'll last much longer?"

His eyes become troubled for a moment. "Panic will set in sooner or later. As comfortable and luxurious as a cabin on the Orient Express is, no one wants to die in one. And being powerless makes a person angry…"

I study him for a while, remembering now how angry he'd become when the first shock of diagnosis had abated. How he'd regarded each treatment as a weapon and turned his fury against the disease. At the time I hadn't known there was panic behind it, but now, in hindsight, I can see. "So, what can we do?"

"About the people in the quarantined carriages?" Joe shrugs. "I don't know, sis. I don't know how much they've been told."

I stop as a thought occurs. "You don't think the murderer is hiding behind the quarantine?"

Joe considers. "I doubt it," he says in the end. "There are only two quarantined carriages, and the train was full, so there wouldn't be any spare cabins. The remaining cabins are visited by stewards and doctors…and there is, of course, the danger of infection." Joe shakes his head. "If he was there, he'd have been found, or at least noticed, by now."

We are at Carriage 16 now, which is guarded by stewards, but it seems that they have been informed via intercom by someone at the Bar Car to expect us. We are allowed through to 16F.

In our cabin, I breathe out. I hadn't realized I was tense, nor do I know why being in a cabin beside the scene of a brutal murder should relax me, but it does.

Joe doesn't waste any time. "Why do you suppose the Mayfields are describing two entirely different men?"

"Witness accounts are notoriously inaccurate, Joe."

"If they glimpse a man running from a crime scene, yes. But this bloke lived with them—it doesn't make sense."

I sigh. "No, it doesn't. The drawings are too different to be excused by a mere variation in perspective or taste."

"So, what do you think they're trying to achieve?" Joe paces, which in the tight confines of our cabin is quite the feat.

"Maybe they don't want Harrington or whoever killed him to be caught."

"Why?"

"They're working with the killer?" I suggest a little hesitantly.

"Or maybe they just want to be the ones to catch him… without Fleischmann's posse."

"Why would they want that?" I demand.

"I dunno." Joe opens the little washroom and finds his toothbrush. I should note here that my brother is obsessive about dental hygiene. He claims to have been traumatized in high school by a chemistry teacher with breath like a decomposing horse. Joe squeezes out toothpaste and talks to me while brushing his teeth—it is an accomplishment in articulation and my own powers of comprehension.

"Let's assume Harrington is the killer—he's killed someone in his cabin for whatever reason and is now hiding. If he is caught by the posse," he gurgles, "he'll be arrested for murder, and the Mayfields won't be able to get the Lower Slaughter Civic Society's money back. And if he is the victim, perhaps they think whoever killed him now has the Civic Society's money."

"Do you think they'd really derail the investigation for that? We're talking about murder."

He spits out the toothpaste and waves his toothbrush about as he continues. "Who knows? Perhaps psychopaths dream of traveling on the Orient Express as much as cops and spies or whatever these people are."

"You think they're all psychopaths?" Joe seems to be getting carried away.

Joe smiles. "No…probably not. But you've gotta admit the old girls are at least a little bit batty, Bob Whitman thinks he's James Bond, Sartori is like a fourteen-year-old playing TV detective, the duchess is straight out of an episode of *Midsomer Murders*. Rees and Singh seem reasonably sane, but, as I said, who knows…"

"You've left out Duplantier," I remind him.

"Because you fancy him."

"Grow up!" I'm careful not to protest too much—Joe has used that against me before.

Joe grins. "In that case…Duplantier is not telling us everything… He's been far more interested in all this from the beginning than his status as a retired French policeman warrants. I like him, but there's something odd there."

I recall finding Duplantier trying to get into 16G the night before the crime scene was discovered and the fact that he failed to mention that to the posse. Maybe because it was a mistake, and he didn't get in.

"What?" Joe asks, looking at me sharply.

I tell him.

"How do you know he was trying to get in rather than coming out of 16G?"

The notion jolts me. "Well, it was…he said… I don't, I don't know."

Joe puts his arm about my shoulders. "Don't look so crestfallen. We don't know that he wasn't doing exactly what he said he was doing—I just want you to be careful."

"So, what now?" I ask.

"How would I know?" Joe replies.

"If you were writing this, what would we do next?"

His head tilts to the right as he thinks. "We'd probably canvass the passengers, find out if anyone saw or heard anything…"

"Then that's what we should do." I stand.

"Whoa there, Nellie…we can't just knock on doors and interrogate people."

I squint at him. "Sure…but we should call on Flex and

Herds and reassure them. They're probably worried. And then, after that, we could reassure that lovely Irish couple we had dinner with. She was taking photographs of everything, remember… And after that we could reassure some other people…"

Joe laughs. "How many people do you think will let us in when they know there's a murderer wandering about?"

"Ben and Felix will, the Fergusons, maybe, and we might not need to be let in for the others. We could talk to people in the dining car when they feed them."

"You think they'll let them out to eat?"

"I think Fleischmann will decide it's the only way to keep them from mutiny."

Joe shrugs. "Ben and Felix's cabin is in Carriage 14, between us and the dining car." He reaches for the door handle. "It'd probably be rude not to drop in, seeing as we'll be passing."

Chapter 15

Ben Herder opens the door on the first knock. We watch his face transform into a bearded beam. "Oh…hello.…"

"There's a murderer about." Joe says disapprovingly. "You should have at least asked who it was."

"Sorry, Grandma," Ben replies.

"The murderer is hardly going to announce himself as such."

Felix Shannon stands up to receive us.

Joe and I slip into the cabin before the carriage guards notice that we've stopped.

"What are you doing here?" Ben asks. "I thought we were all still confined to quarters."

"We've come by to murder you both and toss your bodies out the window," Joe says, taking a seat.

Felix glances at the window and then at the substantial stature of his fellow podcaster. "You might have a bit of a struggle squeezing Ben through."

"We came to ask you a few questions," I begin.

"About what?"

Suddenly I'm at a bit of a loss.

Joe decides to help out. He begins to tell the podcasters what's been happening.

"Hang on a minute," Felix says. "We should be recording this…"

Joe shakes his head. "We'll do an interview when we get back to Paris. Until then the entertainment value of this mess will have to give way to actually getting to the bottom of it."

"Just on the phone then," Felix negotiates, pressing Record on his device.

Joe hesitates, but I agree to their terms, "Whatever."

Joe brings them vaguely up-to-date: Harrington, Maxim's death, the missing passports, the incident room in the Bar Car, and the various passengers whom Fleischmann has deputized. The podcasters can barely contain their excitement.

"So the steward, Maxim, was killed by the same person who did in your neighbor and the other steward?" Ben eyes the recording equipment stored in the luggage racks; he's clearly itching to start making a show then and there. "But this time he made no attempt to hide the body?"

"The alternative would be to believe there are two or three unrelated murderers aboard the train," Joe says.

"Is that impossible?"

"Too coincidental for a novel, but I suppose it could happen in real life."

"What if they're working together?"

Joe rubs the back of his neck. "I guess…but we're after more than speculation."

"How can we help?" Felix offers. Ben nods enthusiastically.

"What have you heard? You've been running around vox popping the passengers. Have you come across—"

"A double, no—a triple murderer?" Felix's brow arches. "They don't usually introduce themselves by occupation."

"I was going to say someone odd or suspicious," Joe says firmly. "Someone who doesn't seem to fit?"

"Man!" Ben exclaims. "You're clutching at straws."

"Well, did you?" I put my support firmly behind my brother. Interrogating passengers had been my idea, after all, and I realize now that I probably haven't thought the details through.

Felix sighs. "There were a couple of guys who reacted very badly to the idea of being recorded or photographed. Became quite heated about it."

"Names?"

"Bloke wearing a turban thing and his Welsh mate."

"Why were you trying to interview them?" I ask.

Ben thinks briefly before answering. "I overheard them talking about the murder in 16G. They were saying something about a Frenchman and the missing body." Ben looks at Felix. "Flex and I thought they might have some insight, so we leaned in with a microphone." He shakes his head. "The things they threatened to do to Flex."

Joe glances at me. Singh and Rees. It had to be. "When exactly was this?" Joe prods.

Felix answers. "Not long after you left the bar this morning."

So, before we were gathered for Fleischmann's posse. Singh and Rees had been previously acquainted, as least well enough to discuss the crime and, I supposed, Duplantier. That wasn't particularly revelatory, of course…We had all been encouraged to mingle at dinner the night before. Rees and Singh might even have been seated together for the meal.

"When you guys record an interview, what happens to background noises and conversations?" Joe leans back against the doors of the enclosed washbasin.

"The software removes or at least minimizes it," Ben replies.

"Can you reverse that?"

"Yeah…I think so."

"Could you do that and send me the files? Please."

Felix regards us both sharply. "What are you hoping to hear?"

"Not sure, just generally eavesdropping, I guess."

Ben shakes his head. "There are hours of recordings…"

"We could go through them," Felix volunteers. "Send you anything we come across that's interesting…"

Joe nods slowly. "Okay, Angels. Your mission, should you accept it, is to listen for any gossip or conversation about the murder or Harrington himself, or… What was he calling himself, Meri?"

"Blackwell," I reply. "And Napoleon knew him as Cheval."

"So be alert for the names Harrington, Blackwell, or Cheval." He pauses a minute and then pulls out his phone and begins texting. "I'm sending you guys a list of other names. If they come up, take note."

I lean in and look at what he's typing. Our fellow members of Fleischmann's council…Joe doesn't trust them.

"First rule of literary crime-solving," he says, winking at me. "Have a look at everybody who has an interest in the deceased."

"But all these people were recruited by Fleischmann," I protest. "They didn't necessarily have an independent interest."

"Even so. Anyone who's ever watched a crime show knows that perpetrators like to insinuate themselves into the investigation."

"God, Joe! This is serious!"

"I know, Meri. We've got to use what tools we have. The construction of crime fiction doesn't come from nowhere. It wouldn't work if it didn't inherently make sense on some level. The safest place for the killer to hide is probably in the investigation. They can keep an eye on what we know or discover, and they may be able to influence us away from themselves."

Ben and Felix agree, lending their vast knowledge of crime novels to support Joe's claims.

Joe curses, staring at his phone. "It won't send—we must be in another dead spot. Do either of you guys have a pen?"

Flex pulls out his own phone. "No need to resort to sharpened rocks. I'll just take an image of the screen."

"Right!" Joe announces, once the list has been captured. "We better move on." He points at Ben. "Be careful; there is actually at least one murderer aboard."

The podcasters agree, more enthusiastic than concerned. "You too. We're all waiting for the new book."

As we leave the cabin, I glance toward the head of the carriage expecting to be caught by the guards stationed there, but the post is empty.

"What happened to the guards?" I say quietly. "There were two here before."

Joe's jaw hardens. "Damn, I hope… It couldn't be…"

He strides down the carriage to the restroom near the

guards' post, pulls his sleeve down over his hand, and opens the door. I stand behind him bracing myself for another horror, but there is nothing. The restroom is empty and spotless.

"Thank God for that!" Joe murmurs.

I nod, breathing heavily in relief. "Then where are they?"

"Come on." Joe grabs my hand. "Perhaps the guards in the next carriage will know where they went."

At that moment two stewards run in. They barely register our presence. "Make way! *Perdoni!*"

A couple of cabin doors open in their wake, and passengers peer out.

"What's happening?"

"Can we leave?"

"Who the hell just ran past?"

"I think you should all stay in your cabins for the moment until we find out what's going on," Joe says.

"And who are you?" One of the passengers, a large man with long blond hair, steps into the corridor and eyeballs my brother. "Who the fuck are you to tell us what to do? And why are you wandering about freely when we're told to stay in our boxes?" He grabs Joe's shoulder. "How do we know the stewards were not running away from you?"

"Hey! Let go of him!" I snarl.

"No! I might just have caught the bloody murderer."

"I admire your initiative, mate." Joe addresses the would-be hero calmly. "But you've jumped the gun a bit. How about you let me go and we go see if the stewards need any help?"

The man hesitates. Other passengers are emerging from their cabins now, and the corridor becomes congested.

Joe turns with the man's hand still on his shoulder. "Come on—before it becomes impossible to move."

I maneuver myself in between Joe and the man trying to capture him, hoping the proximity of a female will give him pause with respect to whatever it is he's considering. It is enough to allow Joe to break away from his grip. Joe takes my hand and pulls me with him as he plunges through the crowd in the corridor in the direction that the stewards had run. Our friend with the long blond hair follows, shouting "Hey, stop!"

As we try to navigate the congested moving train, I can sense the beginnings of panic taking hold as formerly isolated passengers feed off each other's confusion and anger.

"Meredith, Joe!" Duplantier is in the next carriage and calls to us over the heads of passengers. Joe essentially drags me through to him.

"What's going on?" Joe says, drawing me closer in an attempt to shield me from the jostling.

Duplantier leans in and explains quietly. "The passengers in the quarantined carriages. They are no longer cooperating."

Chapter 16

Duplantier pushes us both into a cabin; its occupants seem to have vacated it to join those in the corridor.

"Napoleon! What are you doing here?" I ask.

"I search for you and your brother," he replies. "We received word in the Bar Car that there is a disturbance in the end carriages, and I am concerned."

"What exactly is happening?"

"Some of the confined passengers, they barge the stewards. They attempt to escape the quarantine."

"Were they successful?"

"Partially. In consequence, we have another dilemma… Are all the stewards who assisted in restraining these passengers now to be quarantined too? And if so, are there sufficient stewards remaining to manage the needs of the other passengers on the Orient Express?"

Joe curses. "This is getting a little out of hand. What do you reckon Fleischmann will do?"

Duplantier shrugs. "We have a problem."

I have a sudden mad thought, an idea, and it seems to me, at that moment anyway, worth a try. I push back into the corridor, with Joe and Napoleon Duplantier behind me, and raise my voice to address the passengers in earshot. "Ladies and gentlemen… Ladies and gentlemen! It seems there has been a breach of quarantine which risks contagion." The crowd hushes and is hushed as my fellow passengers strain to catch my words. "At the moment you are safest in your cabins until we have fully assessed the risk."

"How do you know?" The long-haired hero from the other carriage objects. He probably means well, but he's annoying.

I step back against the window, leaving a small space. "Why don't you head down and check? Of course, you should be careful about contact with anyone on the way back…"

People begin hasty retreats into their cabins, closing and locking the doors behind them. And the objector, too, withdraws.

Joe glances at me. "Geez, Meri. You are a bloody genius!"

Duplantier nods. "Well played, madame, well played."

"It'll only work for a little while, but it may calm things down until Fleischmann figures out what to do," I reply, relieved that the ploy worked—if it was a ploy. Nothing I said wasn't true, I suppose. Everyone, including each of us, is probably safest in a locked cabin. I try not to think about it. "We should tell the passengers in the other carriages the same thing."

We do so, though it's barely necessary as word has spread quickly. We make our way back to the Bar Car in search of information or direction or even just reassurance. The car is abuzz as Fleischmann barks orders. Duplantier translates quietly for our benefit.

"Apparently, the breach has been contained, but at least half a dozen stewards have now been exposed. They are discussing what to do with them and how to prevent the next breach."

"Right," Joe says quietly. "Fleischmann has enough to worry about."

Duplantier nods. "A murderer seems the lesser concern in the circumstances."

Fleischmann catches sight of us and beckons.

"Did you retrieve your medication, Mr. Penvale?"

I might look a little startled, because, to be honest, I'd forgotten the pretext on which we had left the Bar Car, but Joe doesn't blink an eye.

"Yes, I'm sorted, thanks." Joe lowers his voice and briefly tells Fleischmann about the disturbance in the carriages and the manner in which the passengers had been persuaded to return to their cabins. Fleischmann nods approvingly at me.

"Mr. Rees, Mr. Singh, and Mr. Whitman are working on a plan to keep the passengers calm," Fleischmann informs us. "We are fortunate to have their experience."

"In what exactly is their experience?" Joe asks.

"I am told it is civil contingencies and strategic interventions."

Joe turns to me briefly and mouths, "They're spies."

I try not to react. But I think Joe is probably right.

"Herr Fleischmann," I begin. "Is it usual for there to be so many 'experienced' people aboard the Orient Express?"

Fleischmann regards me thoughtfully. "Why do you ask, Ms. Penvale?"

"I'm wondering if the passenger list might somehow be associated with the murders."

"How so?"

"I don't know," I admit. "It just seems a coincidence… or extremely unlucky on the killer's part to choose to ride the Orient Express when so many people, equipped and motivated to catch him, are on board."

Fleischmann exchanges a glance with Duplantier. "The Express has always been popular with those in the investigative professions. It is the romance of the train's history, you see…or what people imagine to be its history." He shakes his head. "I cannot say that the number of passengers with a background in pursuing criminals is more this time than any other time." He shrugs. "We usually have more writers traveling with us, but on this journey, it is just Mr. Penvale."

Joe smiles. "Penelope Mayfield writes poetry. She's been extensively published in the *Lower Slaughter Bugle*."

Fleischmann blinks at him.

"Herr Fleischmann, how did you come to select this group of people to deal with the murder in 16G?" I ask.

"I directed Maxim to look through the passenger manifest for policemen or investigators, anyone who might have experience with law enforcement." He shakes his head slowly. "It was probably wrong to ask passengers to assist, but we are, as they say, making it up as we go."

"Is that kind of detail listed in the manifest?"

"Not generally," Fleischmann concedes, "but finding out about people is Maxim's talent. The more we know about our passengers," he explains, "the easier it is to ensure they have the best time possible. Experienced stewards like Maxim watch for details, ask the right questions, strike the right conversations…

And they make notes against the passengers' names. It is why I asked him to find me the passengers who might be able and willing to assist."

The word *willing* catches my attention. "Was there anyone who was able but not willing?" I ask.

Fleischmann inhales sharply in what I imagine is the contained man's equivalent of throwing up his hands. "Only Maxim could have told you that."

I gather my courage and speak frankly. "Herr Fleischmann, how unwell are the infected passengers? Will we reach Paris in time to help them?"

Fleischmann looks weary now. "I hope so. I am told two passengers are struggling, but we will be in Paris in the morning."

"And if they attempt to break out of the quarantined carriages again?"

"We must try to contain them."

"And what if we can't?" Sartori leans into the conversation. "Another attempt or two and all the stewards will be infected." He's agitated. Perhaps a little scared.

"We'll have to deal with that when we come to it." Elle Baird speaks up now, and I notice they have all been listening.

"The problem is we're fighting on two fronts," Whitman declares. "A murderer on the loose and this bloody disease."

"There is a way to eliminate one of those battles," Sartori ventures carefully.

"Not until we actually find the murderer." Abigay regards Sartori as if he is an idiot.

"What if we uncouple the quarantined carriages and leave

them here?" Sartori says evenly, though I detect something akin to satisfaction in his voice.

The silence that follows is borne of shock; at least I hope it is. Surely no one would even consider abandoning a couple of carriages of sick passengers in the mountains.

"Hear me out." Sartori takes the floor. "Paris is less than twenty-four hours away—we can get help back to them very quickly. And we can concentrate on making sure nobody else is murdered before we get to Paris Central."

"Are you out of your mind?" I can't keep silent any longer. "If we uncouple them they'll have no power. Look at where we are! They'll freeze."

"I think Herr Fleischmann will agree that the carriages are insulated enough to prevent that for at least a day or two, and we would, of course, leave them with all the blankets and food and water they could require." Sartori is confident now, taken with the cleverness of his own plan.

"Yer aff yer heid, you doaty nyaff!" The Duchess of Kinross's fury sends her into full brogue.

Abigay seems similarly outraged by the proposal, as are Whitman and Singh. The Mayfields and Rees are conspicuously silent.

Fleischmann tries to put an end to the debate. "Uncoupling and abandoning carriages is not a strategy I am willing to countenance. We will leave no one behind."

"We can send help for them within hours…"

"Even so. It is not our policy to—"

"Then the murderer on board is not the greatest threat to the survival of your passengers, Herr Fleischmann!" Sartori is disappointed, frustrated that his plan is being rejected so out of hand and with it his opportunity to be the hero of the hour.

"Steady on there, mate," Joe intervenes. "You're getting a bit hysterical, aren't you? We're not talking about the Black Plague, and there are plenty of medications on board. And as you said, we'll be in Paris in less than a day."

"Perhaps we should not be so hasty." Clarice Mayfield makes herself heard. "If the passengers in quarantine continue to attempt escape, we will eventually be overwhelmed, and I guarantee the person who killed Gregory Harrington will take advantage of the bedlam. Perhaps this young man's suggestion is safest for everybody."

"Clarice, what are you saying?" Penelope gasps. "We cannot possibly just cut two carriages loose!"

"I think you'll find it's three carriages now," Rees points out.

"What if Harrington or his murderer is in one of those three carriages?" Joe demands. "We'd be leaving sick people trapped with a murderer in the snow! And let's not forget that the natives have not exactly been friendly."

"Please." Fleischmann raises his voice. "This is not a question for discussion. The Orient Express will not be leaving anybody behind!"

"Given that is the case"—Singh's voice is metered and soothing—"may I suggest that we defer our attempts to solve who killed the steward and the passenger in 16G until we are back at Gare de l'Est?"

"Are you suggesting we carry on as if there isn't someone murdering passengers and stewards?" Whitman demands.

"I am suggesting that we deal with the most immediate threat first."

"And which one is that? The virus has not yet killed anybody."

Fleischmann seems to make a decision and stands to address us all. "Ladies and gentlemen, thank you for your assistance, for responding so generously to my request for aid, but it seems events have come in front of us and now it may be time to take a different approach."

"What do you mean, Herr Fleischmann?" Abigay drums her fingers on the table impatiently.

"I mean that our most immediate problem is getting back to Gare de l'Est without any further contamination of passengers or staff, whilst maintaining security and the best service we can manage under the circumstances."

"And the murderer?"

"I assure you that no one wants justice for Maxim and Jean more than I do, but they too would put the safety and comfort of our passengers first." I notice the lines on Fleischmann's face for the first time. "This killer seems to be some kind of phantom—catching him is less important than ensuring there are no further victims of him, or the virus."

"Perhaps it would be best"—Duplantier stands in solidarity beside the beleaguered manager of the train—"if all passengers, including ourselves, were to remain in their cabins in order to maintain some kind of social distance."

The suggestion is met generally with expressions of dismay and protest.

"No way!" Sartori is on his feet. "You can't just send us to our rooms like misbehaving children. It's too late for that! We're all a part of this now."

On some level I feel for Buster Sartori. He is desperate to be a part of something, to belong. Fleetingly, I wonder if he is really a private investigator. Perhaps he's a just a mystery fan with a private investigator's license embracing the chance to emulate one of his crime fiction heroes. I'm pretty sure you can get a license online. On the other hand, people are being killed, and he is, in fact, behaving like a thwarted child.

"Herr Fleischmann," Aled Rees says more reasonably, "allow me to assure you that we are your allies in this. We have all been well and truly exposed to each other, so it is too late for social distancing in that respect. But if you feel that we should cease our investigations and return to our cabins, then of course we will do so."

"Poppycock!" Clarice is not having it. "Penny and I will be sitting ducks in our cabin! Do I need to remind you that if Gregory Harrington is still alive, he knows we can identify him?"

"We have all seen the sketches, so I suppose we can all identify him and whoever the other guy is," Joe mutters.

Elle laughs out loud. Duplantier smiles and whispers something to my smart-aleck brother, who looks up sheepishly. "Sorry—just trying to lighten the mood."

"How about this?" Elle Baird steps up with a solution. "I'll swap my accommodations with the ladies. I'm sure they'll be comfortable in my stateroom, and you know I'd like to have the experience of traveling in one of the wee cabins."

"And have you slaughtered in their place?" Bob Whitman objects immediately. "No! I will not hear of it!"

"Oh, Bob, we have no reason to believe the murderer is after Clarice and Penelope… I offer the swap merely to put their minds to rest."

"It's too great a risk. Absolutely not!"

Elle rolls her eyes. "Well, then, they can take your stateroom and you can sleep on the couch in mine. Will that do?"

Whitman sighs like a man snookered, which I suppose he is. "Is that acceptable, Herr Fleischmann?"

"Yes, of course."

"So we're agreeing to this?" Sartori demands, incredulous. "We're just going to give up and let a triple murderer get away with…well…murder while we go hide in our cabins."

"We'll be in Paris in less than twenty-four hours, Mr. Sartori," Fleischmann says calmly. "And the murderer is, like ourselves, trapped on board. When we arrive at Gare de l'Est, the gendarmerie will bring the killer to justice."

"You do know that confining us all to our cabins will have no impact whatsoever on the contagion." Sartori makes a final pitch. "We're all sharing restrooms, for one thing, and we've been breathing the same air all afternoon."

"That's true." Rees seems torn. My guess is that he agrees with Sartori without wanting to be seen to agree with Sartori. Because he considers Buster to be an idiot. I'm speculating, of course, but it's not fanciful. "If the goal here is to protect us from the virus," Rees continues, "well, that train has left the station…literally."

The Duchess of Kinross proposes a compromise. "Herr Fleischmann, what if you were to concentrate on running the train and managing the contagion while we remain here to discuss the matter of the murders, until say…" She glances at her watch. "It's now six thirty p.m. Nine or ten o'clock? After that we will retire happily to our cabins and reconvene at six tomorrow morning to compile what findings and theories we may have for handover to the gendarmerie."

"We are serving dinner on trays in the cabins at seven," Fleischmann says almost to himself, no doubt weighing up the logistics of the proposal.

"We could have our trays in here while we consider the evidence," Elle replies. "I'm sure that wouldn't be too much trouble." She steps closer to Fleischmann, using the power of her presence to best effect. "To be honest, Herr Fleischmann, it would help to be able to divert our minds from the personal danger of the situation we find ourselves in. And, naturally, if we can identify the murderer or even just come up with some useful information before we arrive in Gare de l'Est, then our reputations and the actions of the management of the Orient Express will remain beyond reproach."

"With respect, there is no point in taking half measures." Duplantier addresses Elle and Fleischmann. "If we are to be free to investigate the murders, then we must have the freedom of the train, including leave to question passengers or staff and perhaps the ability to apprehend a culprit."

"You cannot force passengers to answer questions," Fleischmann replies.

"I am, we are, aware. But some, possibly most, will be willing to talk to us."

Fleischmann looks uneasy.

"We will, of course, treat any person with whom we speak with the utmost courtesy and reassurance," Duplantier promises. "Herr Fleischmann, we have been well selected. There is enough experience in this room to conduct this investigation with discretion and efficiency."

"They'd probably welcome some distraction if they are to be confined to their cabins," Elle adds. "And, so would we."

"It will be difficult to justify having abandoned this investigation if there is another murder," Whitman points out. "And I imagine the other passengers will expect that you are doing something about all the threats to life on board, not just the disease."

Finally, Fleischmann nods. "Very well, as long as you do not breach the quarantine and you do not claim to have any authority beyond my approval."

A general murmur of agreement.

"In that case, I will wish you luck," Fleischmann says, "and ask that you keep me informed. You understand that if there are any complaints, I will have to retract the freedoms you seek."

"Yes, of course."

The manager of the Orient Express departs to deal with the other catastrophe unfolding on his train.

For a moment we say nothing, as the weight of the responsibility we have not just taken on, but demanded, settles upon us. The best chance to catch the murderer is before we get to Paris, before he has a chance to disembark and disappear into the night.

It's Joe who looks up from his laptop long enough to first suggest a way forward. "Why don't we plot a timeline for Mr. Harrington? When he was seen, where, and so on. It may shake something loose."

Elle Baird heartily endorses the idea. Rees and Singh concur a little less vocally. A general acquiescence follows. Abigay places half a dozen sheets of paper end to end and draws a line. "Okay, where do we start?"

"What about when the Mayfields last saw him?" Joe hands Abigay a felt-tipped pen.

"Fine. When was that, ladies, and where?"

"July and in Lower Slaughter, of course," Clarice says primly. "This all began in Lower Slaughter."

"And you didn't see him again until we were on this train?"

"Actually, we never saw him on the Orient Express," Penelope points out. "It was when we went to his cabin to confront him that we discovered that he had been killed or indeed killed someone in there and fled."

I notice a slight crease between Duplantier's eyes as he tries to unpick Penelope Mayfield's assumptions.

"So you cannot be certain that the man in 16G was Gregory Harrington? But let's assume he was; then we still cannot know if he was the murderer or the murdered."

Clarice regards Duplantier with disdain, clearly annoyed that he would doubt what she and Penelope seemed to have decided were the facts. "We may not have seen him, but young Mr. Penvale did. Tell him, Joe!"

"The man I saw wore a beard," Joe replies uncomfortably. "He didn't really look like either of the drawings Meredith made from your descriptions."

"Let me assure you, Joe Penvale, that under that beard he was indeed Gregory Harrington."

Diplomatically, Duplantier moves on. "So you saw him at—"

"About ten p.m.," Joe says. "We were just about to go in to dinner…"

"Hang on," I murmur as the conversation I overheard with a glass against our cabin wall comes sharply back to me. "He was returning from dinner. I overheard Maxim tell Herr Fleischmann that he had signed on for the first sitting."

"That would explain why he was entering his cabin as we were going out," Joe says.

"Yes, but don't you see?" I say excitedly. "There are at least two people to a table. He would have had to have been seated with someone."

"By George, she's right!" Elle exclaims.

"Well done, you," Abigay chimes in.

Even Rees and Singh are interested.

"The kitchen will have a record of who sat where," Singh says, nodding. "And then perhaps we'll be able to talk to some-one who has had a recent interaction with the passenger in 16G. It might give us some sorely needed insight."

"You keep this up," Joe whispers in my ear, "and I might have to write you into the story after all."

"You could call it *Meredith Penvale Investigates*," I murmur without looking at him. "Or *The Amazing Meredith Penvale…*"

Joe chuckles. "Shall Meri and I go see the chef and find out who Gregory Blackwell, as he was named on the passenger list, was seated with for dinner?" he asks Duplantier.

Duplantier nods. "I think your sister has earned that right." He glances at his watch. "Is fifteen minutes time enough to question the chef?"

"Make it half an hour," Joe says. "He may need to look up records, and he'll be the middle of preparing the dinner trays, I expect."

Duplantier agrees. "We will not worry for half an hour then, but you will be careful?"

"We will," I assure him, pleased to have a reason to stretch my legs a little. Despite the glamour and the horror of the journey so far, I am starting to feel the confinement of the train, the need to simply walk. I can only imagine how restless all the passengers restricted to their cabins are becoming.

Joe and I pass the bar as we exit the carriage in what we hope is the correct direction. Frank is cleaning up another broken glass. I pause to speak to him.

He looks up sheepishly. "I'm defending my title as clumsiest barman in Europe," he mutters as he wipes down the bench.

I smile. "You may well retain it, but only because no one in their right mind will allow Joe behind a bar."

"Hey!" Joe says, but that's the extent of his protest.

"Can I make you both a drink, bro?" Frank offers. "I promise I'll be careful."

"No thanks, mate," Joe says. "You don't happen to know where exactly the kitchens are, do you?"

"Are you hungry? I could—"

"No—thanks, though. We just want to have a word with the chef."

"Is this part of the investigation?" Frank asks.

I nod.

"Well, there's actually a kitchen at either end of the train. One has been sealed off with the quarantine carriages, and the other is feeding the rest of the train. But at this time, you'll probably find the chef in one of the dining cars doing sums."

"Sums?"

"Chef Galichet must manage all the receipts and figures for the dinner service…that sort of thing. There's not a lot of room in the kitchens to sit with a calculator, and so he usually does this sort of work in the empty dining room."

"Okay. Thank you, Frank."

"Mind how you go." He begins to make coffee now. A blast of steam from the high-tech espresso machine threatens to melt the wax on his mustache, and the coffee tumbler seems precariously placed in his hand.

"You too," I reply sincerely.

The Bar Car adjoins the dining cars. It is in the third that we find Chef Galichet, a man whose girth threatens to outstrip his height. Dressed traditionally in whites and a tall chef's toque, he smells of truffles and wine. He seems a little startled when Joe and I walk in, and considerably more so when he learns that we wish to speak with him. I open with Herr Fleischmann's imprimatur, explaining that he has charged us with looking into the murder of the passenger in 16G, as well as that of the stewards.

Galichet sighs heavily. "A terrible business. But what can I do for you? I am a simple cook."

"We are looking for a passenger who was seated in the first dinner sitting yesterday. That passenger shared a table with Mr. Harrington," I explain.

"He was traveling as Gregory Blackwell." Joe corrects my mistake.

"Oh, yes. That's right—Blackwell. He was in 16G."

Galichet nods. "Yes, yes, I can tell you that…" He shuffles through the papers on which he is working and finds what appears to be a map of the dining cars with names against each table. He studies it for a minute or so. "Mr. Blackwell dined at first sitting, which begins at seven p.m. He was seated with Paula Atkinson—she too is traveling alone." He squints at the paper. "Madame is gluten intolerant and allergic to shellfish. Monsieur Blackwell requested that he not be served alcohol." Galichet shakes his head sadly at the waste.

"Do you have a record of her cabin number?" I ask.

"No cabin number," he says firmly. "Madame Atkinson has the Paris Suite."

We thank the chef and leave him to his figures and accounts.

"We're going to be back earlier than expected," I say, vaguely disappointed that our hall pass is about to end.

"No, we're not," Joe replies. "We have still to speak to Ms. Atkinson."

"I'm not sure we should do that."

"Why not?"

"Because we were simply sent to find out the passenger's name and report back. We can't just wander off on a folly of our own."

"*Folly of our own...* Why have you suddenly become Jane Austen?" Joe laughs at me.

"It's a legal term," I reply tersely. "It means doing something that is completely unauthorized."

"Authority...we're not in the army, Meri." Joe is already setting off toward the Grand Suites at the front of the train.

I can't very well return to the bar alone, so I follow.

Chapter 17

The carriages are quiet. It's a little unsettling to know that there are people in every cabin we pass, isolated, fearful, angry…or possibly just asleep.

Joe and I move quickly and as quietly as possible, aware that passengers confined to their cabins might find footsteps in the corridor alarming or at least irritating. When two stewards emerge from 10E it does not initially, from the end of the carriage, strike either of us as out of place. But within a couple of steps, we recognize Flex and Herds in stewards' uniforms. For several seconds we struggle to comprehend the various anomalies. Why on earth are the podcasters dressed as stewards? And what were they doing in a cabin we know is not theirs?

"What are you two doing here?" Joe is the first to speak, or shout in a whisper if such a thing is possible. "And what the hell are you wearing?"

Ben places a finger on his lips. Felix looks left and right to check that we haven't been observed and then beckons us into 10E. The cabin is set up as a day sitter, but still it's a tight fit with the four of us. The compartment is untidy, clothes strewn on the floor, a green plaid jacket crumpled on the couch.

I hear Joe swear under his breath. "That's Buster Sartori's jacket!" he says. "This is his cabin, isn't it?"

The podcasters look at each other, smile, and nod triumphantly.

"What the fuck are you guys doing here?" Joe's questions are becoming more profane.

"We thought we'd check out the people on the investigation," Felix replies. "These uniforms were the only way we could get around the train more or less unnoticed."

"What?"

"There's a cabin full of extra uniforms in the carriage that houses the gift shop. We came across it when we were exploring when we first came on board," Ben says quite gleefully. "We went back after dinner and borrowed a couple."

"Why in God's name would you—"

"Flex wanted to see the Orient Express from the eyes of a steward, do an investigative piece." Ben shakes his head. "That's why we took them, anyway. Of course that was before stewards started getting killed."

Flex nods. "Still, we walked through the Bar Car about twenty minutes ago and nobody tried to stop us. You two didn't even look up. Nobody did. Which, incidentally, is exactly what we expected."

Joe starts to say—actually, I don't know what he might want to say. He doesn't get out more than a couple of infuriated sounds.

"You told us to listen for mention of the Bar Council. We

couldn't find anything, so we decided to take a more direct route."

"Are you stark raving mad?" I chime in now. "You can't break into people's cabins!"

"One of them might be a murderer!"

"Anyone on this train might be the murderer!"

Joe finds his voice and tries to reason with them. "Look, fellas, this isn't a game. What if Sartori came back and caught you?"

"It's not like they can throw us off the train," Ben points out. "And you said you wanted us to look into the people on the investigation team."

"I said listen for their names in background conversation, not break and enter! Whoever it is, they've already killed three people—"

"Look, Joe, it occurred to us that with all of you holed up in the bar, it would be the perfect time to see if any of your investigative colleagues are hiding anything." Felix is unrepentant. "It's what Poirot would do."

Joe clenches his fists in his hair.

"We're going to have to report them," I say. "Herr Fleischmann will have to have them restricted somehow."

Flex and Herds react immediately. "What? You'd do that?"

"Yes, we would." Joe stands with me. "For your own good. You're breaking the law, regardless of whatever jurisdiction we're in—actually, how did you get the door open?"

"Felix lifted a master key from one of the stewards."

"Bloody hell! You guys are your own friggin' crime wave!" Joe holds out his hand.

"What?"

"Give me the master key. Now."

"Or what?"

"Or we'll turn you in," Joe says so frostily that even I believe him.

Slowly, resentfully, Felix fishes a key out of his pocket and hands it over. "Last time we try to help you out, Penvale."

"We appreciate that you are trying to help," I say, trying to smooth things over, "but if you are discovered, you'll be arrested when we eventually disembark."

The podcasters finally seem abashed, but just barely.

"I guess we got a little carried away," Ben concedes.

"How many cabins have you already broken into?" I ask.

"Including this one? Two," Ben replies.

"We started with yours," Felix adds.

"Ours?" Joe is incredulous. "You thought Meri and I might have killed three people?"

"Wouldn't that have been a twist?" Ben sighs wistfully.

Felix nods. "It's how I would have written it."

"But we didn't find anything incriminating," Ben continues. "So, unless you two are about to confess, we're looking at a less satisfactory ending…"

Joe shakes his head. "Idiots."

"Look, guys," I intervene. "Joe and I need to get on. You two need to return to your own cabin and stay there."

"And if Napoleon or Abigay recognizes you as you go back through the Bar Car, you're on your bloody own!" Joe adds.

Ben shrugs. "I think you're wasting a great opportunity, but you've got the master key now, anyway."

Felix points at Joe. "You're an ungrateful bastard."

"We'll make it up to you," Joe promises. "I'll give *Death of the Reader* an exclusive when we get back to Paris."

"Yeah, yeah, we'll hold you to that."

We leave 10E after checking that the corridor is clear. Felix is the last out, so Joe hands him the master key to lock the door and, despite the podcaster's best efforts, ensures the key is returned before we part ways.

Joe curses as I try to keep up with his long stride. "We've just wasted ten minutes dealing with the Hardy Boys."

I smile. "You can't help but admire their initiative, though—hey, slow down, Joe."

"We were supposed to report back to the Bar Car five minutes ago. We're going to have to hurry."

***

The Grand Suites are identified via engraved brass plaques on their doors, so locating the Paris Suite is not particularly difficult.

I knock.

"Who is it?"

"Ms. Atkinson, it's Meredith Penvale. I'm here with my brother, Joe. We're members of...of the task force looking into the murders on board. We were hoping to talk to you."

"What task force? I've not heard anything about a task force!" The voice on the other side of the door is more annoyed than fearful.

I turn to Joe, unsure how to proceed.

"You're perfectly correct, Ms. Atkinson." Joe speaks at the

door. "We should have thought to bring some form of formal authorization. We'll say goodnight—"

The door opens before he finishes. "Come on, then—you'd better come in."

"Are you sure?"

"Quickly, before I change my mind."

We step into the Paris Suite, which is every bit as grand and exquisite as Elle Baird's Istanbul Suite, though it is more chic than lavish in style.

Paula Atkinson is a small woman, birdlike with sharp features, darting movements, and a high, chirping voice that punctuates in a kind of pecking rhythm. She shows us to the plush sofa. "I expect the murderer wouldn't try to gain access to my suite by reminding me of the murders," she says. "Can I offer you a drink? The butler is no longer available to me, but there are bottles of all sorts of things in the drinks cabinets." She looks pointedly at a full glass and a half-empty bottle of scotch. "I was just having a drink myself…to pass the time, you know. It's a long time to be shut in by yourself."

"We wanted to ask you about dinner on your first night aboard—" I begin.

She flaps her hand in my direction. "Oh, yes, I made the mistake of opting for the early sitting. I believe the late sitting was where the party was, but I was hungry, you see." She pulls various bottles of alcohol out of the cabinet and places them in front of us. "Help yourselves—I don't care in the least. I was just having a little drink myself. This lockdown nonsense wouldn't have been so bad if Alfredo had managed to get on board."

"Alfredo?"

"My lover. He was to join the train at Venice, and then I wouldn't have cared if we'd not been allowed to leave the suite until Istanbul." She refreshes her glass. "I met Alfredo at Madonna di Campiglio—he is just wonderful on skis, graceful, you know."

"We really wanted to know more about the man you had dinner with yesterday." I try to stem the patter about Alfredo. "Mr. Blackwell?"

"Oh, Greg—why do you want to know about him?"

A couple of beats as we consider how much to tell her. Then Joe takes the lead. "Well, he's gone missing," he says, clearly deciding on at least a degree of transparency. "His cabin was the first crime scene."

"The one with all the blood?" Paula sits and leans toward us.

"Yes, that's the one. We're hoping that knowing a little more about him might help us find him, one way or another."

Paula's eyes are bright, excited. "Imagine that! And I had dinner with him…"

"What did you think of him?" I ask, trying to get Paula back on track.

"Oh, well, he was perfectly pleasant, I guess, charming even. But clumsy."

"Clumsy?"

"Yes, yes! He dropped three glasses and his knife and fork before dessert! The waiters were very nice about it—cleaned up and replaced the glasses in seconds. He retrieved his knife and fork himself and tried to keep them. I think he was embarrassed, but the waiter would have none if it! Fresh cutlery before he could say 'never mind'! I was inclined to feel sorry for him, but really, he was like a butterfingered bull in a china shop!"

Okay, so our murderer was clumsy. Perhaps that's why the crime scene was such a mess. But I'm not really sure that the revelation helped us in any way. "What did you talk about?"

Paula shrugs. "This and that. He said he'd had a hard year but that he'd turned his life around. I was a bit worried he'd found God." She shudders. "You don't want to have dinner with someone who's recently found God."

Joe laughs, and she raises her glass to an ally.

"Anyway," Paula continues, "he said this trip was to celebrate his new beginning. Honestly, when he said 'new beginning' I was terrified he was going to say he'd been 'born again in Christ' and start bibling at me...but he didn't."

"That's very helpful." Joe thanks her, though I really can't see how it's helpful.

"Oh, there's more!" Paula exclaims as we begin to stand. "Are you sure you wouldn't like a drink? I think he was vain."

"Vain? How so?"

"Well, in that contrived-to-look-like-he-doesn't-care way. His beard was ungroomed, bushy like an old man's, but I'm sure he was wearing a wig or a toupee. You see that, don't you? Men who can grow beards but are completely bald on top... It's nature's cruel irony at play, I think. Anyway, his hairline was too precise. It's a giveaway."

Joe says nothing. I can almost hear the cogs turning in his head, though I couldn't tell you why.

"Thank you, Paula." I stand up now. "You've given us a lot of insight into Gregory Blackwell. We should really go." I nudge Joe with my foot to bring him back from wherever it is his thoughts have taken him. "Maybe don't let anyone else in," I say to Paula. "I know being on your own is getting to you, but we'll be in Paris soon. There is a dangerous man on board."

Paula smiles. "I wish!" She holds up her hands. "Kidding, kidding. I get it. I'll be careful." She looks around at the beautiful suite. "I may have to find a book to read or something."

Joe reaches into the inside breast pocket of his jacket and fishes out a slightly dog-eared paperback. He hands it to her. "Let me know what you think of the ending. I suspect the author was really drunk by the time she got there."

Paula takes the book and pours herself another scotch. "To be fair, I might be too."

Chapter 18

When Joe and I walk into the bar, Duplantier is beginning to become a little concerned by the length of our absence.

"You're late," he says, glancing at his watch. "Did you have difficulty finding the chef?"

Joe shakes his head and confesses. "He identified the guest with whom Blackwell had dinner, and we made a bit of a detour to speak with her. She gave us some interesting—"

"What do you mean, you spoke to her?" Buster Sartori gets to his feet. "You were just supposed to get a name—what the fuck!"

"Hold on there, mate," Joe says calmly. "We got the name from Chef Galichet: Paula Atkinson. She has the Paris Suite. We thought we'd save a bit of time and—"

"You can't do that!" Sartori is shouting, gesturing wildly. "That wasn't what we agreed. Now the rest of us won't be able to use the element of surprise. You've wrecked it for the rest of us."

"Surprise? Come on, man; she didn't do anything other than have dinner with him."

"How do you know she wasn't his accomplice, that they weren't working together?"

"Well…"

"Did you search her suite? I would have searched her suite. He might have been hiding in there all this time and, if he was, I would have found him!"

"There was no one hiding in her suite," Joe says wearily.

"How do you know? Did you look in the en suite…under the bed?" He jabs his finger at Joe's chest, though he stops short of actually touching him. "He'll have gotten away by now—you've effectively warned him. This whole thing is bad enough without having to clean up after amateurs!" He turns to Duplantier. "Are you going to let them get away with this?"

"If Madame Atkinson was Monsieur Blackwell's accomplice," Duplantier replies, "it would be very stupid of him to have dinner with her shortly before he commits murder."

Elle Baird agrees. "He's been clever enough to evade us all so far, so why would he be glaikit enough to dine with an accomplice in full view of the record?"

I am, to be honest, unsure. As much as Buster Sartori is overreacting, he does have a point. Maybe Joe and I have messed up.

Sartori isn't finished with Joe. "It seems to me that you've been involved whenever the killer has slipped through the cracks."

"What the hell do you mean by that?" Joe demands.

"You conveniently slept through the first murder in the adjoining cabin." Sartori counts his grievances off on his fingers. "You didn't notice the guard disappearing from the door of 16G, you didn't see anything when Maxim was killed, and now you make sure we don't apprehend the killer in his accomplice's suite!"

Joe stares at him, clearly stunned.

I notice other members of the Bar Council, who until now have been ignoring the exchange, look up. Their expressions range from disdain to interest. It's the latter that alarms me.

Duplantier intervenes. "There are a number of problems with this theory of yours, monsieur. My cabin also adjoins 16G; I also heard nothing and noticed nothing. Maxim had already been gone too long when we sent Monsieur Penvale to fetch him—it is improbable that the murderer of our steward lingered to be seen, and I cannot say that I would have approached the questioning of Madame Atkinson any differently. Furthermore, I know that the apartments of all passengers traveling alone were searched by the stewards when the passengers were confined, for their own safety."

I watch the others. Rees, Whitman, and the Mayfields are not entirely convinced by Duplantier's defense. I can see skepticism and suspicion in their eyes. Needless to say, Sartori is also not convinced.

"They're your buddies—you're just covering for them. If they're not working with the killer, they might as well be! We should at the very least exclude them from this investigation!"

"Mr. Sartori," Elle Baird says, sounding very much like a duchess, "it would hardly do to begin fighting amongst ourselves. The Penvales have made a very valuable contribution to our efforts, and it behooves us to maintain a level of unity and cooperation."

For a moment Sartori simply gapes at her. And then he almost visibly shakes himself. "No! I'm not putting up with this! It's ridiculous…" He faces Duplantier. "You have no idea what you're doing! Aussie Joe here does what he wants because he's famous… for writing about murder, mind you. Lady Muck," he gestures furiously at Elle, his face reddening with every word, "tries to tell us how to breathe. The two old biddies from Hogwarts don't even know what the man who lived with them looked like, and G-man here…" Whitman enters his focus now. "He thinks we don't all know he's having an affair with the Duchess of Yoga! If we're all going to do what we want and conduct private investigations without the knowledge of the team, I might as well go!"

He storms out of the bar.

"Extraordinary!" Elle is the first to break the wake of his tirade.

"How rude that man is!" Clarice says coldly. "Hogwarts, indeed!"

Joe exhales. "Look, guys, I'm sorry. Speaking to Ms. Atkinson straightaway was my idea. I didn't even consider she might be a suspect rather than a witness."

"Everybody is a suspect," Singh says flatly. "But Buster is overreacting. Give him a few minutes—he'll calm down."

"We should search Ms. Atkinson's suite, for what it's worth," Rees says, looking sternly at Joe and me. "Sartori was right about that."

"Clarice and I will go," Penelope Mayfield volunteers. "Two old biddies won't alarm the poor woman at least."

Clarice agrees. "And now that Mr. Whitman has so kindly given up his suite for us, Ms. Atkinson is our neighbor. I wouldn't mind freshening up a little."

Duplantier checks his watch. "Shall we all take fifteen minutes to do so? Dinner is due to be delivered when we return, and we can discuss who else we might want to question while we eat."

There is a general agreement. I suspect a few members of Fleischmann's council may wish to conduct their own investigations unhampered by the group. Considering what Joe and I have done, it would be hypocritical to object, and who knows—a bit of independent sleuthing might unearth something overlooked by the group. We are, after all, not an official task force.

As everybody disperses Duplantier pulls Joe and me aside and questions us about our meeting with Paula Atkinson.

We sit down with him and recount the conversation, Paula's insights and impressions. Duplantier listens carefully.

"She is probably correct about the wig…his beard too. It might have been a deception if he was traveling in disguise. Monsieur Cheval, when I last saw him, had the abundant auburn hair and no beard or mustaches."

Joe responds, "Which basically means that nothing she told us is of any use in identifying Blackwell-Harrington-Cheval, assuming, of course, he is our killer and not the first victim."

Duplantier stands suddenly. "I must try to find Herr Fleischmann and update him before we resume."

"Oh…okay…" We watch him leave the bar.

Joe opens his laptop.

"You're going to write now?" His ability to compartmentalize amazes me.

"The ghosts are talking to me—I've got to get it down."

"The ghosts of…?"

"Stories past." He smiles. "They become anchored to the places in which they existed in literature."

"You're beginning to sound a bit crystal-and-aura-loopy."

He laughs.

"What are they saying, your ghosts?"

"They're squabbling. Christie's people want to keep things civil; Hitchcock's think we need more action, a gunfight or two."

"I didn't know Hitchcock wrote a train book."

"He didn't, but he directed *The Lady Vanishes* and *Strangers on a Train*, and somehow Ethel White's and Patricia Highsmith's characters have become his."

"Typical." I yawn. "You're…they're talking about your manuscript, right?" I clarify. "Not what's going on here…"

"All related, I guess. They did mention that you should have your hair set."

I fold my arms on the table and drop my head into them. "I need some sleep."

"You've got about ten minutes." I feel his hand on my shoulder. "Go ahead and power-nap, Meri—I'll keep watch."

The last thing I hear is the muted tap of Joe's fingers on keys, and the first thing when I open my eyes, strangely rested…or at least no longer having to struggle to keep my eyes open.

"How long have I been asleep?" I ask.

"Only about half a page." Joe closes his laptop. "Do you feel any better?"

I nod and stretch my neck. "Yes. I'm not sure why…but I feel quite wide awake."

"Exhausted hysteria." Joe smiles.

"Where's the gang?" No one seems to have returned.

Joe shrugs. Even Duplantier has not come back.

Frank comes out from behind the bar with two cups of strong coffee. "Thought you could both use a bit of caffeine."

"Whatever they pay you, mate, you're worth more." Joe drains his cup in two large gulps.

I'm not far behind him. I could just about mainline coffee right now, though I decline when Frank offers up another cup. It's now been twenty minutes since Duplantier dismissed the class. Where the heck is everybody? Have they all just given up and had an early night? Honestly, right now that doesn't sound like such a bad idea.

"Let's go look for them." Joe stands up.

I agree. Something has to be going on.

We tell Frank what we're doing in case someone returns before we do, though in reality they couldn't do so without passing us in the corridor.

Joe hands the barman his laptop. "Would you mind keeping an eye on this until we get back?"

"Sure. I'll put it behind the bar." Frank smiles and waves us off. "Don't worry; I'll hold the fort, bro."

It is unsettlingly quiet, just the constant background of the train in motion, more a sensation than a sound. We don't come across the congestion until we reach Carriage 16. There are a number of stewards in the corridor, Fleischmann himself, and what appears, at first glance, all our fellow members of the Bar Council. They speak in whispers, so we do too.

"What's happened?"

Fleischmann and Duplantier step aside so we can see. Buster Sartori is in a pool of blood at the open door to 16F—our cabin.

Chapter 19

gasp.

Duplantier places a finger on his lips. "We try not to alarm the passengers."

"I think it might be too late for that."

"Even so." Duplantier beckons us closer. "He has been stabbed in the neck, like Maxim and the other steward."

"What the hell is…was Sartori doing here?" Joe asks.

"I expect he was trying to search your accommodations."

"Because he thought we were hiding the murderer?"

"By the looks of it," Whitman says, peering over Fleischmann's shoulder, "the murderer was in 16F. Buster surprised him and paid the price."

"He may also have been in 16G or my accommodations," Duplantier says. "Or he may simply have walked down the corridor and surprised Monsieur Sartori."

"If you hold the door open"—I avert my eyes from the private investigator's body—"I could probably tell you if the cabin has been disturbed since we left it."

"Wouldn't it be better if you stepped in and had a proper look?" Elle Baird says encouragingly.

I grimace. "It doesn't seem right to just step over Buster's body."

Joe shrugs. "I don't mind." He moves past me and almost leaps over the corpse into the little cabin. He looks around for a moment. "I don't think so," he says in the end. "The cushions are stacked to one side of the seat as we had them. There's my half bottle of water on the table, and," he says, checking the washroom, "our toothbrushes are where we left them. It's impossible to say for sure, of course, but if anyone has been hiding out here, they didn't touch anything."

"Wasn't there a guard outside 16G?" I say, frightened now that there may be yet another body to discover. "Where is he?"

Fleischmann shakes his head. "With the extra personnel required to maintain the quarantine, and to deliver food to all the cabins, I decided that placing a man outside 16G was a luxury we could not afford. Needless to say, I regret that decision now."

"Is everybody else accounted for?" I stretch to see as I try to do a head count.

"Everyone seems to have found their way here except Clarice and Penelope Mayfield," Whitman replies.

"They may still be in the Paris Suite," Joe says, "but we should check that they're all right."

Fleischmann immediately sends two stewards to the Grand Suites to retrieve the old ladies. "We must clear this corridor and maintain calm," he says quietly.

Duplantier nods and directs us to return to the bar, leaving

Fleischmann and his stewards to move Sartori's body out of the corridor. I presume he will be placed in some makeshift morgue with Maxim and the other slain steward. The image it conjures is grim and deeply sad. My God, how could this be happening? We are escorted back to the Bar Car, and I am relieved to see Frank, alive and well. I hadn't till then been aware that I was worried about him. Somehow, on a crowded train, the killer manages to find his victims alone, to appear in those few moments that there are no witnesses, no one to help or cry for help. Joe slips his arm around my shoulders. "Are you all right, Meri?"

"The killer was in our cabin, Joe, or at least near it. What if one of us had gone back to freshen up or collect something…"

"I know." He tightens his grip a little. "We'll be in Paris in the morning."

"If there is anyone left," I murmur.

He smiles. "Come on, Meri; you're the positive twin, remember? Buster stormed off to conduct his own investigation. Maybe he was on to something, and it got him killed. We just have to work out what he was doing outside our cabin, or at least in Carriage 16."

"Doesn't this unnerve you, even a little, Joe?"

"That he was outside our cabin?" He shakes his head. "Buster was clearly of the opinion that we were engaged in some conspiracy with Napoleon. It's not surprising that the first thing he would do is search our cabins. I expect he thought we'd all be in the bar for a while."

"But how did the murderer know Buster would be poking about our cabins at precisely that moment?"

"He might not have known, Meri. The murderer might have slipped back to 16G to retrieve some incriminating evidence that we have all so far overlooked. Perhaps Buster stumbled over him and not the other way around."

We take a seat opposite Abigay Williams while we wait for the word on the Mayfields. Rees and Singh have their heads together, and Elle is talking to Frank at the bar. Bob Whitman, as always, is at her elbow, and the barman seems shy in the presence of the duchess. Duplantier sits by himself staring out the window.

I excuse myself and move to sit next to him.

"Are you all right, Napoleon? You seem shaken."

He sighs. "If by shaken you mean responsible, yes, I do feel that."

"Responsible? For Buster?"

"Yes, I should have not allowed Monsieur Sartori to leave, or at least I should have sent someone after him."

"How could you know—" I begin my defense.

"Three people had been killed before him, Meredith," he says wearily. "I became so focused on catching Cheval that I failed to be vigilant."

"As did we all, Napoleon, most of all Buster himself." I touch Duplantier's arm to make sure he's paying attention to what I'm saying. "For the record, short of tying him up, I don't think you could have kept him from leaving the bar."

"You are very kind, Meredith, but I did not even try. Indeed, I was relieved not to have to deal with him for a few minutes."

I wince. "You were not alone in that." I follow his gaze to the window. It is dark so the glass offers not a view to the world outside but a reflection of what is inside the Bar Car. I realize now that Napoleon Duplantier is not gazing at the window out of some melancholy, but because he is surreptitiously watching the people in the Bar Car.

"Do you suspect one of us?" I ask bluntly.

Duplantier does not take his eyes off the window. "Of killing Monsieur Sartori?" I watch his reflection flinch a little. "Only you and your brother remained in the Bar Car. The rest, on my suggestion, stretched the legs."

I want to inquire further into his thinking, but we are interrupted by the return of the Mayfield sisters. Clarice is leaning heavily on her stick, while Penelope seems short of breath. They look around the car. "Whatever is the matter? We were having quite a nice visit with Paula."

Duplantier informs them that Buster Sartori has been killed.

"Oh, my Lord! Where?"

"Carriage 16."

"Oh, thank goodness!" Penelope blurts.

The exclamation is met with a kind of heavy silence.

"I mean that we were on the other side of the train," Penelope clarifies. "I know it's selfish of me, but I do not want to confront the murderer personally. With Clarice's heart and my lumbago…"

"Of course," Duplantier says kindly. He proceeds to explain to the Mayfields what has happened in their absence. I listen carefully, as there are things that Joe and I still don't know. Apparently, it was Rees who first came across the body of Buster Sartori, only a minute or so before Singh also came down the corridor. Rees remained with the body while Singh fetched Fleischmann, who was at the time speaking to Duplantier. They attended the scene with a number of stewards in tow, and then the Duchess of Kinross and the ever-faithful Bob Whitman arrived on their way to the Grand Suites. And then finally, Joe and I showed up.

Throughout, the Mayfields gasp and exclaim. Clarice asks Duplantier to repeat some parts as her "hearing is not as good as it was."

"This is shocking, isn't it, Penny?" Clarice says in the end.

"Yes, shocking!" Penelope agrees. "We were beginning to suspect him, you see. I suppose it couldn't be him now?"

"Suspect? Why in heaven's name would you suspect Buster Sartori?" Elle Baird voices what we are all wondering.

"Well, he's that type, isn't he, Penny?"

"Yes, definitely that type. Always big-noting himself, desperate to have people regard him as a renowned detective."

"We thought he might have murdered Mr. Harrington for the attention, or the chance to save the day." Clarice sniffs contemptuously. "Like those people who join the fire brigade and then set fires so they can swoop in and be heroes. There's not much point being a private eye if there's nothing to investigate."

"Have you been persuaded that Mr. Harrington is dead?" I ask the sisters, intrigued. They have until now insisted that Mr. Harrington was the murderer, rather than a victim.

Clarice nods. "He must be. We'll never get the Civic Society's money back now, but at least he has met some sort of justice. We can be comforted by that, I suppose."

Joe grimaces.

"Whyever are you pulling faces, young man?" Penelope demands.

Joe doesn't backpedal. "It just seems a tad harsh to be comforted by murder."

Clarice pauses. She takes a deep breath, and when she speaks again, her voice has a barely perceptible shake. "You are right, of course. I am a foolish old woman overcome with the dreadfulness of it all. It's just that Penny and I will have to tell the Civic Society that we have failed them, that the nursing home will not be built and...oh..." She pulls a handkerchief from her handbag and sniffs into it. "It's all too bad, just too bad." She and Penelope huddle together, the latter glaring at Joe.

And now, naturally, Joe feels bad. I can tell by the way he plunges his hands into his pockets like a sulky twelve-year-old. "Of course... I didn't mean..."

The awkwardness is relieved by the arrival of dinner trays. We are invited to eat in the dining car since it is not being used and there are no tables in the Bar Car. As the gleaming silver plate covers hint at something more than sandwiches, we accept and retire to Étoile du Nord.

When the covers are lifted, it is apparent that service on trays does in no way compromise the presentation or quality of meals on the Orient Express. We are presented with risotto and warm, freshly baked bread rolls, embossed butter, green salad with dressing on the side, and, for dessert, chocolate mousse and poached pears. Even so, the stewards apologize as they place the trays before us. Having not eaten since breakfast, we are ravenous, and for several minutes I can think of nothing else but how delicious every mouthful is. I close my eyes to savor the firing of each and every taste bud.

I hear Joe laugh, and reluctantly I drag my attention from the wild mushroom and black rice risotto to raise an eyebrow at him. "What?"

"Nothing," he says, grinning. "But I suspect no man will ever make you as happy as risotto does."

Duplantier looks up. "You do your own sex a disservice, *mon frère*, to suggest we will be defeated by rice porridge."

I laugh…more at the notion of calling the exquisite dish before me "rice porridge" than anything else. "You'll excuse me if I don't comment—I want to eat before something else happens."

"Ever the pragmatist," Joe says, speeding up his own intake—just in case I'm right, I imagine.

Duplantier holds up a finger. "*J'ai oublié.* The woman in 12C would like to see you. A Madame Lesley Bocquet."

"Me?" I am surprised.

"No, no—not you, Meredith," Duplantier replies. "Joe Penvale."

Joe keeps eating.

"She hopes you will call on her at the earliest convenience," Duplantier prompts.

Joe nods.

"Who is she, Joe?" I ask.

"An acquaintance, I guess."

"What is she doing here?"

Joe shrugs. "Clearly, I am irresistible."

"So, she followed you onto the Orient Express?"

"She might have become…you know…obsessed with me."

"Are you serious?" I'm aghast, almost despairing. On top of everything else we're contending with, Joe produces an actual stalker.

"I think it's best just to ignore her."

"Dammit, Joe! Is she dangerous?"

"Compared to what?"

"Joe!" My God, he can be infuriating!

Joe rolls his eyes. "Don't overreact, Meri. If I ignore her, she'll probably get in a huff and never speak to me again. So let's do that."

I turn to Duplantier since Joe is determined to be an idiot. "When exactly did she speak to you, Napoleon?"

"She had stepped out of her cabin to use the restroom when I was walking past in search of Herr Fleischmann. She seemed quite startled to see me, so I introduced myself and assured her I am not a murderer."

"And what did she say?"

"That her name was Lesley Bocquet…it is a beautiful name, no? She wondered if I had encountered a passenger called Joe Penvale." Duplantier glances almost apologetically at Joe. "I told her that I had indeed, and she asked me to tell you that she was on board, and she would like to catch up with you."

"And she told you all this," Joe says, "without trying to shoot, stab, or strangle you?"

"*Naturellement!*" Duplantier replies.

"Then I think it is clear that of all the issues competing for our attention at the moment, Ms. Bocquet is the least of our concerns."

"What if she is the murderer?" I hear myself asking. "What if it's been her all along?"

"All the more reason not to accept her invitation, I would think." Joe turns and meets my gaze. "Look, Meri, trust me. Lesley is not dangerous, but it would be best if I avoided her."

"Did you know she was on board?" I demand, remembering the occasions when Joe seemed to be ducking for cover for no apparent reason. "Have you been avoiding her this whole time?"

Joe sighs. "I have caught sight of her once or twice and have tried to make sure she didn't see me."

If we hadn't been in the circumstances we were, Joe and I might have argued about avoidance strategies and their failure to resolve anything. But at the moment, my brother's haphazard love life is more an annoyance than an issue. I can tell that he is holding something back, but I don't ask. It's personal. If he wants to tell me about Lesley Bocquet and why she followed him onto the Orient Express, he will. I suspect their relationship is not as casual or as fleeting as he claims, though considering he has spent most of the last eighteen months in treatment, it's hard to know when he had time for any kind of secret liaison.

"Yeah, all right. Though if you're not interested, you should put the poor woman out of her misery."

Joe begins on his chocolate mousse. "I'll talk to her once we're off this train. I promise."

And so, I let it go.

We return to the bar after dinner, but we are all starting to flag. No one travels on the Orient Express to sleep, I guess, but this group of passengers has probably slept less than most. We go over what we know again, mapping a timeline from the moment Blackwell stepped onto the Orient Express in London. Dinner with Paula Atkinson; a brief, curt interaction with Joe as he returns to 16G; and then the discovery of the blood-spattered cabin just after breakfast. The murder of the steward stationed outside 16G at about midday, and then Maxim between four and four fifteen p.m. The inspection of the cabins—the lack of fingerprints, the missing overnight bag, the disturbed items on the table, and the clean space below the lower bunk. And, finally, the killing of Buster Sartori between eight thirty and eight forty-five p.m. The drawings of the man described by each of the Mayfield sisters, as well as a third sketch I made of the man Joe and I saw walk into 16G. I don't think any one of us is truly kidding themself that this mystery will be solved here in the Bar Car, but maybe behaving like it will, crowding our minds with timelines and sightings and suspects, is a distraction sorely needed, as we begin to feel progressively more isolated from the world.

Abigay yawns. Frank serves coffee, but he too is beginning to look tired. I feel sorry for the barman. I wonder if he'll be relieved soon; I feel like he's already worked a very long shift. For a while we go over and over what small amount of evidence we have. And tempers begin to fray and unravel.

Duplantier finally calls an end to the proceedings.

"Ladies and gentlemen, our discussions, I fear, have reached their useful end. Let us retire for the night and reconvene in the morning to collate our findings for conveyance to the authorities. We will all be glad to see Paris, I expect."

I am so relieved when the suggestion is met with enthusiasm.

I feel bone-weary, and the thought of sleep is tantalizing and almost desperate.

As a precaution, stewards escort us to our cabins and the Mayfields to Bob Whitman's suite. He moves into Elle Baird's apartments. As we open our respective cabin doors in Carriage 16, I am caught by a sharp concern about Napoleon Duplantier. He is, after all, leading the Bar Council, and he does not share his compartment. The one consistent feature of these murders, three of which have now taken place at or in association with the cabin between us, has been that the victims were alone when they were attacked.

"Napoleon," I say, stepping over the floor where Sartori fell, though the body has been removed and the area cleaned of blood, "are you sure it's safe for you to sleep alone?"

Duplantier looks vaguely nonplussed, and Joe starts to laugh.

"Meri, that has to be the world's most unsubtle pickup line! Whatever happened to 'do you come here often?'"

I feel the blood rising in my face as it dawns on me what I've said. "No, that's not what I meant… Joe shut up!" I begin blithering about my entirely valid and platonic concern. The steward is grinning now, and I want to kill Joe myself.

Duplantier smiles. "You make a very sensible point, Meredith. I am comforted that you and your brother share a cabin, and I assure you I will take extra precautions. I thank you for your concern, *mon amie*, but you must not worry—I will sleep with one eye open!"

The steward clears his throat. "I could stand guard—"

"Merci, but no," Duplantier says immediately. "You and

your brave comrades appear to be in the most danger of all. Let us not give him a chance to do more."

Joe and I add our agreement.

Still mortified, I wish Napoleon Duplantier a good night and return to 16F. Joe wishes Duplantier good luck and closes the door. He locks it and drops his laptop onto the lower bunk. "You can get changed first?" he offers, climbing into the bed. "Just be quick or I'll fall asleep waiting for you." He turns to the wall to give me some privacy. As I said, getting dressed quickly is my superpower, and the reverse is also true. I am in pajamas, cat-washed, moisturized, and teeth brushed in under five minutes. I climb onto the upper bunk wondering at the discipline and dedication of the stewards who quietly converted our cabin into a sleeper in the midst of all this mayhem.

I stare at the ceiling while Joe changes and brushes his teeth. "You know, I really miss showers."

"You had one a little over twenty-four hours ago," Joe informs me through a mouthful of toothpaste.

"I know, but it feels like it was a month ago. I'm sure I could think more clearly if I could just shower. Wet washcloths are not the same thing as hot running water."

Joe sighs. "I wonder what Buster Sartori knew or discovered that made him our latest victim."

"You think he learned something about the killer?"

"He took off to conduct his own investigation."

"He was killed outside our door. His investigation took him to us!"

"He might have been trying to get into 16G…or 16H."

It takes me a moment to work out what he's saying. "16H?

You're saying he might have been trying to search Napoleon's cabin?"

"Maybe."

"That's absurd." Even as I say it, I'm not sure it is in fact absurd.

"Can we account for where he was when the murders were committed?"

I try to think, but my brain resists. *Go to sleep*, it screams... *Tell Joe to shut up and go to sleep!* "I'm not sure we can account for anyone during the murders," I mumble in the end.

"True." Joe seems to be on a bit of a roll. "Certainly for the murder next door. And the steward placed on guard. What about Maxim? Where was Napoleon then?"

"I can't remember. I think we dispersed to stretch our legs and so forth when you went to fetch him."

"On whose orders?"

"We weren't ordered to do anything, but I recall the break was Napoleon's suggestion."

"Interesting. He also suggested we break after Buster Sartori stormed out."

"Can we please talk about this in the morning?"

I hear the creak and shuffle of Joe climbing into the lower bunk. "Yes, okay."

Once again, I drift off to the soft pad of Joe's fingers on the keys of his laptop.

Chapter 20

It is still dark when I wake, regaining full consciousness abruptly. My heart is pounding. Something is different. Joe is already up and at the window. And then I realize what has changed, what woke me. The train is slowing down.

"We're not there already, are we?"

I can hear as well as feel it now. The brakes. I slip down from the upper bunk, cursing as I stub my toe on the ladder in my rush to join Joe at the window. We couldn't possibly be in Paris already, surely.

"I reckon it's just the French border," Joe says. "They'll check the paperwork before we're allowed to cross."

I breathe out. Of course. We would have made the same stop on the way out, but we clearly slept through it then. I peer out the window. I am surprised by the lights ahead of us.

"Our passports are missing," Joe says. "This might be awkward."

The Orient Express comes to a stop.

For a moment the desire to disembark is overwhelming.

Perhaps Joe notices, because he presses my hand. "Not long now, Meri. We'll be pulling into Gare de l'Est before you know it."

The searchlights catch us both by surprise. They flood the carriages and rouse anyone who might have slept through the stopping of the train. And then the sound of helicopters.

"What the devil's going on?" Joe scrambles for his clothes.

"What are you doing?"

"Something's going on, Meri. Whatever it is, I'd rather not deal with it in pajamas."

"I expect it's just a fuss about the missing passports," I reply. "They'll sort it out and we'll be on our way again soon. This is, after all, the Orient Express."

"Still, we should be ready."

I climb back up to the upper bunk. "You be ready. I'm going back to bed."

I lie down, determined to go back to sleep, but Morpheus refuses to open his arms to me. Joe takes a seat by the little table under the window and watches.

"I don't suppose they're going to let us disembark here," I ask.

"I can't see any ambulances," Joe says, "so I doubt it."

"What do you suppose is going on?"

"No idea." Joe shakes his head. "Maybe this is just normal for a closed border. It was still open when we came through the other way."

That makes sense. It's nothing out of the ordinary. We should just go back to sleep. But I cannot sleep now. So I just lie there, listening to Joe breathe as he watches.

"Do you want to tell me about Lesley Bocquet?" I ask to relieve the tension of waiting for the train to move again.

"No."

"Come on, Joe. It's just me."

"There is nothing to tell."

His tone makes it clear that no amount of teasing or cajoling will change his mind. I give up before he becomes annoyed.

"What on earth?" Joe presses his face to the window. "Bloody hell!"

A gunshot, and then a volley of gunshots. I hit my head on the ceiling sitting up too quickly. "Joe!"

He stands up and helps me down. We both huddle by the window. I can see flashing lights now. Searchlights swing along the length of the train. A new concentration of lights appears at the end of the train. "What happened?"

"I think some passengers tried to jump off the train."

"They shot them?" I gasp.

"No—I think, I hope, those were warning shots." He hugs me. "Better get dressed, Meri. Looks like the world is about to go nuts."

I glance at my watch. Half past four. Six hours since we went to bed. I've negotiated multimillion-dollar contracts on less. I pull on a pair of jeans, a sweater, and my sneakers. I packed them in my carry-on luggage a lifetime ago for tromping around Venice before reboarding the train. It's not quite up to the dress standards of the Orient Express, but it may be time to let standards slip. I grab a hair elastic from my toiletry bag and tie back my hair. "Okay, I'm ready. What now?"

I catch Joe smiling in the pass of a searchlight. "You've got your Ninja face on."

"Shut up."

"It's not a bad thing," he says, opening his laptop.

"You're going to write now?" Even for Joe, this is insane.

"Of course not," he says, plugging a USB into the machine. "We haven't had coverage for a while, so I can't back up to the cloud, and I can't always take the laptop with me." He pulls out the USB and slips it into his pocket. "Just in case."

"When did we lose coverage?" I ask. While I take photos often, I don't really have social media nor do I surf without reason, so I haven't noticed that we've been offline all this time.

"Since we first found 16G, in my estimation. The email you sent with my manuscript attached still hasn't gone."

"That's odd, don't you think?" I whip out my phone and try to connect, somehow needing to see for myself. "The whole route of the Orient Express can't be a blackout spot. And surely we were covered when we approached Venice…or now at the border." A familiar rotating circle tells me that my phone is not connecting.

Joe shrugs. "Not so odd. The Orient Express probably doesn't want to risk passengers posting pictures of bodies and so forth. And I expect Italy and France want to control any information of an infected train shuffling between Paris and Venice. They've probably blocked the signals or something."

"Is that even possible?" For God's sake, people post from war zones!

"I don't know," Joe replies. "Maybe you can turn the train into a giant moving Faraday cage. Anyway, I suspect we can take it as a given that anybody who might be inclined to help us knows what's been going on."

Considering what's happened in the last day and a half, you wouldn't think that not having internet would be a particular concern, but the realization unnerves me. If we are invisible, we are unprotected by all the laws and rights we've always taken for granted. That someone would be intentionally making the Orient Express invisible terrifies me. "God, it sounds like Hitchcock's people are winning."

Joe looks at me. "Meri...breathe. We'll be okay."

I give myself an internal shake and force myself to smile. "Of course we will. I have my Ninja face on."

"Right, then." He grins. "Let's grab Duplantier and then make our way back to the Bar Car."

I agree. Napoleon has been in regular conversation with Herr Fleischmann. He might understand what is going on.

There is another volley of gunshots.

"Warning shots," Joe says firmly.

I nod. Just warnings. Fucking Hitchcock.

We are not alone when we emerge into the corridor. Other passengers have naturally been woken by the stopping of the train and the floodlights and gunfire. And there are now many anxious people in Orient Express robes in the corridor. Duplantier, fully dressed in a three-piece suit, is trying valiantly to reassure our fellow travelers.

"Nobody has been shot. It is merely to highlight that passengers should not yet leave the train."

"Who on earth highlights disembarking procedures with machine guns?" a woman in pink flamingo pajamas snaps.

Others echo the sentiment. The word *outrageous* is bandied about, and Duplantier is beleaguered. Joe and I maneuver to stand beside him in some proximate show of support. It doesn't turn out to be the best idea.

"Hey, why are you all dressed already? Did you know this was going to happen?"

"Of course not," Joe replies for all of us.

"You are the people who've been in the bar while the rest of us have been locked up!" It's our friend with the long hair from yesterday's thwarted rebellion. I'm not sure what he's doing in Carriage 16. "Laughing at us all while you drink and call the shots."

"And it just so happens"—Pink-flamingo-pajamas adds fuel to the fire—"that they have the cabins either side of where six people have been murdered!"

"Six?" Joe begins. "That's just—"

Long-blond-hair reaches out and grabs Joe by the throat, slamming him against the windows with such a crack that for a heartbeat I am convinced another shot has been fired. But it's Joe's head against the pane. Duplantier and I move immediately to Joe's aid, but someone pushes me in the opposite direction. And suddenly it's a fight. I don't know if all the other passengers are against us, or if some are trying to help, or if some are simply hitting out at anyone in frustration. I find myself on the floor with a hysterical woman slapping at my head. I can't see Joe or Duplantier. Then someone pulls off my assailant, and someone else offers me a hand. I look up into the face of Siobhan Ferguson, the travel writer I'd met in the Midnight Bar the first night on board. She gets me up, doing her best to protect me from further assault. Her husband, Noel, seems to have subdued Long-blond-hair with some kind of choke hold, and the remaining passengers seem to have calmed somewhat. In fact, some must have returned to their cabins, as it seems fewer people are in the corridor. Duplantier is with Joe, who is touching the back of his head gingerly.

"Joe…"

"I'm all right. Just a bit of an egg on the back of my skull."

"What should I do with this eejit?" Noel asks.

"Let him go," Duplantier says, staring at the man in disgust. "If I hear from you again, I'll arrest you myself, as soon as we cross the border. *Comprenez-vous?*"

Noel Ferguson releases him, and under Duplantier's threat and the silent glare of us all, he retreats, backing away into Carriage 17. A couple of passengers go with him, while others mumble apologies or disclaimers and return to their cabins.

I turn to Siobhan and Noel. "Thank you."

"Indeed," Duplantier agrees, shaking Noel's hand. "Your arrival was well timed."

"Grateful for your assassin-type skills," Joe adds. "Did you say you were in finance?"

Siobhan laughs. "Noel does jujitsu to keep fit… I never thought it would come in useful."

"What are you doing here?" I ask. I recall their cabin is in a different carriage.

"We came out of the cabin to see if anyone knew what was happening"—Siobhan takes my hand—"and we heard the shouting."

"So naturally we ran toward it," Noel mutters, indicating that the decision might have been Siobhan's.

"Do you know what's happening?" There is the slightest tremor in Siobhan's voice. "Why are they shooting?"

"I expect some people tried to get off the train."

"Feck! Since when is that punishable by firing squad?"

"They were just warning shots," Joe says. "Let's hope they worked."

"People are starting to panic." Noel puts an arm around his wife, and they look at each other for a moment. "Maybe we should have gone to Disneyland."

Duplantier smiles fleetingly. "Surely it's not so bad yet?"

"What should we do?" Siobhan asks.

"You are probably safest in your cabin," Duplantier replies. "Particularly if we are to see more skirmishes. Hopefully we will be on our way soon, and then it is only hours till we pull into Gare de l'Est."

Noel's eyes narrow. "What are you lot doing? The eejit with the hair said you were congregating at the bar—"

I tell him honestly. "Herr Fleischmann gathered everybody with investigative or legal expertise to advise him on how to handle the missing passenger and the state of 16G."

"Right, we heard about that. It's going well, is it?"

"Not particularly," Joe concedes.

"What's the problem?"

"An excess of bodies, though not one is the bloke from 16G."

Noel nods sympathetically, as if we were talking about traffic in London.

"I don't suppose either of you noticed a man about this tall"—I indicate against Joe—"with a full dark beard and blue eyes and…" I try to remember the details Joe had given the others.

"He was pigeon-toed," Joe finishes, demonstrating the man's walk.

Noel rubs his chin. "And when would we have seen this pigeon-man?"

"The night we came on board."

Noel shrugs. "I don't notice as much as Siobhan, and she doesn't notice as much as she photographs."

Siobhan pulls out her cell phone. "I've taken hundreds of photos in the last couple of days. It'll take an age to look at each one."

"We should get back to the bar and see how many of us are still standing," Joe cautions as I consider looking through Siobhan's record of our journey for the man in 16G.

Siobhan glances at her husband. "Here," she says, holding out her cell phone. "Let's swap. I'd look through and send you any pertinent images, but we have no coverage. This way you can look through my images when you get a chance for your bearded pigeon-man, and I can take photos with your phone… Please tell me you don't use something ancient with a terrible camera?"

I laugh as I hand her my latest-model Samsung. I'd bought it for this trip. Before that, I'd used a five-year-old iPhone that was losing its functionality and had a crack in its lens. "Thank you, Siobhan. I'll take good care of it." At the very least, a photo might establish that we're all talking about the same person.

We exchange passwords and I am aware of how much trust we are putting in each other with this trade. Not that I intend to look at anything in Siobhan's phone aside from her photographs, nor do I have anything on my phone that I was particularly concerned about Siobhan seeing, but still it feels strange.

"I've been thinking about upgrading to one of these," Siobhan says, smiling as she examines my phone. "This will give me a chance to try it out."

"It took me a little while to learn to drive it properly," I warn.

Duplantier clears his throat. "If you are ready," he says politely, "we should make our way…" He trails off with a glance in the direction of the Bar Car.

"Of course," I reply. "This is not really the time to be chatting in the corridors."

"Should we walk you back to your cabin?" Duplantier offers.

Joe laughs. "Noel just saved us from the mob… I don't think he needs our protection."

Noel flexes his biceps, clearly gratified as well as amused. "I expect we'll be all right."

I believe him. There's a quiet confidence about the Irishman, an unflappability that's reassuring.

And so we take our leave of the Fergusons, wishing each other luck. The corridors are not as congested as they were a short time before, but there are a few people looking tentatively out of the large windows and speaking in urgent, hushed tones. It's difficult to make out exactly what is outside the train because it is still predawn, and any vision is compromised by the glare of the spotlights directed toward the carriages of Orient Express.

Joe pauses to look out anyway. "This is a little bit fucked," he says under his breath.

"*Vraiment*," Duplantier replies. "That it is."

Chapter 21

I don't say anything, unnerved that, for the first time, Joe sounds uncertain that we'll come out of this. He doesn't say that, of course, but I remember that edge in his voice. I've heard it before. People think that illness, impending death, makes the sufferer truthful somehow. It's why, legally speaking, weight is given to deathbed confessions or declarations, over and above utterances made without mortal fear. My recent experience, however, is that even in the shadow of death, honesty is compromised by bravado, by the need to convince yourself and those you love that all is not lost; pain is downplayed, despair denied, and optimism flung over everything in an attempt to contain panic. And so, fear escapes only occasionally, breaking through the frantic positivity in another guise. And in time you recognize it, but you too are pretending everything will be okay, so there is a kind of pact not to acknowledge how bad things are, out loud at least.

I decide to join the denial club. "We'd best get back to the bar, so we can sort this out before we pull into Gare de l'Est."

The fact that the train is stationary should make it quicker to traverse the carriages, but it doesn't. We are aware of doors being cracked open to see us passing. Some passengers step out to ask us what we know, what we've seen, what we think. We try to avoid extended conversation by pleading that we too are just passengers, and, for the most part, that works. Occasionally, we are challenged about the fact that we are walking the corridors at all. Joe replies that we are searching for an unoccupied restroom, and we manage to get by with a pretext of urgency, though one woman suggests archly that we wait to use the one on the end of our own carriage.

We also encounter stewards moving in the other direction as they deliver predawn cocoa to each cabin with promises that we will be on our way again soon. I notice that the stewards keep each other in sight as they hand over the trays.

"Napoleon!" A passenger catches sight of us through the open door and hails the Frenchman. He is tall and solid—the kind of physique that's gym-built. His head is shaved or he's very bald, and his accent, thick even in a single word utterance, is Eastern European.

Duplantier stops and turns. He sees the man who called his name, and then he smiles—half a beat too late, I think. Perhaps he's simply tired, which he probably is, but it may be that he isn't all that pleased to meet this man here.

"Alexei" is all he says.

"Napoleon Duplantier, how is it I did not know you were on board, my friend?"

"I have never been able to explain your lack of knowledge, Alexei. It has always perplexed me."

Alexei laughs. He takes the tray from the steward. "Stop here a moment, join me for a drink, and we will rectify my ignorance."

We fully expect Duplantier to tell the man that he has no time to stop to catch up, and so it is a surprise when he nods.

"Why don't you continue on to the Bar Car?" he says to Joe and me. "I'll catch up with you shortly."

"Are you sure?" The words are out before I can suppress them.

"Run along, little girl." Alexei smirks. "You will barely have time to miss him."

Duplantier glares at Alexei, but he doesn't walk away.

"Come on, Meri," Joe says, "I need to talk to you anyway."

And so we leave Duplantier to reacquaint himself with the man he calls Alexei, however strange the timing, and continue toward the Bar Car.

The dining cars are busy with stewards returning for more trays and others going out. We make our way through silently. It's in the third dining car that Joe grabs my arm.

"Let's just stop for a bit. I need to talk to you."

"Can't we do that in the bar?"

"Some of the others may be in the bar already. Come on, let's sit for a bit." He takes a seat at one of the tables and motions me to the chair opposite.

I sit down and lean forward toward him, assuming he wants to talk about Alexei and why Duplantier acceded to his demand that they have a drink now.

"What do you think this Alexei character has over Napoleon?" I ask. "You could have knocked me over with a feather when Napoleon agreed—"

"Actually, that's not what I wanted to talk to you about… though I agree it's odd and we should talk about it, but later."

I glance quickly around the carriage. The stewards are too preoccupied with their own duties to pay any attention to us, and from where we sit, Joe can see anyone entering in one direction and I can do so in the other. It is as good a choice for a private conversation as possible under the circumstances.

"Okay…what's up?" I pull up suddenly. "Are you feeling okay? Are you—?"

"I'm fine, Meri. This is not about me." Joe shakes his head irritably, as if the question is ridiculous, as if there is no reason for me to worry about him. But there's no time for that argument right now.

"What then?"

He exhales. "I think I might have worked out why there were no fingerprints in 16G…maybe."

"What do you mean?"

"Well, I could be seeing things that aren't there because for the last year everything has been about chemo and blood tests and radiotherapy… Maybe that's all I can see now."

"Sorry." I'm confused now. "What on earth are you talking about?"

"My life, our lives, have been all about me and my illness for so long." Joe seems anxious. Really unsure. "I'm just worried that it's become the lens through which I view the world now."

I smile. "Maybe it is. But maybe you noticed something important anyway. How about you tell me and let me decide whether you're on to something or just really self-involved… or both?"

He hesitates.

"Come on, Joey; we haven't got time to stuff around."

He nods. "Yeah, okay." Joe brings his head close to mine. "Do you remember that first round of chemo I was on… Oxi-something and some other drugs—they called it Folfox."

"Yes, I remember." It had been the first and toughest round and not something I could forget.

"Do you remember the side effects?"

"Yes…skin reactions, cold sensitivity, hair loss…but, Joe, what has that got to do with—"

"Do you remember what happened to my hands?"

"I remember you couldn't bear cold or metallic surfaces—"

"Yes, but it was more than that. My nails discolored, the skin on my hands and feet cracked and peeled. And I lost my fingerprints."

"Yes…" I had actually forgotten, till now. Joe's hands and fingers had become shiny as his skin became taut, and his fingerprints disappeared. We hadn't noticed the swelling until then, distracted by more attention-seeking side effects. The biometrics on his phone would not work. He became a butterfingers, with previously stable items now slipping through the smoothness. I finally begin to follow.

"You think the passenger in 16G has undergone chemotherapy?"

"Recently." Joe holds up his hands. "My fingerprints are back."

I say nothing for a moment, contemplating. "It's a bit of a coincidence, don't you think?"

"How do you mean?"

"Well, that the person in the cabin next to ours not only has cancer but happens to have been treated with the same poison."

"Not really." Joe shrugs. "There are hundreds of different cancers, but Folfox is used to treat many of them. And considering the average age of people who can afford a berth on the Orient Express, or who have saved up for this particular bucket-list item, I reckon a significant proportion may have cancer, or have had cancer. Perhaps the bloke in 16G is celebrating too, or perhaps this is his last hurrah."

"Okay," I reply tentatively. "You're right, of course, but what does that tell us?"

"Well, it could explain a few things. Remember Paula Atkinson thought the man she had dinner with was wearing a wig. So maybe the chemo induced hair loss as well. It could be the passenger in 16G doesn't have a hair on his head as well as no fingerprints. It would explain the lack of any fingerprints or follicles in the cabin."

I shake my head, still reluctant to accept the idea. "Yes, but could someone suffering cancer have murdered two men and disposed of a body without help?"

"The stewards were stabbed in the jugular from behind… no struggle, relatively little strength required. As for the cabin and the missing body, I don't know. Perhaps he did have help." Joe defends his theory. "This would explain Blackwell's clumsiness at dinner. Without prints, things slip out of your hands bloody easily and… Meri?" He's looking at me closely. "What's wrong? You look like you've seen a ghost—"

"Not quite a ghost." I grab his shirt and draw him closer. I'm on board suddenly and absolutely. "Frank."

Chapter 22

The barman?"

"Yes, he's bald, and he's clumsy." It starts to fall into place now. "He paints his fingernails, Joe. When he's not wearing gloves."

"He couldn't possibly be both staff and a passenger... someone would have recognized him," Joe points out. "And he's a Kiwi... Surely someone would have mentioned if Blackwell or Harrington was a Kiwi."

"The Express changed crew at the French-Italian border as we were going through. It would have been easy to slip in as one of the new crew then. An unfamiliar face would not have been remarkable..." I pause, trying to hear Frank's voice in my head. As far as I can tell Frank's accent is flawless, but I'm Australian, not a New Zealander. It strikes me that the Kiwi accent is a clever choice in terms of disguise when you're speaking to an Australian. There's an immediate antipodean connection, a familiarity but not so much that I might pick up the odd slip in inflection, and it hides him from all those chasing an English or

European criminal. "Frank speaks with a New Zealand accent at the moment. It's not a hard accent to pull off when you're not actually speaking to Kiwis. I've heard you do a reasonable Kiwi accent."

"But he's been in the room, listening to us all discussing the murders…" Joe's voice is becoming more alarmed than dubious.

"Yes."

"I don't know, Meri. You think he killed Maxim, and the other steward and Sartori in between making cocktails?" Joe swears. "We have to tell Napoleon."

I shake my head. "No…this could all still be a coincidence. He could just be a clumsy man who likes manicures. I want to be sure before we accuse anyone of being a murderer."

Joe frowns. "What are you proposing we do?"

"We confront him ourselves. Give him a chance to explain. It's not as if he can go anywhere."

Joe considers it. "If he is our man, then he's dangerous."

"As you said, the stewards were taken by surprise from behind and they were alone. We won't give him that opportunity. And if it does turn out that he's a murderer, we just shout for help."

Joe sighs. "Something tells me it's not going to be that simple, but why not. Let's try it."

To be honest, I'm not sure what has suddenly turned me into Nancy Drew. I am excited about what Joe and I have put together, but I want to be sure. I don't want to look like an idiot in front of Duplantier—of everybody—if we're wrong. Or perhaps it's because as much as I have volunteered Frank as a possible culprit, I do like him. I feel I owe him a chance to defend himself before I denounce him to the Bar Council.

"So how are we going to do this?" Joe asks.

"We have to try to get Frank alone."

Joe glances at the end of the dining car, which leads to the bar. "Let's see who's in the bar—we may be lucky."

We are not. Not entirely, anyway. Frank was still behind the bar, but Elle Baird and Bob Whitman have returned, as have Aled Rees, Ajeet Singh, and Abigay Williams.

"There you are!" Abigay exclaims as we enter. "We're just waiting on the old ladies and the Gov then."

"The Gov?" Joe asks.

"Monsieur Duplantier." Abigay rolls the name on her tongue with flourish.

"Actually, we're on an errand from Herr Fleischmann," I announce, with a glance at Joe to go along with me. "He wants Frank to take a tray of the Orient Express's best scotch and six glasses on a tray to the first carriage."

"What on earth for?" Whitman is the only one who seems interested.

"I believe he's negotiating with border officials to gain us entry back into France."

Elle Baird nods. "You better take a couple of mixers too, just in case."

"I can help you," I volunteer as Frank begins to look uneasy.

"And I'll come along as security," Joe says. "With everything that's happened, we can't be too careful."

For a moment I'm afraid that Joe has overplayed, but the others seem to accept the notion and return to their earlier conversations.

"Where is Monsieur Duplantier?" asks the Duchess of

Kinross. "We are very nearly back in France, and he's essentially the leader of our Bar Council. Let's just hope he has not become a victim of this elusive fiend."

"He stopped to speak with one of the passengers," Joe informs her as I help Frank gather scotch, soda, and a bucket of ice. "He said he wouldn't be too long."

Frank drops the ice.

"Which passenger?" Singh looks up.

"Alexei." Joe's face is hard to read. "An old friend, I think."

Singh frowns but expresses no concern or disapproval out loud.

"And Herr Fleischmann?" Abigay directs the inquiry at us, presumably because we brought the message for Frank.

"I believe he's trying his best to get the train admitted into France," Joe says, "even if he has to get the border officials drunk to do so."

Aled Rees is not optimistic. "There are demonstrations in Paris calling for the Orient Express to be prevented from returning," he says mostly to Singh, though we all hear. "Some groups are threatening to blow up the track. There's a fair bit of hysteria."

"But we left from Gare de l'Est," Elle protests. "How can they—"

"There are claims that the strain we carry is not the Paris variant but something even more dangerous emanating from Italy and brought on board by the Italian crew. Apparently, someone has tried to extort the Italian government with the threat of a new pandemic just before the Orient Express approached Venice. There are even rumors that the train has become a kind of biological weapon deployed against Europe. The world is panicking."

"That's ridiculous," Whitman explodes. He stops abruptly and turns back to Rees. "How do you know all this? The rest of us have been disconnected since the train initially left Gare de l'Est!"

Rees meets his gaze unflinchingly, but he does not explain himself.

"What does it matter?" Elle snaps. "He knows what he knows."

"I want to know why he is getting communication from the outside world while the rest of us can't pick up a signal for love or money." He takes a step toward Rees. "What was it you said you do, pal?"

If Rees has any intention of replying, he does not do so before Whitman continues.

"What the holy fuck is going on?" He raises his voice and advances on Rees. "What do you know about the infection on board?"

There is a stunned silence as we absorb the implication of Bob Whitman's accusation.

Finally, Aled Rees responds. "I believe I declared on our first meeting that I had a background in international and domestic terrorism. Consequently, my devices are equipped with technology that prevents the signal or reception being blocked."

"Well, then, you can call for help." Abigay claps her hands as if she's calling a room of schoolchildren to order. "Let the people know what's going on via social media, or—"

"Great. Let's make a TikTok," Singh mutters.

Joe laughs, but nothing will soothe Whitman. "I demand you hand over your cell phone, Rees!"

"Why?"

"So that we are all privy to the same information. God knows what's happening out there—the rest of us have been essentially offline for a day."

Rees clearly has no intention of relinquishing his cell phone to Whitman. The argument is poised to escalate.

I grab the tray bearing glasses and a fresh bucket of ice, deciding this is as good a time as any to make our exit. Frank follows suit with the bottle of premium scotch and another of water. Joe seems a little torn, but he falls into step behind us, murmuring, "We won't be long."

Chapter 23

The carriage ahead of the bar is a passenger carriage, though its cabins are not occupied. Instead, they are used to house the *Orient* Express's souvenir shop, a kind of post office that allows passengers to mail letters that are conveyed to the local postal service at each stop, and for storage. And it's deserted. It is consequently ideal for our purposes. We walk through until we are nearly at the end of the carriage, and then I stop. Frank pulls up to avoid running into me.

"Is something wrong?" He turns around to notice that Joe is now directly behind him.

"Well, yes," I say as evenly as I can. "We have a couple of questions we need to ask you."

"What kind of questions?" Frank is wary.

I start. "Where are you from, Frank? I don't remember seeing you in the Midnight Bar when we first boarded."

He shrugs. "I was looking after one of the Grand Suites. They were having a private cocktail party."

"Which Grand Suite was that?"

He barely blinks. "Paris."

Paula Atkinson's suite. She didn't mention a cocktail party when we spoke to her, but there was probably no reason she should.

"Why do you paint your fingernails?" Joe blurts.

"I like to treat myself to a good manicure every now and then."

"Still, not many men paint their nails."

"Maybe not back home or in Australia, but this is Europe. It's more open-minded." Frank seems to be hitting every query right back.

I decide to go directly to the heart of the matter. "Did you board this train as a man called Blackwell?"

And there it is. Realization. Panic.

Frank swings the decanter whiskey at Joe and in the completion of the same movement, pushes me out of the way as he makes a run for it. I save myself from falling only to be collected by Joe as he barges past in pursuit of the fleeing barman. I scramble up and after them both. Then suddenly the lights go out, and we are cast into a shadowy world of moving searchlights in the early twilight. The change seems to confuse Frank, and he hesitates before he tries the door.

Whatever interfered with the functioning of the lights seems to have also deactivated the locks, and the door moves. I see Joe launch himself at Frank to tackle him before he leaves the train. He fails.

The door is open. Frank slips out, and Joe goes after him.

"Joe, no!"

Cursing both the barman and my impetuous brother, I

follow. The air outside is glacial, and it is barely light enough to see. The swinging spotlights make me feel like I'm in some kind of prison break film, which is probably not unreasonably far from the truth. As I run after Joe, gunshots pepper the break of dawn. I'm not sure if the movement of the door and our emergence have been seen, or if the shots are indiscriminate, intended to warn that any attempt to leave the train will be met with lethal force. Each report seems to hit me physically in the chest, and I want desperately to return to the safety of the train.

A thud a few feet in front of me, and I see that Joe has brought down the barman. Instructions over the loudspeaker that any passenger should return to the train. The words *final warning* cut through.

Joe now has Frank in a makeshift choke hold. In the struggle, one of the barman's extravagant mustaches has come away and repositioned itself on his cheek. Joe drags him back toward the door. Another round of gunshots. I want to flatten myself against the cement, to cover my ears and ride it out.

I hear Joe. "Don't panic, Meri, they're firing over our heads…rubber bullets, probably. Just get back to the Express."

We reach the door, and I hold it open while Joe drags the barman back into the carriage. And for a moment we stop, exhausted and gasping.

In the background an announcement on the train's intercom system tells passengers not to leave the train in English, Italian, German, and French—the languages that I can recognize at least. Sirens outside the train and more gunshots convey the same message.

It's not till Joe speaks to me that I realize I've frozen, that I'm sitting on the floor with my arms protecting my head.

"Meri, are you all right? Come on!"

He manhandles Frank, who is kicking and biting, into one of the empty cabins. It's full of spare bedding.

I shake off my terror and follow.

"Pick up everything we dropped," Joe instructs.

I do so without really knowing why—bottles, ice bucket, glasses, tray. Luckily nothing has broken, but the ice has spilled out and is melting into the carpet. I scoop what I can into the bucket and take the lot into the cabin.

"Lock the door, Meri." Joe has his hand pressed hard over Frank's mouth.

"Why?"

"In case someone comes through to investigate who tried to open the door."

"And what if they do?"

"We want to speak to Frank first before we hand him over." He talks directly into Frank's ear. "If you have any defense or reason or excuse for killing three people, mate, you'd better talk to us now 'cause I don't think the chaps with guns or your fellow stewards are going to give you much of a hearing."

Frank's eyes are wide.

"Decide," Joe says harshly. "We're only giving you a chance because my sister likes you. I'd be just as happy to offer you up so we can go home."

With Joe's hand still clamped across his mouth, Frank nods. There are tears in his eyes. I have to fight not to feel sorry for him.

I hear running steps outside and place a finger on my lips. Joe keeps his hand on Frank's mouth, and we wait in silence until we can no longer hear any sounds of movement outside the door. If whoever came through noticed the ice on the floor, its importance seems not to have been recognized. Considering the sirens and the bullets, other passengers are probably also trying to leave the train, which is not all that surprising. Still, we keep our voices to a whisper.

"Okay, Frank," Joe says, "now's your chance. But any false move, and I swear you'll regret it."

"I didn't kill anyone!" Frank says desperately as soon as he's no longer gagged by Joe's hand. The New Zealand accent is gone. It's English now, refined. "I assure you, I've never killed anyone."

"But you're Gregory Blackwell?" I press.

He nods.

"So whose blood was in 16G?"

"Mine."

"You look okay for someone who's lost so much blood."

"It was extracted over a couple of months. I brought it on board in my hand luggage, and after I'd been seen at dinner, I returned to my cabin. I removed my disguise, read Chaucer for a while, and splattered the blood about my cabin."

"Where's the disguise now?" Joe is, as always, interested in details that seem irrelevant to others.

"I threw it out the window before I climbed into the space under the lower bunk," Frank replies. "I thought that my fingerprints would eventually identify the mysterious Gregory Blackwell as Cheval, Harrington, Zelic, Browne, etc., and the blood would convince people I was dead."

"Why did you want people to think you were dead?"

"Rebirth, reincarnation into a new life."

"You'd better start making sense soon," Joe growls, his arm still locked around Frank's neck.

Frank responds quickly, cringing. "Six months ago I was diagnosed with hepatocellular carcinoma…it's liver cancer." He pauses, presumably to allow the tragedy of his situation to sink in and take effect. "I've already endured twelve weeks of chemotherapy, and in a week, I'll begin radiotherapy in preparation for surgery." His voice is full of hope. "But staying in one place to receive treatment when you have as many people looking for you as I do is difficult, to say the least."

"People like Napoleon Duplantier?" I ask.

"Yes."

"I can't imagine Napoleon would spend his retirement chasing petty criminals," Joe says. "What did you do—steal the gendarmerie retirement fund?"

I notice Frank flinch at the word *petty*. He sighs. "I shot him in the leg. It was an accident—I had no idea the gun was loaded. It ended his career, and he's more than a bit bitter and twisted about it."

"Bitter and twisted?" I'm skeptical and maybe a little defensive of Duplantier.

"He's very good at being the handsome, charming Frenchman," Frank shoots back resentfully. "You can't imagine that he would become obsessed with revenge over an accident, however humiliating. But he did. You see, it was his gun I picked up—it shouldn't have been out of his control, it shouldn't have been loaded. That's the reason he lost his job…though he likes to think it was my fault, that he retired from the frontline as a wounded hero."

"So all this is to escape Duplantier?" Joe doesn't believe him—I can tell. I'm not sure it sounds right to me either. But Duplantier did say he'd come on board on the trail of Cheval. Why hadn't he mentioned that Cheval had shot him?

Frank shrugs now. "Napoleon Duplantier's just a policeman. An angry policeman, but just a policeman. I'm afraid I've crossed people far more dangerous than he is. People who won't let a grudge go until I'm dead. Some of whom have followed me onto this train."

"Out with it then—who?"

"Well, the Duchess of Kinross… I took her for half a million pounds a couple years ago." There's just the tiniest note of pride in Frank's voice. This is a man speaking of his accomplishments. "I don't think it's a coincidence she's on this train, do you?"

"You think she's trying to kill you?"

"One should always be wary of widows. Have you ever wondered what happened to the duke?" His voice takes on the note of a gossip revealing a salacious offering. "She was staff, you know, before she married him. Quite the age gap… The poor old duke didn't have a chance."

"This is absurd," Joe says. "She takes this trip every year."

"She told you that did she?"

"Who else?" I demand.

"Ajit Singh."

"And what did you do to him?"

"Not him, his sister. I took her for about two hundred and

fifty thousand. Of course I didn't know her brother worked for Scotland Yard. And a chap called Noel Ferguson. Uppity Irishman. I ruined a few of his big clients…they blamed him for some reason."

"And just coincidentally, all these people happened to track you to the Orient Express at exactly the same time?" I challenge.

"I may have left breadcrumbs for them to follow," Frank concedes slyly. "I needed a few of my enemies to witness my demise, so that they could convince the more dangerous ones. Though considering all the murders, perhaps I miscalculated who was most dangerous."

"Is that it?" Jo gives the barman a sharp nudge. "Duplantier, the duchess, Singh, and Ferguson are the only people on board in pursuit of you?"

"Except for the Mayfields," Frank says shuddering. "They're relentless…pursuing me over a debt of three hundred sixty-five pounds for rent and board. But the point is, I'm a changed man. A diagnosis like cancer changes you—you begin to think about life and right and wrong. It made me realize the error of my ways. It's just that these zealots won't give me a chance to start over. And they're pussycats in comparison to the Russians."

Russians… I think of Alexei who had managed to waylay Napoleon Duplantier for a drink despite the circumstances. Could that have been what he and Napoleon had in common? Were Frank's victims beginning to work together? The idea casts the Frenchman in a different light. Was it possible he'd boarded the Orient Express in pursuit of vengeance as opposed to justice? As much as I like him, feel like we're friends, we've only known him a day.

"Why don't you give them all back their money?" I suggest. "That may help...with the people you didn't shoot at least."

"Sadly, I don't have it anymore. Medical treatment is expensive, not to mention berths on this train."

"Berths?"

"Time and money spent in reconnaissance. I wasn't preparing to snatch handbags. Something like this requires planning and timing."

Joe has now released his lock on Frank's neck and is regarding him incredulously. "You're not sorry at all, are you? You're just too sick to stay ahead of them for much longer."

"Maybe," Frank admits. "But I didn't kill anyone. Why would I?"

"To distract people so that you would not be discovered before we reached Venice," I counter. "With every murder we were more panicked. Perhaps we would have realized the crime scene in 16G was staged if we hadn't been looking over our shoulders in fear of who would be murdered next."

Frank shakes his head vigorously. "I had already organized a distraction. One a great deal more effective, less risky, and may I say elegant, than simply stabbing people like some kind of street thug." He smiles smugly now, obviously bursting to share his cleverness. "I switched a few of the COVID tests the Orient Express carries, in case a passenger shows symptoms, with ones that were designed to return a positive result regardless—they're available if you know where to get them. Voilà! Panic, hysteria, distraction...even the odd conspiracy theory."

"You mean no one on the train is actually sick?" I gasp, horrified by what he so proudly claims to have done. "For God's sake, they've closed the borders to the Orient Express! We're all stuck on board! People have been confined to their cabins and treated with antivirals."

Frank becomes defensive. "They may be infected. I don't know. They just haven't actually had a valid test."

"So how did being turned back from Venice fit in with your plans?" Joe's voice is hard, cold.

"I didn't anticipate that," Frank acknowledges grudgingly. "But I knew they'd have to allow the train to stop somewhere, eventually. The point is I had no reason to kill anybody. I didn't kill anybody. That's not who I am."

"On that point, who the hell are you?" Joe demands. "Harrington, Blackwell, Cheval…"

"All of them, none of them. I was born Hugh Booby. Is it any wonder I use any name but… My parents were idiots!"

I rub my face, trying to think. I don't know what I thought would happen, but this is not it.

"Look," Frank begins to plead now. "You can't hand me over to Duplantier and the others. They'll kill me. They'll make it look like self-defense or an attempted escape, but they will kill me. For pity's sake, I have cancer!"

Joe laughs. It's unexpected and to Frank it must seem mad or cruel, but he throws back his head and laughs. "Cancer is not a get-out-of-jail-free card, mate. It's bad luck, but it doesn't count as penance."

"I may only have a few months," Frank begs. The tears are back, and I honestly cannot tell if they are sincere or merely designed to manipulate. Possibly, they are both. "Don't take that away from me too."

Joe meets my eye. An unspoken conversation.

"What are we going to do?"

"I don't know."

"Should we hand him over to the others?" I say out loud.

"They'll kill me, I tell you." That was Frank out loud.

"Just shut up for a moment!" Joe says irritably. "Actually… stand in that corner and put your hands over your ears."

"What? Why?"

"So Meredith and I can talk about you."

"I will not."

"If you don't, we'll have no option but to hand you over. Your choice."

For a moment Frank doesn't move, clearly still contemplating whether Joe is serious. Eventually he shuffles over to the corner and places his hands over his ears.

"Turn around and face the wall," Joe directs. I detect a tiny note of enjoyment. "I don't want you lip reading."

With a look that could curdle blood, Frank turns around. Even so, only a few feet separate us, so I don't how much privacy we have gained. It is possibly just breathing space.

"One of us needs to stay here with him while the other talks to Fleischmann," Joe whispers.

"You'll have to stay," I reply. "Frank's less likely to try to overpower you." Although he is apparently ill, Frank is at least eight inches taller than me, and aside from his lack of follicles, he seems robust.

"But if what he says is true, Napoleon could be dangerous. What if you run into him?"

"He is dangerous!" Frank shouts, his hands still over his ears. "The bastard's here to kill me! Why won't you listen?"

Joe and I both roll our eyes.

"You stay with Frank," I say firmly. And then a little louder, "If he tries to escape, break his legs."

Joe grins. "I've been trying to avoid breaking bones again. The screaming often makes things awkward."

"I'll be careful," I promise quietly. "But regardless of what Duplantier might want to do to Frank, I doubt he'll hurt me. I'm more worried about you with this idiot."

Joe shrugs. "Nobody is getting off this train, Meri…well, not for a while anyway. And I'm the only thing standing between Frank and the people he claims want to kill him. His best bet is to cooperate and ensure I don't have to call for help."

And so we agree to separate, both worried for the other and reluctant, but there seems no alternative.

"Find Fleischmann, but you stay out of Duplantier's reach, Meri," Joe warns again as I open the door. "The irony of you being the one to die doesn't work for me. It's not how I'd write it."

I grab his hand and squeeze it. "Of course, Joey. I swear. And you don't take your eyes off the barman."

Chapter 24

I step out of the cabin, unsure of which direction to turn. To my left is the bar, the others, and perhaps Duplantier by now. To my right, more passenger carriages and the head of the train. I decide that Fleischmann would more likely be stationed at the front of the train, the part closest to the border between Italy and France, as he negotiates with the border officials.

The corridors are mostly deserted. I presume the gunshots have sent people back to their cabins, away from the larger windows in the corridors. Occasionally a door opens and someone sidles out, crouched and tremulous, to glimpse what's happening on the other side of the train.

"Didn't you hear the shots? I thought they'd boarded and were taking us all out one by one." A young man in knickerbockers and a knitted Fair Isle vest squats by a window. "You'll want to get down."

"I think they were only shooting at the doors," I reply reassuringly. "We're safe as long as we don't try to leave the train."

A flash of impossibly white teeth as he laughs. "Safe? I think you have very low standards when it comes to personal security, miss."

"It's all relative, I guess." I step past him. "Good luck."

He wishes me the same and returns to his surveillance of the heightened activity outside.

The compartment doors in the next carriage are all tightly shut and so I make my way through quickly. I spy Napoleon Duplantier coming out of a cabin as I enter the following carriage. He must have passed through the bar and past the cabin in which we have Frank held captive. Maybe he came after us. He doesn't notice me at first, preoccupied with locking the door with his picks. I freeze. And somehow that very act of stillness is what seems to alert him to my presence.

Duplantier looks up. He seems startled. "Meredith!"

"What are you doing?" Internally I hear Joe asking the same thing of me, but I continue regardless. "Don't tell me you've got the wrong door by accident again."

"I would not insult your intelligence."

"Whose cabin is that?"

He says nothing.

"Is there anyone in there?" I demand. I'm angry with him, though I'm not sure why. The fact that he has lied to me is hardly relevant if he has boarded this train intent on murder.

"Meredith, I've been looking for you and Joe. We should return to the bar. I can update you—"

"Who is Alexei?" I cut him off. "Whatever made you stop to chat with him? What could be so important?"

"A criminal. He is a criminal. I needed to find out why he was on board."

"Why? You're no longer a policeman."

Duplantier smiles faintly. "It's not always easy to stop, Meredith." He takes a breath. "There are things I need to tell you and the others. We should return to the bar."

"Sure… I'll just get Joe and meet you there." I walk toward him, my mind working frantically. Could Frank have been telling the truth—at least about this? Was Duplantier intent on vengeance, on killing the man who had ended his career? Could he have killed Maxim, the other steward, and Buster Sartori? Why? I try to remember where he was when they were killed, but it's useless; I'm confused. However, I do remember that he found Buster's body. And that I found him trying to get into 16G the first night aboard. "But first, tell me whose cabin this is."

"It belongs to the Mayfield sisters."

"Have you managed to lock it again?"

"No."

"Napoleon, would you mind stepping back, please?"

"Why?"

It's my turn to say nothing.

"Meredith, please—"

"Step back, Napoleon."

He shakes his head, exasperated, and finally complies with my request. And when he does, I move quickly, turning the handle and swinging the door open.

The cabin is a mirror image of our own and is in its day sitter form. The bodies are seated on the plush couch, leaning toward each other so that their heads in death are cheek to cheek, the blue jackets of their uniforms soaked in blood. Felix Shannon and Benjamin Herder. The scream is stuck somewhere in my chest. I am mute with horror and fear and fury. Flex and Herds, their eyes open as if they are surprised to be dead, look unseeingly back at me.

Napoleon's voice through the fog. "I think we should keep this to ourselves, Meredith… We could—"

I turn slowly.

"*Je vous prie de bien vouloir accepter mes sincères condoléances,* Meredith. I know they were friends of yours…"

I notice then his left hand, latex-gloved and relaxed at his side. The small pistol in its grip.

I explode into action, charging, pushing past him and running, with no doubt that it is for my life. I want to scream to call for help, but I cannot make a sound. Felix and Ben… They were barely more than boys—enthusiastic, excited boys with heroic dreams. They were innocents. Why would Duplantier have killed them—what possible reason aside from evil?

Duplantier is coming after me. I can hear his limping gait, and strangely I am grateful to Frank for having shot him, for giving me a chance to outrun him.

I get to the next carriage well before him. A couple of passengers are peering out of their cabins.

"Get back," I say hoarsely. "Danger!"

They slam doors on the threat and on me.

All except one.

"Meredith, in here!"

I turn to see the quivering face of Clarice Mayfield in the gap of the partially open door of the restroom. She beckons me in, and I don't hesitate. Penelope is in there too. She puts her arm about my shoulders and places a finger on her lips. I am aware of the smell of lilac powder and relief. I want to cry for my friends—the ones who've been killed, and the other I've just lost to the fact that he's a killer. But I must not make a sound, so I clamp my hand over my mouth and wait. The restrooms on the Orient Express are as large as the cabins, and without the need for beds or other furniture, they are in comparison spacious, so we are at least not on top of each other.

Penelope Mayfield braces the door, and we wait.

I realize that Duplantier must have come after the old ladies—picking the lock on their cabin. Did he find Flex and Herds in there? Had the podcasters continued their break-and-entry investigation despite our warnings? Had they stolen another key? Or was the key they surrendered to Joe not the master key at all? Had Duplantier found them in there and killed them because they witnessed him commit the same break and entry they had just committed?

My head is starting to swim. Clarice rubs my hand gently, warmly, and I feel the pounding ease a little.

We can hear Duplantier in the corridor now. He calls my name. "Meredith, you don't understand. It's not what it seems. Meredith!"

I'm struck that he sounds like a cheating lover caught out. I think about how much Joe would love that, how he would play with the similarity and use it to write about passion and the common root of light and dark. But it only makes me feel sick that someone so evil would seek to cajole me into giving him an opportunity to lie again. That he thinks I'm so stupid...

The limping gait passes our door as we hold our breaths. Will he notice the restroom is occupied? Will he try to force the door? And where are the stewards? Why will no one come to help?

We wait several minutes after Duplantier's footsteps have faded into silence before Clarice speaks. "My darling girl, did he hurt you?"

"No…but he killed my friends."

Penelope nods. "We were returning to our cabin when we heard the shots. We weren't sure where they were coming from, so we hid in here. Lucky…"

I realize suddenly that at least some of the gunfire we assumed was border control warning passengers trying to escape was the execution of Flex and Herds. I wipe away my tears. There's no time to mourn the death of the podcasters.

Clarice hands me a handkerchief. I want to sob into it, blow my nose, but it's embroidered and scented with lilacs, and so I just dab my eyes prettily and hope the flood of tears does not drown us all.

"I wonder what those boys were doing in our cabin," Penelope says. "That villain will no doubt claim he was shooting them in the act of doing something criminal. That's what they do when they shoot people of their heritage."

"Australian?" I say, confused now.

"No—not that heritage. He'll probably say they were terrorists. It's wrong, but that's what the world is these days. When we were young, it was just the Irish, of course…"

I blink, incredulous, shocked. Would he try something so outrageous? Maybe he would. Maybe people would believe him.

"My God, it was Napoleon all along… Frank is telling the truth."

"Frank?" Penelope asks.

"The barman. He's your Mr. Harrington, also Blackwell and Cheval."

"No, we would have recognized him."

"He's been ill—cancer—so he may have changed a great deal, and he's been wearing a fake mustache and beard…and I guess—"

"The barman's eyes are brown. Gregory's eyes were blue." Clarice is still unconvinced. She seems quite stricken.

"Contact lenses can change eye color, and chemotherapy can affect your vision, so perhaps he saw the opportunity to disguise himself further. He said he was Gregory Harrington."

"He just volunteered this information?"

I tell them how Joe and I pieced together the lack of fingerprints, the account of Paula Atkinson about the man with whom she'd had dinner, and the clumsy hipster barman. "It's only because the same thing happened to Joe when he was on similar chemotherapy drugs that we were alerted."

"You didn't say a thing," Penelope says mournfully.

"It seems so obscure that we wanted to test the theory, talk to Frank first."

"My dear, what a terrible risk! You should have come to us first. The man is a murderer!"

"No…he isn't!" I find myself defending the barman. "Napoleon Duplantier…" I shake my head, still struggling to believe what's just happened. "Frank just wanted to escape his past, so he faked his own death."

"You feel sorry for him?" Penelope's question is more thoughtful than accusatory.

"No. What he's done is appalling. But he didn't kill anyone. Apparently, at some point he shot Napoleon, which is why Napoleon limps, but it was an accident. It was Napoleon's gun, and he didn't know it was loaded."

I hear myself valiantly arguing Frank's case, and to be honest I don't know why. I am aware of a feeling of loss with respect to Duplantier…a harsh disillusion. But this insanity, this trail of destruction, was initiated by Frank. He virtually invited the people he'd wronged to follow him onto the Orient Express to witness his death—and, in the process, two stewards, Buster Sartori, Benjamin Herder, and Felix Shannon were killed, and we were all imprisoned on this train. Two carriages of passengers have spent the past two days, and another a day, believing they'd been exposed to or even contracted a very dangerous strain of coronavirus. Perhaps I'm defending Frank because he is fighting the same disease that so nearly took Joe, or perhaps it's just because it's the truth. I hope it's the latter, but I suppose it doesn't matter.

"Where is he now?" Clarice glances at her sister.

"Who?"

"Harrington." She licks her lips and swallows. "We should render assistance to your brother."

I am, to be honest, touched by their bravery, their concern for Joe. But I decline. "No, I think it's more important that I find Herr Fleischmann and let him know that Gregory Blackwell-Harrington-Cheval is alive and posing as his bartender. That it's Duplantier from whom we need to be protected." I take a breath. "I've wasted enough time. You should stay here—Napoleon can pick locks, so keep bracing the door… I'll find Herr Fleischmann."

"No!"

I'm a little startled by the sharpness of Clarice Mayfield's response.

Penelope continues for her, more gently. "My dear girl, you cannot wander the train on your own when there is an armed murderer on the loose. The conductor will be at the head of the train—it was in that direction that that fiend Duplantier was headed. He may even have killed the conductor and his men by now. We should find your brother and Mr. Harrington."

Their concern for me, I can understand. The strategic use of going to Joe and Frank, less so. I wonder if they are afraid of being left alone should Duplantier return here…of course they are. Two old ladies could hardly brace a door against the onslaught of an enraged, determined, wicked man. "Perhaps we should go to the bar. Tell the others and enlist their help."

"Perhaps we could collect your brother and Gregory on the way?"

There is something about their insistence. I'm not sure why I push against it, but I do. "They're probably safest and most secure where they are…at least till we inform everyone what's happening." I step toward the door.

Clarice sighs. And then she looks up at me, smiling. I extend my hand. "Come on; let's go."

The blow is so completely unexpected that I think I am more stunned by the fact that it was delivered than by its impact. It's followed by a shove before I can recover. I fall heavily with no thought or time to prepare, and I catch the corner of the porcelain washbasin as I go down. The crack seems loud, and on my hands and knees, I can see blood dripping onto the tiles of the restroom floor.

Chapter 25

I battle against losing consciousness. My hand slips in my own blood, and I find my face hard against the tiles. For a moment I use the cool surface to regroup, to try to understand what's happening. Clarice and Penelope are whispering. Clarice nods, and Penelope searches in the handbag, which has hung on the crook of her arm throughout. She pulls out a six-inch, thin-bladed dagger—like an ice pick—and I recognize now that I have to fight for my life. Terror clears the fog in my brain. I kick out, collecting Penelope in the shin, and her knees buckle. I scream for help, which is risky, considering the number of murderers who seem to be on this godforsaken train.

And then they scream too.

"Get the knife off her, Penny!" Clarice shouts. "Oh, my Lord, she's going to kill us!"

I almost stop, bewildered. I don't have the knife, Penelope does... And then I am struck by the rat cunning of the Mayfields, the calculating cleverness. They are setting up a defense, even as they murder me. But I have not the wherewithal to shout a counterargument. I just scream again as Penelope raises the knife to plunge. I stay on the floor, hoping her knees are arthritic or she has lumbago—whatever that actually is—that might restrict her ability enough to reach me. But she is agile and spry.

I grab her wrist as the knife descends and stop its piercing momentum, all the time still calling for help while Clarice shouts that I am trying to kill them. It's surreal and desperate; my head pounds and the blood in my eyes makes it hard to see. Part of me just wants to give in, to be overcome. But Joe is in my head demanding I keep going. And I remember how he fought when everything seemed lost, how he rallied at every setback, and I try to summon that strength.

Clarice comes away from the door to help her sister. I can feel myself beginning to weaken, and the tip of the blade presses now against my chest. Damn it, no! I twist and wrench Penelope's wrist sideways. She swears. Despite the circumstances, I am startled to hear those words coming out of her mouth… If she hadn't been trying to kill me it would have been completely incongruous. As it is, it is only partially bizarre.

Someone is banging at the door.

Penelope pulls away from me and places her shoulder against the door. She continues to curse, but now it's under her breath.

Clarice cries, "Take the knife before she stabs me!" It's still in Penelope's hand.

A thud and then another, and the door finally flies open, propelling Penelope Mayfield to the other side of the restroom with its momentum. My relief is short-lived. Napoleon Duplantier stands in the doorway.

"Meredith!" He offers me his hand even as I cringe away from him. "*Mon Dieu*—you're hurt. Please don't be afraid of me."

Behind him I can see Penelope retrieve her dagger from the floor and lift it to strike.

Duplantier must have seen something in my face because he turns in time to stop her lunge. Clarice now attacks him with her stick, raining blows as he struggles with her sister.

"Meredith, run!" he shouts. "*Dépêchez-vous!*"

I go, leaving him to hold off the crazy old ladies and still not quite sure of who has killed whom. And I scream for help. For me, for Napoleon, for all of us.

The cabin doors stay firmly shut, and after the past day and a half, I can't blame the passengers behind them for not giving up their relative safety to respond to yet another threat.

I run headlong into Joe.

"Meri! Are you all right? What happened?"

I shake my head. How do I tell him? How do I explain it? All I can manage is "Napoleon…I don't know…help…"

"Right." He grabs me by the shoulders, looking closely at what I assume is the gash on my head. "I tied Frank up with the curtain ties. You go check on him; I'll help Napoleon."

"Mayfields," I gasp. "They tried to kill me."

"The old ladies?" He's clearly skeptical. "How hard did you bang your head?"

"They're not…" I can't seem to finish.

"Okay," he says. "I'll watch out for the old biddies."

"Restroom, Carriage 7… Napoleon has a gun," I stammer. "He…" I blanch against the memory of Flex and Herds, bloody and vivid in my mind. "I think he shot…" I hesitate, no longer sure of anything.

"It's okay, Meri." Joe interrupts me before I can find a way to tell him his friends are dead. "I'll be careful. You check on Frank and raise the alarm."

And so we part, sprinting in opposite directions. I stop briefly at the empty cabin and look in. Years working on farms and cattle stations means Joe can tie an effective knot—Frank is bound hand and foot. There's no chance he'll escape on his own.

"What's going on?" Frank begs. "What the fuck is happening?" His eyes widen. "Do you know you're bleeding?"

"The Mayfields attacked me."

Frank pales.

"I have to go alert the others," I say.

"No, you can't leave me alone! If those old witches find me, I'm as good as dead."

"That seems to be a theme with you," I reply, fed up now with his constant pleas for protection against the consequences of the nightmare he created. "Joe and Napoleon are trying to hold them off—I need to get help. Be quiet or they might just work out where you are!"

I slam shut the door and run toward the Bar Car. I am breathless again when I burst in. Rees and Singh and Elle Baird are deep in conversation over the timeline. Bob Whitman is watching the duchess from a seat by the window. Abigay Williams is eating bacon and eggs, presented beautifully on Orient Express china, garnished no doubt with truffles and caviar and served alongside a silver pot of tea.

"Help!" They all look up at me now. Baffled, expectant.

"Blackwell is Frank the barman, Duplantier may have shot two passengers, and the Mayfield sisters tried to kill me!"

Bob Whitman stands up. "What now?"

"Meredith!" The Duchess of Kinross moves quickly toward me. "You're hurt. You must come and sit down."

I shake my head. "There's no time. Joe and Napoleon need help!"

"Help? Why?"

"They're fighting the Mayfields." I know I sound like a lunatic, but there is no time to explain in full. "Please…someone needs to help them."

"Where are they?" Bob Whitman is at the doorway, ready to take action, and for that alone I suddenly like him.

"Carriage 7, the restroom. Please hurry."

Whitman is off before the word *hurry* is out of my mouth. Abigay Williams is close behind him and then Singh and Rees. And I am relieved. The posse has become a cavalry. Elle Baird waits with me, stops me from following them all.

She applies a napkin soaked in whiskey to my forehead.

"Whoa! That stings!" I pull away.

"It's quite a cut," the duchess says, frowning. "How exactly did you sustain this injury, Meredith?"

I tell her.

Elle cups her hand over her mouth as she listens. "Those two sweet old ladies? Bloody hell! But why, Meredith? Why would they attack you?"

"They wanted me to take them to Frank… They were so insistent, I started to wonder, and then…" I shrug. "Then they became themselves."

"But they're old, frail…"

"They did not seem that way in the restroom." I stand anxiously. "Perhaps we should fetch Frank, bring him here."

"Perhaps we should." Elle is quick to agree.

"He thinks you're trying to kill him, you know."

"Me! Why ever would I want to kill him?"

"He says he defrauded you of half a million pounds."

Elle stops, caught. "Well, there is that, I suppose, but I just want to see the roaster arrested. That's why I brought Bob along. It would have given me the utmost pleasure to hand him over to the carabinieri in Venice. But I'm not an assassin." She smiles. "What did he tell you?"

I hesitate and then decide that Elle Baird is not easily hurt. "He suggested you might have had a hand in the demise of your husband…" I say awkwardly.

I'm relieved when the duchess laughs. "Oh, my, he's painting me as a black widow, is he? A bit cliché but somewhat sexy, I suppose." She shrugs. "No, sadly, Henry caught coronavirus in the early days, before we had any way to fight it. I met Mr. Blackwell when I was beside myself with grief. He was posing then as a Dr. Allsop, whose lab was working on a vaccine. I gave him quite a lot of money in Henry's memory." Her face crumples fleetingly before she regains her composure. "Stupid, stupid, stupid! Henry deserved better." She sighs. "You'll understand that I have been a bit jumpy about the infection on board."

I hadn't actually noticed that she'd been anxious, but I see it now in her face. An edge of controlled terror. And so I tell her, as we head for the cabin in which I left Frank, that he fabricated the COVID crisis on board to introduce an element of distraction to his scheme. That as far as I know, no one on the Orient Express is actually sick.

She stops, grabbing my arm and looking into my face. I see relief in hers and a kind of outraged chagrin. "The fucker!" she says finally and with feeling. "I hate him, but I can't deny he's canny."

"Yup." I quicken my pace, mildly worried that he's *canny* enough to have escaped his bonds. We can now hear the shouting from the seventh carriage.

"How long can it take six grown men and a DCI to subdue two old ladies?" Elle mutters.

She has a point. I open the door behind which I hope Frank still lies bound hand and foot. He does.

"Frank, you remember the Duchess of Kinross." He squirms visibly.

"Your Grace, I might leave you to keep an eye on the elusive passenger from 16G," I continue. "I want to go see what's taking so long in the next carriage, and we do need to find Herr Fleischmann and tell him his train is not contaminated." I look from Frank to Elle. "I'm choosing to believe Frank's fear of you is fabricated, or at least born of guilt. Please don't kill him."

Elle nods gravely. "I will try. I may slap the numpty around a little, of course."

On cue, Frank begins to whine.

I smile at the duchess. "Of course."

Chapter 26

More than those who left the bar are in the corridor of Carriage 7. I jostle my way in as I become aware of why aiding Joe and Napoleon is taking so long. The noise has finally brought passengers out of their cabins. It seems that even the most terrified will try to help two old ladies being attacked. And so, well-meaning passengers are trying to save the Mayfields. The noise has also brought stewards to the fracas and, as I arrive, so too does Verner Fleischmann.

One of the stewards blows a whistle. The blast pierces through the confusion, the exhausted panic, and seems to shock everyone into silence.

"Ladies and gentlemen," Fleischmann says, his voice loud and calm and smooth. "If you would just step back into your cabins, we will sort this matter out."

"The old ladies were being mugged!" a passenger volunteers helpfully.

Fleischmann nods. "If you'd just move back into your cabins, we will resolve everything."

In seconds the corridor is vacated by everyone but Fleischmann, the stewards, and we of the Bar Council. "Perhaps if we all move back and clear the restroom," Fleischmann suggests.

"We have a problem." Joe's voice comes from inside the restroom.

I weave past Singh and Rees toward the door.

"What's the problem, Mr. Penvale?" Fleischmann asks.

Duplantier replies from just inside the door. "Madame Clarice Mayfield has a gun pressed against Joe's head."

I dodge the steward who tries to stand in my way and look into the restroom. Joe is on his knees. There's an abrasion on his cheek but no other injuries as far as I can see. Clarice stands over him with the gun—a pistol much like the one Duplantier had held earlier—resting against his temple. She stands confidently, strongly, and without her stick. The bun in her hair has come loose, and she no longer seems as old as she managed to convince us all. I swallow, terrified, as I see that Joe is not particularly frightened. His eyes are darting about the room in search of God only knows what, but he is, in this frame of mind, liable to do something stupid and get himself shot. Duplantier stands against the wall, his eyes fixed on Clarice. Penelope is on the ground, unmoving. I can't see any blood or obvious wounds, but I from where I stand, I cannot tell if she's breathing. I feel sick. Would Clarice take my brother's life in payment for her sister's?

"Madame Mayfield," Duplantier begins softly, "there is no point to this, no escape to be had."

"I'm not trying to escape, Mr. Duplantier." Clarice's voice is different, no longer soft and tremulous. "I'm defending myself. You and Mr. Penvale attacked me and my sister."

"Come on, pet." Abigay has moved to stand beside me. The men stay back, perhaps on the grounds that Abigay and I would be less threatening to a fraught old lady with a gun. "We should see about getting your Penny some help." Then carefully, "What happened to her?"

"Mr. Duplantier tried to murder her," Clarice hisses.

"He pulled her off me and she hit the back of her head on the cistern," Joe corrects.

I freeze, willing him to just shut up. Bloody hell, Joe! Why would you argue details with someone holding a gun to your head?

"Why are you threatening poor Joe?" Abigay croons. "He didn't do anything to you, did he, love?"

Clarice says nothing.

"Why not let the lad go?"

I think frantically. What can I offer her? "Clarice," I say, trying to keep my voice steady, "you haven't really committed a crime yet, not one that can be proved without my cooperation. Let Joe go. I won't say anything about our altercation, and when we are finally allowed to disembark, we can all go happily back to our lives."

Clarice looks surprised. "What did Gregory tell you?"

"Meri," Joe interrupts, "you don't understand…"

"Shut up, Joe! He said that he owes you three hundred sixty-five pounds… He doesn't have it anymore, but I could pay his debt. Just let my brother go."

Though the gun remains trained on Joe, Clarice's eyes

are bright, thoughtful, and they are focused on Napoleon Duplantier. Why? It dawns on me too late that she means to kill the Frenchman. But Joe must have felt a movement, some tensing of the muscles in her wrist because he reacts just as she moves to aim the pistol at Duplantier. He hooks his arm around her knees and drags, shouting "Duck!" The gun goes off. The report is so extraordinarily loud it seems to reset the beat of my heart. The bullet hits the wall of the restroom and ricochets to shatter the mirror above the washbasin. Clarice drops the gun as she falls. It skitters toward the door. She grapples with Joe to retrieve it, and in the process seizes the knife that lies on the floor near Penelope.

Duplantier reaches the gun first, and my initial instinct is relief despite what I know. The stewards move in now, though I'm not sure how they manage to do anything with so many people in the confined area.

Clarice Mayfield is arrested, as much as you can be arrested by stewards, anyway. She is restrained and suddenly fragile and old again, leaning heavily on the stewards and calling for her sister. Duplantier too is placed into the custody of the stewards. He accepts being so apprehended with what I've seen to be an unfailing dignity.

But Joe protests, even as he bleeds. At some point in the scuffle, Clarice Mayfield has stabbed him in the thigh. I am distracted by Joe, but the memory of Napoleon saving me from the Mayfields competes with the memory of him walking away from the bodies of Flex and Herds with a gun in his hand.

A steward is sent to fetch the closest passenger who is also a doctor, while Fleischmann restores calm and order.

"Why are you arresting Napoleon?" Joe demands.

"Your sister reports that he killed two passengers," Fleischmann replies.

Joe looks at me. "Which two passengers…"

I swallow. He doesn't know. "Ben and Felix."

Joe pulls back, and a different pain enters his face. "Where?"

Duplantier answers, his wrists in cable ties. "They were in the cabin of Mesdames Clarice and Penelope Mayfield. I discovered them slain. I am sorry for you, Joe. I know they were your friends."

"You had a gun," I accuse.

"The gun was on the table. I took it so it could do no more harm. I should have unloaded it, but I did not want to compromise the evidence."

I remember the latex glove.

"What were you doing in the Mayfields' cabin?" I am not yet able to let go of what I'd believed.

"I had intended to search it. Their descriptions of Monsieur Harrington, so discordant, seemed to me contrived rather than a factor of age as they would have had us believe. And I wonder why they do not want us to know what the man they are seeking looks like."

"God, Felix and Ben must have been searching the cabin, too." Joe rubs his face. "The stupid bastards didn't give us the master key." He scrabbles in the pocket of his jacket and fishes out the key he confiscated from the podcasters. "This is probably just the key to their cabin. Dammit, why didn't I check?"

"Joe, don't move too much," I mutter, anxiously inspecting his wound, which is bleeding but not gushing—with luck it is the legendary "flesh wound" of no threat to life or limb. Where the hell is that doctor? I keep talking to keep him distracted, something at which I've become adept. "We used this key to lock Buster Sartori's cabin after we shooed them out of it."

"Felix supposedly locked the cabin... He might have just closed it...we didn't check."

"So you think they used the master key to get into the Mayfields' cabin?"

"I expect they were continuing their investigation of those conducting the investigation." He closes his eyes briefly. "They would have loved how meta it was."

Clarice pipes up, addressing Fleischmann in her manner. "Considering what's been going on on your watch, Conductor, we can hardly be blamed for defending ourselves against two strange men invading our boudoir!"

"Your boudoir, madame," Duplantier says coldly, "showed no evidence of a struggle."

Clarice smiles faintly. "Oh, dear, perhaps it wasn't us after all. My memory is not what it once was—I get confused sometimes—and you were holding the gun, were you not, Monsieur Duplantier?" She looks at me. "I'm so sorry if we frightened you, dear. We were ourselves terrified after being attacked. We didn't know who we could trust." She sniffles. "Oh, where is my handkerchief... Things seem to have become muddled in all the panic."

I am aware of a growing dismay in the pit of my stomach. Clarice Mayfield is very ably setting up her defense. "No," I reply firmly. "You tried to kill me because I wouldn't take you to Joe and Frank."

"Oh, my dear girl, I am so sorry if we gave you that impression. It could not be further from the truth—"

At that moment a steward returns with a woman in tow. She's vaguely familiar.

"*Scusi, scusi.*" A steward clears a way between the Bar Council investigators in the corridor. "I have Dr. Bocquet to see to the injured."

I'm startled by the name. Could it be—

She smiles at Joe. "Joe! What on earth have you done to yourself now?"

"Stay back!" I warn.

"Meri, it's okay…" Joe begins.

"But she's been stalking you! You don't know—"

"Stalking you?" Lesley Bocquet is clearly aghast, and possibly amused. "You said I was stalking you? Is that why you've been avoiding me?"

"No. Well, yes and no." Joe groans. He turns to me. "Dr. Bocquet recently joined the team of oncologists looking after me… I knew it must be bad news, something unexpected and terrible if they sent her to fetch me back, and I just wanted to enjoy this, have you return to your own life, before it all fell apart again… I'm sorry, Meri…"

I feel weird, numb. But Joe was well. They said he was clear… What the fuck happened?

Dr. Bocquet is looking from him to me and back. Her expression is inscrutable. "Joe, I don't know what you think oncologists do, but I assure you we don't chase our patients across the world to drag them back to treatment."

My head is beginning to pound again. "I don't understand."

Lesley Bocquet addresses Joe, her hands on her hips. "You invited me to join you and your sister on the Orient Express, remember? I decided last minute, so you'd already flown out for Paris, and you weren't answering my calls, but I figured I could just catch up with you on the train…"

Joe's face—relief and mortification combined. "I forgot," he says in the end. "I thought if you'd come to get me, it was because there was something really wrong, and I didn't want to know. Not yet."

"So you avoided me and told your sister I was stalking you?"

"It sounds a lot more stupid than it seemed at the time."

I watch the exchange, incredulous. I'm speechless, struck dumb with fury. At Joe. What if it had been as he feared? How could he not respond to a call from his doctors? How could he risk everything for a holiday? I turn away from him so that I don't punch him.

"I'm sorry." Joe's voice. I don't know if he's talking to me or Dr. Bocquet. I still want to punch him.

Clarice interrupts. "What about my sister? That terrible man tried to kill her—she needs medical attention."

Dr. Bocquet takes over. She asks if the Orient Express has an infirmary. On being told that it has, she sends a steward to fetch a neck brace, and once that has been fitted to Penelope, instructs the stewards on transporting her. She inspects Joe's wound, calls it a scratch, and applies an appropriate dressing. Apparently, the knife only penetrated a couple of centimeters and missed all major arteries and blood vessels. It is to her credit that I cannot tell if she's angry at my idiot brother.

While this is going on, I talk to Fleischmann. I inform him

that the man we have all been chasing has been hiding in plain sight as Frank the barman. I tell him that the positive COVID tests were fakes, brought on board by Frank and planted.

Fleischmann face drains of color. "Are you sure?"

"It's what he says."

"And you believe him?"

"Perhaps it's best if you hear it from him." I glance back at Rees and Singh, still hovering, Bob Whitman a little farther down the corridor, and Abigay with Joe. "Maybe you should all hear it directly from him now."

Fleischmann follows my gaze, and then he nods. "Yes. It's time we looked at all the cards. Where is Frank?"

"Carriage 5. The Duchess of Kinross is keeping an eye on him."

"We shall all return to the bar," Fleischmann decides. "If we can establish that there has been no virus contamination on board, they might open the border and we can return to Gare de l'Est."

Chapter 27

Frank and Elle are the last to return to the Bar Car. The barman is barefaced now, his extravagant artificial facial hair removed. He is clearly frightened. The duchess is disdainful. Duplantier and Clarice Mayfield are still in restraints made of cable ties, but they are seated amongst us with stewards on either side. Other stewards are standing unobtrusively but ready to keep order should Fleischmann's chosen investigators lose control…or turn out to be killers.

We are still stationary, halted in a kind of jurisdictional limbo at the border between Italy and France. Outside the train, the military surrounds us, as it did when we were stopped short of Venice.

"Be careful, Hugh." Clarice Mayfield's voice is sharp and clear, as it was in the restroom. The caution is more threat than concern. "Let me explain."

Frank looks away. I can see the quiver in his throat. His old landlady terrifies him.

I sit beside Joe, though I'm still furious with him.

He leans over and whispers. "I'm sorry, Meri. I only wanted a break. To not think about it for a while, to write. It didn't occur to me that Dr. Bocquet would just want a holiday… I invited all the doctors, a couple of nurses, but I didn't think they'd actually come."

"Well, I'm sure she regrets it now," I mutter.

Joe smiles and grabs my hand. "Story of my life."

Fleischmann asks Joe and me to speak first. To tell them all what made us suspect Frank. Joe explains his experience with chemotherapy, particularly the effects of a drug called capecitabine, which caused his fingernails to turn black and his fingerprints to disappear. How that, along with Paula Atkinson's claims that Blackwell was wearing a wig and dropped tableware incessantly, as well as the lack of any fingerprints at all in 16G, made him wonder whether the missing passenger had been receiving treatment for cancer.

"You have cancer?" Elle sounds quite stricken.

"*Had*…as far as I know and with any luck," Joe replies calmly.

I take over, telling them that I had noticed that Frank was incredibly clumsy, that he painted his fingernails, and I was sure that we hadn't seen him at the Midnight Bar that first night on board. And so Joe and I had made the leap that perhaps Frank the barman was Blackwell hiding in plain sight. But because we knew it was a leap, we'd decided to speak to him first.

Rees can't remain silent. "That was hideously naive, even foolish, wouldn't you say?"

Joe shrugs. "It seemed a long shot. After all, he'd been serving us drinks for hours and none of you recognized him."

"Joe speaks the truth," Duplantier says quietly. "I did not know this man is Cheval, and if Mesdames Mayfield recognized him as their boarder, they did not say so." He looks Frank up and down. "You are much changed, monsieur. Even your eyes are a different color."

"Cancer can do that." Joe rubs a hand through his hair. Perhaps he's remembering the lack of it. "And contact lenses. Anyway, we decided to talk to him first, to give him a chance in case his only crime was having cancer. Call it a sentimental failing on our part."

We then recount what the barman told us, with all the detail that we can recall, including his accusations. When protests are raised, Fleischmann decrees that Joe and I be allowed to finish before we argue about the truth or otherwise of Frank's tale. The revelation that the COVID tests were switched, that the outbreak on board was fabricated as a distraction, stuns every-one into silence. Fleischmann promises that the positive tests are being closely examined as we speak, and that if it is found that they are indeed fakes, all the relevant authorities and disease control bodies will be informed immediately.

I tell them about coming across Napoleon Duplantier in my search for Herr Fleischmann, what I saw in the cabin of Clarice and Penelope Mayfield, and then the gun in Napoleon's hand. My eyes are on the Frenchman, and I am surprised to see him nodding as I speak, even as the others gasp and draw the same conclusion that I have…had… I'm not really sure anymore. He does not interrupt or demand that he be allowed to defend himself. Indeed, he seems more interested in hearing my account in full.

And so, I go on, telling them how I ran, how I was given refuge in the restroom by the Mayfield sisters. I go over our conversation and their insistence that I take them to Joe and Frank, how they turned vicious when I refused, attacking me while screaming that I was the aggressor.

Clarice speaks up immediately, claiming that I am confused or outright lying, that it's all a misunderstanding or that I am manipulating the situation.

"Penelope and I are victims!" she says, her voice trembling. "We tried to help you, Meredith. I cannot understand why you would say such things." She points at Duplantier. "That man might have killed you if we hadn't taken you in. That's what we do, Penelope and I, open our home and our hearts… It's what we did with Gregory Harrington. Why are young people so ungrateful, so treacherous." She finishes, sobbing, and I can feel everyone beginning to feel sorry for her. I'm beginning to feel sorry for her!

Joe nudges me. He too can see what's happening. Forgetting for a moment the wound to his thigh, he stands and then grabs the back of the settee to stay upright.

"Why did you kill Felix and Ben, Clarice?" he asks.

"Who?"

"The two young men; they were kids, really, that Napoleon found in your cabin. You shot them."

I can see Clarice internally debating whether or not to deny shooting them outright, despite her prior admission to the same before Joe, Duplantier, Abigay, me, and possibly others within earshot. She decides to hedge her bets.

"That was nothing to do with us. It's clear the cabins on this train are not secure. That's down to you, Conductor." Her head shakes a little as she exhales. "But I remind you that these men broke into our cabin. If we had encountered them, we would quite understandably assume that they were responsible for the other killings and terrorists with some cause intent on adding Penelope and me to the body count. If Penny shot them, it would be in self-defense as we were running away."

"So why exactly were you running from Napoleon Duplantier if you believed you'd shot the murderers?" Joe presses, ignoring the provisos and disclaimers that counter her confession.

"We were beside ourselves. We didn't know who to trust."

I feel the change in the room. Not quite skepticism but a kind of neutrality is restored.

"Since we've no evidence that Napoleon killed anyone," Joe says, "perhaps the restraints should come off."

Fleischmann nods. Clarice's hypothetical justification has worked in the Frenchman's favor. A steward steps forward and cuts the cable tie.

Rees crosses his arms. "So the barman killed Sartori and the stewards?"

"No!" Frank finds his voice. "I didn't kill anyone. I'm a conman, a fraudster, *un escroc, un truffatore, ein fucking schwindler*! I don't kill people!"

"And innocence may be your greatest con," Elle Baird says. "A man cold enough to leave people's lives in financial ruins could well be able to stick a knife in a steward's neck."

"But why would I? What would be the point?"

Again, I get the feeling that there is something Frank isn't saying, something he needs encouragement to reveal. So I try to provide that encouragement.

"The point is that we know you boarded this train with the intent of escaping your victims... Perhaps you—what's the word?—escalated."

"No." He stops and licks his lips. "The killers boarded this train at Paris."

More than one. I step toward him, trying to interrupt his line of sight. "Who?"

"Several months ago, I boarded with two spinsters in Lower Slaughter—respectable old sisters. They took a shine to me."

Immediate protests, but Fleischmann calls for quiet and directs us to let him finish.

"I had the run of their cottage. They cooked for me, fussed and doted...flirted, even."

Clarice scoffs loudly at this.

"I nearly felt guilty," he continues regardless. "It was like living with your unmarried aunts." He swallows. "I happened to be home one day when they were out, and so I did a bit of exploring... These old ducks sometimes leave money about the place."

"See the kind of scum you are listening to," Clarice hisses.

I move closer to Frank. "Go on."

"They have a cellar. Very neat like the rest of the house. I looked around for... well, whatever I could find. And in the process, I took the lids off three large barrels stored down there. They smelled odd, you see." He gags involuntarily at the memory.

"There were people in there...corpses. In apple cider vinegar, I think." He screws up his face. "I didn't taste it, of course."

"So, what did you do?"

"I scarpered! Got the hell out of there."

"You didn't go to the police?"

"Of course not! Even if going to the cops would not have put me in personal danger of arrest, this was knowledge that could be financially useful."

"You mean blackmail."

Frank shrugs.

"Filthy, ungrateful liar!" Clarice screams. "We tried to look after you. He's making this up. There's nothing but gooseberry wine in those barrels!"

It occurs to me suddenly that if what Frank is saying is true, which for some reason I think it is, the Mayfields have had months to dispose of the bodies in a manner less culpatory than pickling in their basement.

"I took photos, and footage," Frank says smugly. "Three barrels, three bodies in their basement. The darkest fucking TikTok you've ever seen." He leans so that he can look past me at Clarice. "You and your sister are monsters! I suppose if I'd stayed, I would have ended up a human gherkin too!"

I am, to be honest, uncomfortable with allowing Frank to take the moral high ground, but I want him to tell us everything he knows. Clarice looks wounded and more dangerous for that.

"We treated you like family," she spits.

"That's all very well." Elle Baird glowers at Frank. "So the ladies have a history that belongs on an episode of *Midsomer Murders*. But why would they kill Maxim and the others? That doesn't make sense."

"I can explain Maxim, perhaps." Duplantier stands, no

longer in restraints. "I searched the cabin of Mesdames Clarice and Penelope Mayfield—"

"Why?" Singh seems not entirely convinced of Duplantier's innocence. "Why were you searching their room?"

"I could not understand why they would give such different descriptions of a man who had lived with them. The difference was too great to be a natural variant. It seemed to me that they did not want us to discover this Mr. Harrington, and I wondered why."

"So you broke in?" Singh remains dubious.

"I picked the lock…there were no breakages." Duplantier fishes inside his jacket and extracts two British blue passports from the interior pocket. "I find these, the passport of Madame Clarice Mayfield and that of Madame Penelope Mayfield. You will recall that we had dispatched Maxim to bring back the passports so that we could make a study of everybody on the train, including, one supposes, ourselves. And had we done so, we would have discovered that the sisters Mayfield are not nearly as old as they have presented themselves. Indeed, Madame Clarice is in her midsixties and Madame Penelope is two years younger."

"Pretending to be a little older, or even a little younger, than you actually are is hardly a crime," Elle points out. "Why would they murder someone to hide that?"

"The ladies make much of being elderly…the *grand-mères*, sweet, frail, poisoners, if anything." Duplantier glances at Joe and me in fleeting acknowledgment of our conversation the first night on board. "But we would never suspect them of physical confrontation, of stabbing a man."

The passports are handed around the group. The birth dates therein show that Clarice turned sixty-five just three months ago and that Penelope is sixty-three. The pictures are undeniably them, but less shadowed and lined, no glasses, and hair colored and worn loose.

"But the other steward…"

"They may have wished to enter 16G to search it or even collect something Blackwell had left."

"They came in and took my duffel bag!" Frank declares triumphantly. "At the time I wondered what had happened to the steward on guard—"

"How would you know what we did?" Clarice's lip trembles. I can see the dismay in her eyes as everything unfolds.

"I was under the bottom bunk; there's a space big enough to hold a man."

I interrupt. "We checked that."

"When I realized there was no guard, I got out of there… once the Manson sisters had left, of course." Again that self-satisfied smile, a man impressed by himself. "I was under the bunk when the room was first discovered and when the boss and Maxim came in to talk about what to do. I had intended to stay there a bit longer, but when Bonnie and Cly—uh, well, Bonnie and her sister, dropped in, I thought it was time to get out. I put on the steward's uniform I'd stowed in the space and pushed what I'd been wearing out the window."

"And your beard and dinner suit and so forth."

"Pushed them out the window the night before."

The route of the Orient Express, it seems, is littered with a trail of evidence. I must admit a kind of grudging admiration for the planning involved to pull off what Frank nearly did. It is extraordinary.

Abigay speaks directly to Clarice now. "It's over, love. You can see that, can't you? The only real question is whether you'll be arrested in Italy or France. So how about you tell us about Buster Sartori…else Frank here is going to be telling your story."

Clarice closes her eyes for so long I begin to wonder whether she's passed out. And then she speaks. "Penny killed him. It's always been Penny—she is…impetuous. I shouldn't have covered up for her…but you know, I'm her big sister. And of course, I too was in fear for my life."

I want to glance around to see if anyone is buying this, but I don't want Clarice to stop talking. "Why? Why did she kill Buster?"

"He inquired after her age, and she thought he might be *onto us*, as they say." She exhales and gazes down at her hands. "She said he was constantly watching her. Penny could be paranoid about things like that."

I think of poor heartbroken Buster Sartori, determined to both punish and win back the wife who left him. Had his interest in Penelope been nothing to do with any suspicion about the murders? Had a killer caught his eye?

Clarice is not finished. "And, he was a very unpleasant man—terrible manners." She looks to the room for support. "None of you liked him. The only wonder is that Penny killed him first! Of course I tried to dissuade Penny… I always did. But she is a violent woman, and there is only so much one can do."

"Why did you both give such absurd descriptions of your Gregory Harrington?" Duplantier asks. It was what made him suspicious of the Mayfields, so I expect he is particularly interested in that detail. And in hindsight, perhaps we all should have paid more attention to the discrepancy rather than ascribing it to the frailty of age. The Mayfields had used our assumptions to hide right before us.

"If he had been found and apprehended by the group, then we would never have got back the money he owed us."

"Three hundred sixty-five pounds in missed rent?" Joe remains dubious. "And the funds swindled from the Lower Slaughter Civic Society."

Clarice presses her lips together.

Joe groans. "The Lower Slaughter Civic Society doesn't exist, does it? Damn!"

Some of the others look at Joe strangely, perplexed by his reaction. I know that my brother is lamenting the loss of "material." I expect the travails of the Lower Slaughter Civic Society had made it into his manuscript. He could still use it, I suppose, but it's possible he considers that the creative ownership of the idea belongs to the Mayfields, and so using it would now amount to theft. It's ridiculous, but he is a writer. They seem to live by highly idiosyncratic moral webs.

"You do not spend thousands in fares in the hope of retrieving three hundred sixty-five pounds." Duplantier's scrutiny is still fixed on Clarice.

"Well, Monsieur Duplantier, you spent a similar amount to retrieve nothing at all. In fact"—she looks from Duplantier to Elle and then to Singh—"none of you are going to get your money back, and I doubt you ever thought you would. And still you purchased a ticket and came on board. What did you intend?"

I shake my head. Clarice Mayfield is not going down easily, and clearly, she's willing to throw her sister under the bus…or train.

There is increased activity outside. Fleischmann answers our questions before they are asked. "The carriages we have quarantined are being retested. If there is no evidence of an outbreak on board, the Orient Express will be permitted to continue on to Gare de l'Est. Finally."

In the ensuing relief, Fleischmann gives instructions about the confinement of our prisoners. Frank will be placed under double guard in an empty cabin. He reminds Fleischmann to organize an ambulance to meet the train, because he is not a well man. Clarice begs to be confined with her sister in the infirmary.

"How could I possibly escape?" she says, holding up her hands in their restraints. "You can tie my leg to her bed if you want, Conductor. Penny needs me."

I see Fleischmann wavering as Clarice appeals for compassion.

"No! Please." I act before he can relent. "Penelope Mayfield has had no chance to speak for herself. If she dies, there will be no one to contradict Clarice's account that it was all Penelope's doing. Penelope Mayfield must be protected against her sister."

And that, it transpires, is the straw that breaks the back of Clarice's performance. She launches herself at me, screaming profanities, breaking away from the surprised stewards and bringing me to the ground. Joe grabs her around the waist and tries to pull her off, but she is incoherent with fury and clearly strengthened by that. Duplantier pulls me up and away from Clarice, protecting me as best he can, while Whitman and Singh help Joe hold on to the twinset-clad dervish.

It is only then we realize that the train has begun to move.

Chapter 28

The Orient Express pulls into Gare de l'Est. The platform is teeming with all sorts of authorities and officials, the consuls of a number of countries, ambulances, the media, and of course the gendarmerie. I watch the activity, relieved that we are finally back. There is much that needs to be done before we will be allowed to disembark, I imagine. But even so, it is comforting to know that we are back where we began.

Before me, Joe's laptop, the beginnings of his new novel. The man himself is asleep, his head on the white linen draping the dining table at which we sit, as the past two and a half days, everything that's happened, and the fact that he has forgone sleep to write crash down on him.

There are only a few chapters of his manuscript written, of course, but I can hear the voices of the ghosts he claims walk the corridors of the Orient Express. He has turned 16G into a classic locked room mystery, but already I can see the back and forth between Christie-esque mystery and Hitchcockian thriller. But whatever this crazy, metafictional, autobiographical tale is, it is good. Clever, compelling, and contemplative. And funny, because it is Joe. If anything, it's better than the book that launched him into literary stardom. And I am convinced now that Joe will be fine, that he will reclaim everything.

I had earlier sought out Dr. Bocquet to apologize, for myself and for Joe. She had been gracious.

"It is nothing. I understand why he did it."

"I'm not sure I do," I'd confessed. "He told me you were obsessed with him—I thought you were deranged."

She'd laughed. "I'm an oncologist, Meredith. When our patients are sick, we are hope. The path back to life and health. They look to us to save them. And when they are well, they are terrified of us. We become the harbingers of sickness and death. It's not something of which we are unaware."

"But doesn't it offend you? Joe owes you his life; it seems so wrong that he would treat you this way."

"Not really." She'd dismissed my protestations with a shrug that was both resigned and unconcerned. "Most of all, we want our patients to fight. If we have to become the face of what they fear, the focus of that fight, that's okay. Whatever it takes, really." She'd been so kind. "Joe did everything we could have asked of him this last year and a half. Let's allow him one stupid act."

"If only it was just the one."

She'd laughed. "Your brother's reaction, while wrong-headed and, well, bonkers, is understandable…and will make an amusing anecdote in time. I'm glad I was doing nothing more than trying to accept his invitation to join you on the Orient Express."

I watch Joe as he sleeps, wondering about the shadows that

now make him jump. I'm glad his doctors are so forgiving, so human. Siobhan Ferguson comes into Étoile du Nord and smiles when I wave her over. She slips into the seat beside me, and I hand her back her phone.

"How ya getting on? Did you find anything useful in my photos?" she asks quietly with a glance at Joe.

"I didn't actually have a chance to look," I reply sheepishly. It seems a poor way to reward her trust. "But the man Noel was after, the one who defrauded his clients, has been caught. He was hiding out as a barman called Frank. He'll be handed over to the gendarmerie shortly, I presume."

Siobhan sighs. "You know about that, do you? I told Noel that trying to track him onto the Orient Express was mental."

"Frank said that Noel had reason to…to want some kind of retribution," I reply carefully. "The gendarmerie will probably want you to make a statement or something."

She nods. "Fitting way to finish a holiday on the Orient Express, I suppose."

I laugh.

"So, there was really no COVID outbreak on board?"

"No."

"Feck!"

I agree. The use of the world's collective post-pandemic PTSD to create mayhem and distraction is both brilliant and cold. If anything, it worked too well, and the extended time on board became Frank's undoing. If we had been allowed to disembark in Venice, he would have disappeared, and it would have been assumed that Blackwell and whoever else he is had died in 16G.

"I don't think Frank has much left of all the money he took from people," I tell Siobhan apologetically.

"Noel never expected to get anything back from that gombeen," she confesses. "He just wanted to drag him off to the guards or some such rubbish. I was hoping he'd just start enjoying himself and forget about the eejit."

"How did you know he'd be catching this exact train?" I'm curious as to how Frank organized his witnesses.

"Noel received an anonymous message from someone who claimed to be another victim of O'Hara—he knew him as Finn O'Hara. Whoever it was attached an image of a ticket in the name of Gregory Blackwell. That was it." Siobhan shakes her head. "Noel took it to the guards, of course, but they wrote it off as a prank. And to be honest, I thought it was too. I was sure one of Noel's clients, who had invested with O'Hara and blamed Noel for not stopping them, was trying to get their money back."

"Where is Noel?" I ask.

She points behind me. I turn. Noel Ferguson is at the table at the end of car with Elle Baird and Ajeet Singh. Frank's victims, those he hoped would spread the word of his death. They had that in common.

Siobhan stands up. "I'm going to go pack up our cabin… I know, I know, it'll probably be hours before we're allowed to step off, but I'm keen to be ready." She gives me a hug. "If I don't see you, all the best. And tell Joe I'll be waiting for the book to come out. I've put our details into your contacts if you want to be in touch."

I assure her that I will. Joe seems to mumble a groggy farewell, but it's difficult to tell if he's awake.

On the platform I can see Penelope Mayfield being transferred via stretcher into an ambulance. There is a young policewoman accompanying her. Clarice Mayfield is also on the platform in restraints and flanked by a burly policeman. I breathe out. Knowing they are off the train is a relief.

I nudge Joe…he'll want to see this. "Joe, they're taking the Mayfields away."

He opens his eyes in time to see at least a passing glimpse of the ladies from Lower Slaughter who killed five people between Gare de l'Est in Paris and Venezia Santa Lucia in Venice. It's a newspaper headline-writer's dream.

"Well, that's that then," Joe says finally. "Have they taken Frank away yet?"

"Not that I've seen. Perhaps they're still questioning him on board."

More stretchers are carried onto the platform now, sheets drawn up over faces, keeping the dead anonymous for now. The stretchers are lined up beside each other, ready for the coroner. Those on the platform keep a respectful distance, and we look upon a scene that is staggering in its sadness, its sense of futility. I reach for Joe's hand. We knew four of the five men who now lie on those stretchers. Maxim had been the smiling face that welcomed us onto the Orient Express and we'd worked, or tried to work, with Buster Sartori. And two were our countrymen, our friends: Flex and Herds.

Joe swears quietly. "I hate to say it, but it's how the damn fools would have wanted to go."

I smile faintly. Joe's right. If they had to die, this is how Ben and Felix would have wanted to do so, slain in the midst of a

mystery they were trying to solve. Both victims and red herrings. And on the Orient Express, no less. It is a thin comfort,
however.

"I'll miss those idiots," Joe admits, shaking his head.

For a time, we continue to watch, to grieve in silence. The
stretchers are taken away one by one, until the platform is clear.

"I'm going to have to get in touch with our travel agent." I
try to take Joe's mind off the loss of our friends. "All our book-
ings are for and from Istanbul…perhaps there's a flight."

Joe's brow furrows. "Do you mind if we hang around Paris
for a while?" he says. "I want to get as much of this written
while the ghosts are still speaking to me. They may not follow
us to Istanbul."

I shrug. "Okay. The gendarmerie, and quite possibly Interpol,
will probably want us to hang around for a while anyway."

"Are you sure you don't mind?"

"Not at all. You write, talk to ghosts, and whatever else you
need to do. I'll visit the galleries and be inspired. And we'll be
here in case there is anything we can do for Ben or Felix…or
poor Maxim."

Joe nods. "What happens when you die abroad?"

"I don't know. The travel insurance might repatriate them.
Otherwise, I think it's very expensive."

"Maybe I can help with that."

I rub his forearm. "We can ask."

"Do I hear that you will stay in Paris?" Napoleon Duplantier
takes the seat that Siobhan vacated. He smiles at me.

"For a little while," I reply. "Joe wants to write. Perhaps we'll
ride the Orient Express again one day and make it to Istanbul."

"You're on!" Joe promises. "Why don't you come too, Napoleon? We'll call it a reunion."

Duplantier laughs. "That we shall, Joe. Perhaps, like the Duchess of Kinross, we will take this journey and meet every year."

"They're taking Frank off," I warn, my gaze glued again to the window.

"For someone who didn't kill anyone, he sure caused a lot of trouble," Joe says as we watch the barman being handed to the gendarmerie. Frank is no longer wearing the uniform of the Orient Express but is dressed in jeans and a pullover.

"I wonder where he got the clothes."

"He probably stole them," Joe replies.

Duplantier disagrees. "Herr Fleischmann would have found him the attire most innocuous. It would not do for a criminal to be photographed wearing the uniform of the Orient Express."

"You know he asked me to ghost-write his autobiography?" Joe shares suddenly.

"What?" My mouth feels like it's hanging open at the sheer gall of the man. "Really? That's—"

"It would probably sell," Joe concedes.

"You didn't say yes?" I gasp.

"No. I'm a novelist, not a biographer." Joe regards me like I'm a lunatic for even asking. But he admits, "I didn't have the heart to inform old Frank that I'm already telling his story, on my terms with a *work of fiction, resemblance to actual people is purely coincidental* disclaimer."

Joe and Napoleon digress into a conversation about the parameters and legalities of fiction. I half listen while I watch

Frank, now devoid of his fake mustache and goatee. He looks pale. I can see his lips moving, and I have no doubt that he is already trying to charm anyone and everyone who might be able to help him.

"He didn't mean to shoot you, you know," I say with no idea why I feel the need to do so.

"Perhaps," Duplantier replies. "But he did load the gun, so he intended to shoot something."

"He loaded the gun?" I stare at Duplantier, and then I realize that of course he did. "Oh. I'm sorry, Napoleon. I don't know why I would believe anything that man says."

Duplantier waves away my apology. "Monsieur Cheval is an extraordinarily persuasive liar. It is his gift. He has an instinct for how to most effectively manipulate. But he does not lie, as far as I know, when he says he has killed no one but himself. Although it is perhaps his innocence in this respect that is accidental."

"Who exactly is Alexei?" The fact that Duplantier stopped to speak to the man in the midst of it all still bothers me. "You said he was a criminal, but why did he want to speak to you?"

"Alexei Pasnikov—a minor gangster. He runs after the bigger criminals. Alexei gave Cheval a large amount of money. Money that belonged to his Russian masters."

Joe nods. "Frank did say the Russians were after him."

"Alexei followed me onto the Orient Express, hoping I would lead him to Cheval. I stopped because I was concerned that he might be the murderer. I wanted you and your sister to continue without me to ensure you would be unharmed."

"What if he had been the murderer?" Joe says. "That was risky, mate."

"As it was when you and Meredith spoke with the barman," Duplantier counters. "We were all becoming a little reckless, I think, but I would not have forgiven myself if Meredith had been hurt."

Joe either does not notice or chooses not to react to the fact that Duplantier's concern seems directed particularly at me. An old-world gallantry, possibly. Perhaps I should be offended, but right now I can't be bothered. "So, why did he want to speak to you so urgently?"

"He asks if I will help him if he is willing to give evidence against his masters. He believes Cheval's ruse, that he is dead, and he knows that a terrible price will be demanded from him for the money lost. So he is afraid, and willing to give evidence in exchange for protection." He points to a group of policemen standing separately from those who have Frank in custody. "You see, they wait for Alexei Pasnikov. They will hide him until he speaks to the magistrate."

"Well played," Joe replies approvingly. "We apologize for anything we might have thought about you. Especially Meredith."

I choke and glare at my brother. But Duplantier laughs.

"I would have had similar thoughts if I had been in your place," he replies generously. He stops and continues tentatively. "Perhaps, Meredith, if you have changed your bad opinion, you might join me for dinner tomorrow?"

I am, I admit, a little startled by the invitation. And there is an awkward moment in which I feel like I'm changing gears. I can almost hear them grinding. And I realize I would like to have dinner with Napoleon Duplantier again. Joe sits with his arms folded, grinning like an idiot. Such an idiot!

"Yes, I'd like that, very much. *Merci beaucoup*, Napoleon."

Napoleon nods. "I will call you, Meredith." He stands and takes his walking stick. "I must make sure that the arrangements for Alexei are in place." He kisses me on each cheek and shakes Joe's hand before he makes his way out of the carriage. The limp seems a little more pronounced now, his shoulder dropping and his body leaning as he takes his weight on the stick. It's not surprising, considering the events of the last few hours.

And then Joe shouts after him. "Flat tire."

I can feel my eyes widen.

Duplantier turns, confused. "Pardon?"

"Your nickname." Joe rocks from side to side, beaming. "That's what we'd call you, mate. You know, like a car with a… flat tire."

Chapter 29

DEATH OF THE READER: 2SER 107.3 FM

ABOUT:

Join Flex and Herds as they take you on a Murder Mystery Tour in *Death of the Reader*. From the classic British puzzle in the Golden Age of detective fiction to modern noir, we trace the influences of the genre around the world.

LATEST EPISODE

MURDER ON THE ORIENT EXPRESS...AGAIN

This final episode was recorded on the Orient Express on which Flex and Herds met their own untimely deaths. It is uploaded as a final tribute to the founders of *Death of the Reader*. RIP, fellas.

TRANSCRIPT:

FLEX: You're listening to *Death of the Reader*, Flex and Herds here for your murder mystery world tour. We come to you from that world-famous mecca of mystery, the Orient Express, discussing Agatha Christie's original and the plethora of lesser-known train mysteries which followed and preceded it, including screen adaptations of the same. So, Herds, here we are on the train that began it all.

HERDS: That's right, Flex. You and I are on Poirot's iconic "Stamboul Train," thanks to a very generous grant from the Australia Council for the Arts.

FLEX: Acknowledgment deftly done, Herds. We are indeed very grateful to the Australia Council for their support, let that be clear, for the sake of acquittal, and let us never speak of it again. But we will speak again and often of our gratitude to longtime friend-of-the-show, Joe Penvale, author of the internationally bestselling *Murder Beyond the Black Stump*, who, as it happens, invited *Death of the Reader* to join him on the Orient Express as he works on a new novel in situ. We'll catch up with Joe shortly, but right now, we shall endeavor to *orient* you, loyal listeners—see what I did there—with the train.

HERDS: Very droll, Flex, very droll. *Death of the Reader* is currently most comfortably ensconced in a very swish cabin in Carriage 14 awaiting summons to our first dinner on board.

FLEX: We still have half an hour or so. What do you think, Herds? Shall we explore?

HERDS: Lead the way, Flex!

FLEX: We're now standing in the walkway outside the cabins. To our right are the dining cars, I believe, and to our left, well, who knows. Which way, Herds?

HERDS: Left seems to be just passenger accommodations. Let's see what's on the other side of the dining cars, Flex.

MUSIC

FLEX: So we've just walked through the dining cars and the bar, and we are now in what appears to be the central business district of the train. This carriage is pretty much like all the others, but the cabins are being utilized for other things.

HERDS: We've just walked past the Orient Express mailbox… I think the idea is that passengers post their letters, written while on the train, into it, and they will be stamped and sent off at our next stop.

FLEX: We've stopped briefly at the cabin which is the Orient Express gift shop wherein *Death of the Reader* bought a very expensive pair of cuff links by way of a souvenir.

HERDS: We can wear them in turns or sport one each! I must say that the staff here are very obliging. Antonio, who is responsible for the gift shop, is allowing us to peek into the other cabins on this particular carriage. They seem to be packed with the necessities of elite train travel: linen, extra soaps, and toilet paper... And in this one, champagne buckets and silver trays.... And here we have a cabin full of freshly laundered and pressed steward and waiter uniforms...in all sorts of sizes.

ANTONIO: Just in case one of the staff soils their uniform, messieurs. We cannot have them serving with a stain.

FLEX: Indeed, sir, we cannot. Tell me, Antonio, what lies beyond this carriage of requirement?

ANTONIO: More passenger carriages like those on the other side of the dining cars. And beyond them, near the head of the train, are the Grand Suites and one of the kitchens.

HERDS: There are a fair few people moving through to the dining cars now, and we find ourselves moving against the flow of traffic. We should probably let you get back to the gift shop, Antonio, and make our way to dinner. Thank you for the behind-the-scenes tour.

ANTONIO: My pleasure, messieurs. Welcome to the Orient Express. Enjoy your dinner.

MUSIC

FLEX: Good morning, listeners. You are with *Death of the Reader* on the trip of a lifetime, a special show from the world's most famous train. We have now spent about twelve hours on board. If you joined us from the beginning of this episode, you will have explored the train with us before dinner last night. We didn't record during the meal because it's not the done thing, and we were in any case either speechless with wonder and awe at what was placed before us, or our mouths were engaged in the consumption of the same.

HERDS: It was unbelievable! I fear it may have spoiled all forms of pleasure for me hereafter. My taste buds have peaked.

FLEX: Luckily, our failure to document the experience has been compensated in the Instagram feed of our dining companion, the renowned travel writer and Instagrammer Siobhan Ferguson. We urge you to check it out… There may also be a few images of Herds and me devouring any one of five courses on behalf of all *Death of the Reader* listeners.

HERDS: As was our duty.

FLEX: Now, good friend of the show, Joe Penvale will be joining us shortly to talk about his much-anticipated second book. But first, listeners, we must tell you that this morning has seen life imitate art, even the dark arts, on the Orient Express.

HERDS: Indeed, it has, Flex. To give listeners a little context, Flex and I are sitting in the Bar Car waiting for Joe. A few minutes ago, two old ladies, distinctly Jane Marple in appearance and manner, walked into the bar and announced that there had been a murder in 16G!

FLEX: So, what are we thinking, Herds? Another murder on the Orient Express, or an onboard floor show?

HERDS: I've got to admit, I hope it's the former, Flex. Of course, it's no surprise that Christie's *Murder on the Orient Express* is a selling point for the train, but I'd like to think they wouldn't be so cheesy as to organize a parlor game along those lines. 16G is the cabin beside the one Joe Penvale is in, isn't it? Perhaps he'll be able to enlighten us either way.

FLEX: Speak of the devil, and here he is. Joe Penvale, welcome to *Death of the Reader* once again. It's been a while since we've had you in the studio. Indeed, we've had to chase you onto the Orient Express, no less, to get an interview, so great is the demand for your time these days.

JOE: Hello, fellas. Aren't you glad I gave you a reason to get on board?

FLEX: *Death of the Reader* has always been on board the Joe Penvale train.

HERDS: Boom boom!

FLEX: I reckon we have some of the first tickets ever issued. But enough of the "we knew him when…"—tell us, Joe, what brings you here?

JOE: My sister, Meredith, actually. You know the last eighteen months or so have been a bit rough, so Meri thought this next chapter should be called "The Penvale Twins on the Orient Express."

HERDS: Ah, yes, the delightful Meredith Penvale has in fact just entered the Bar Car. Perhaps she'll speak to us later. So, Joe, have you just given *Death of the Reader* an exclusive on the title of a new book?

JOE: What? No, of course not. I was just kidding. I've barely begun writing—but I promise it will not be called *The Penvale Twins* do anything. That's an entirely different genre.

FLEX: But you have begun writing something?

JOE: Yes.

FLEX: And is the Orient Express providing you with inspiration?

JOE: Yes, in a way. The stories associated with this train and trains in general are certainly coming to mind. They're a kind of a background, unseen but front of mind when you ride the Orient Express. You're haunted by history and story, the imaginations of the writers who've gone before you. The same things that inspired Christie are speaking to me, but there's another layer. When I experience this train, I do so aware of what Christie made of her experience, what Ethel Lina White did with a similar setting in *The Wheel Spins*, or Highsmith in *Strangers on a Train*.

HERDS: *The Wheel Spins*, of course, was brought to screen by Alfred Hitchcock as *The Lady Vanishes*. Let's not forget Christie's other train book, *The Mystery of the Blue Train*, and her short story "The Girl in the Train."

JOE: Yes, all of that.

FLEX: You used the word *haunted*. Are the ghosts of Poirot, Haines, and Bruno, not to mention the wonderful Miss Froy, having a drink in the bar, or, dare I say, hanging about the restrooms of the Orient Express today?

JOE: Can fictional characters have ghosts? They don't actually die after all…if they survive the book, that is. They have an immortality beyond the small, finite lives of their authors.

HERDS: You could argue that immortality rubs off on their authors, though. There'd be few people in the literate world who've never heard of Agatha Christie.

JOE: That's fair. Her words, the products of her imagination, are being experienced by millions of readers every day. I guess that is a kind of immortality.

FLEX: So when a writer like Christie achieves immortality through her work, or even simply extends her literary life into yet another generation of readers, is there also an extension of a less enlightened time?

JOE: I think you may have to explain what you mean.

FLEX: Are readers absorbing not only the glamour and style of the Golden Age but also the class prejudice, the racism, the gender inequity, and homophobia of that era? Here, on the magnificent Orient Express, for example, does one need to reject egalitarianism, or at least suspend it, in order to be so outrageously indulged?

JOE: Yes.

HERDS: What?

JOE: Yes. This is a luxury train…to enjoy the experience you have to allow people to cater to you, to clean up after you, to carry your bags, and bring you drinks. But that doesn't mean you're looking down on them, or that you believe you are inherently deserving of the privilege beyond having paid for it. Golden Age mysteries are just that—mysteries which are a product of their age, with all its lack of enlightenment, its inequities, and prejudices. I expect they are appreciated differently by the modern reader. I hope we can enjoy them while being cognizant of all those crimes they don't raise.

FLEX: But what about what you're writing, Joe? Did you choose to write a book inspired by the Orient Express so that you don't have to be bothered with the problems of today's world?

JOE: I live in today's world, Flex. How could I not be bothered about it? Is it tempting not to think about it and just write a whodunit? Perhaps, but I'm not sure it's possible for me. The modern world works its way in.

HERDS: Before this conversation gets too philosophical, tell us, Joe, what happened in 16G? Are we talking about life imitating art or a slightly tacky exploitation of the Orient Express's history as a setting for murder?

JOE: I don't know what happened, Ben. But something did, and it seems the passenger in 16G has disappeared.

HERDS: We have been reliably informed that 16G was locked and latched from the inside.

JOE: That's correct, as far as I know.

HERDS: But no person, dead or alive, was found within.

JOE: You are well informed.

FLEX: So, what we have here, dear listeners, is a classic locked room mystery on the Orient Express, either a tragedy or a carefully constructed set created for the enjoyment of the many mystery fans on board.

HERDS: Stay tuned as *Death of the Reader* gives you a ringside seat to what unfolds.

MUSIC

FLEX: Welcome back, listeners, as Flex and Herds take you on the Orient Express, the real one, not the creature of literature, upon which we find that life is imitating art. An update from our earlier broadcast—

HERDS: Recording.

FLEX: That's right, Herds. It seems we have no coverage, so we are merely recording the show for broadcast at the earliest opportunity. Which is probably not a bad thing, as the situation here is changing quickly. This morning 16G, the cabin beside that of friend-of-the-show Joe Penvale, was the bloody scene of…something. No body was found, but the passenger assigned to 16G is missing. Shortly thereafter, the steward who was guarding the scene of the crime was found murdered in a nearby restroom. Additionally, the latest deadly strain of COVID has broken out in some carriages, which have been quarantined, and the rest of us have been restricted to our own cabins.

HERDS: We boarded the Orient Express looking for an experience, but this is too much, Flex! We're essentially trapped on a moving, contaminated closed set, with someone who's killing people. To top it all off, all lines to the outside world have been cut, so we could be recording our own eulogies. And the best management can do is send us all to our rooms!

FLEX: To be fair, the management of the train has formed a task force made up of passengers with some vague background in policing to reassure the rest of us that something is being done to find the passenger in 16G and maybe solve the murders in the process. Herds, what do you think? Are we in some kind of parallel universe where passengers are directed to have their tickets ready for inspection and solve a murder?

HERDS: Nothing so ordered or predictable as parallel, Flex. I'd say we're in a skewed universe! The management is naturally and thankfully trying to deal with the sick passengers, and, I presume, since we have no coverage, they are unable to get instructions from people not in the middle of it all.

FLEX: So, who are these task-forcers they've appointed to deal with the murder side of things, Herds?

HERDS: Well, Flex, we met several of them over cocktails in the bar last night. Napoleon Duplantier, who is a retired French policeman; Elle Baird, who claims to be the Duchess of Kinross—not sure how true that is. The American, Bob Whitman, who I think might be the duchess's bodyguard. Also, the two Jane Marple lookalikes who first told us about the trouble in 16G. There are a couple of others, but we have not yet learned who they are. And, our very own Joe Penvale and his sister, Meredith. At this stage, Flex, I'm not ashamed to say I'm hooked, and a little alarmed. We have a murder, perhaps two, on the Orient Express, a missing body, a missing passenger, a locked room mystery, and, in a structural twist worthy of Christie's *Lord Edgware Dies*, more detectives than suspects!

FLEX: There you have it, listeners. Stay tuned to see how *Murder on the Orient Express* unfolds…the second time.

MUSIC

FLEX: Well, listeners, events have overtaken us somewhat. Since we last recorded, the Orient Express has been turned back to Paris. Another man has been killed. A steward was stabbed as he was collecting the passports of all the passengers from a safe. Friend-of-the-show Joe Penvale and his sister remain in the thick of it all and have asked for the help of *Death of the Reader* to solve what are clearly class-motivated murders.

HERDS: It's interesting, don't you think, Flex, that nobody else seems to have noticed that the victims are both stewards but the concern seems to be for the safety of passengers?

FLEX: The capitalist obsession with making everything about themselves. It's tragic on so many levels.

HERDS: Even Joe does not seem to have recognized that we are looking for someone who is motivated by the archaic divisions so often celebrated or accepted in Golden Age mysteries. He's requested that we go through the recordings we have made for the show while on board, in a search for anything suspicious which might have been picked up as background noise.

FLEX: A strategy as desperate as it sounds. Never mind that there are hours of recordings; the idea that we would be in the right place to "overhear" or record something of import would be a coincidence which would not be tolerated in literature.

HERDS: Joe has also given us a list of the other members of the task force, now ensconced in the bar. It seems Joe doesn't entirely trust his colleagues in the purpose-formed Bar Council.

FLEX: What do you think he expects us to do with the list, Herds?

HERDS: He says he wants us to listen for these names as we search through our recordings. But I don't know, Flex. I think really, deep down, he wants us to investigate each of them, find out what we can about them. It seems to me that friend-of-the-show Joe Penvale wants us to do a little sleuthing of our own.

FLEX: And because he's a friend of the show, we can hardly refuse. And perhaps we can infuse into this investigation our insight into the motivations of this murderer who is targeting stewards.

HERDS: Tell the listeners what you've done, Flex.

FLEX: I might have obtained a master key from the steward who delivered our last meal…by that I mean the meal we had most recently, not our final meal. I hope. Let me apologize here on the record, for taking advantage of the man's understandable distraction, but commandeering the master key was necessary.

HERDS: And what are you proposing we do with this master key, Flex?

FLEX: I'm proposing we conduct a thorough investigation into the Bar Council.

HERDS: How exactly?

FLEX: We'll start by searching their cabins. We have the stewards' uniforms we borrowed earlier—we could use them to move about the train without alerting anyone unduly.

HERDS: Whoa! Hold on a minute. May I remind you that one of these people might have killed two stewards? And you want to search their rooms dressed as stewards?

FLEX: It'll be okay, Herds. They'll all be in the bar.

HERDS: They'd better be, Flex, they'd better be.

MUSIC

FLEX: Welcome back to *Death of the Reader* on a trip that seems to involve the death of just about everyone else, on a train that isn't moving.

HERDS: Nonsense, Flex! The dead stewards could well have been readers, for all we know. They might have been fans of the show, in which case, this murderer has been targeting our listeners.

FLEX: And so, it is for their sake we have taken the action that we have.

HERDS: That's right. We're saving our listeners.

FLEX: As you will remember, Herds and I procured a master key from one of the stewards. Since we last spoke, dear listeners, we have been investigating the Bar Council, which has been charged with finding the killer on board the Orient Express. Now any mystery reader worth their salt knows that killers often try to involve themselves in the investigation, and so it seems to us that our murderer may have embedded himself in the Bar Council itself. In the interests of non-bias, we began our investigation with the cabin of friends-of-the-show Joe and Meredith Penvale. You'll be happy to know that despite the excellent twist it might have been, we found nothing. Then we searched the cabin of the American, Buster Sartori. We found several dubious suits but nothing particularly incriminating.

HERDS: Regrettably, we were busted in this enterprise by none other than Joe and Meredith. They put on a show of outrage and concern, and we put on a show of allowing them to confiscate the master key. By the way, what key did you actually give them, Flex?

FLEX: The one to our own cabin. We can lock and unlock it with the master key, so it's superfluous to our needs. Joe and Meredith won't realize unless they decide to use it as a master, which, after the dressing down they gave us about breaking and entering, would be somewhat hypocritical.

HERDS: Absolutely, and so before returning to our own cabin, and while Joe and Meredith were talking to some- one in the Paris Suite, we managed to search the suites of the Duchess of Kinross, and the other American, Bob Whitman, and the cabins of Aled Rees and the Frenchman Napoleon Duplantier. All but Duplantier were on that side of the train.

FLEX: We can report that Aled Rees appears to be the most boring man on earth. His cabin contained a change of clothes, a toothbrush, and a couple of French newspapers dated the day we all boarded in Paris. He's reading a book called *Tax and Trade in the European Union*. The duchess and Whitman have neighboring suites and seem to be playing a game of musical beds. Whitman's effects, identified by name tags inside the collars of his shirts, are in the duchess's Grand Suite, next to a yoga mat and bolster cushion.

HERDS: Flex's mum does yoga, so he was able to identify the paraphernalia.

FLEX: Not sure which one of them is the yogi, but the duchess certainly looks more flexible than Whitman. I should say, as the son of a yogi, that while yoga is undeniably a cult—

HERDS: Undeniably.

FLEX: …and the first murder, at least, has a ritualistic quality to it, *Death of the Reader* does not believe these are yoga-related murders. Of course that doesn't mean the woman calling herself the Duchess of Kinross is not involved. As a duchess she is certainly vested in the classist system.

HERDS: Whitman appears to be sleeping on the couch, so perhaps this cohabitation is not romantic. It could be that they are merely co-conspirators discussing who they'll kill next.

FLEX: There was someone or some *two* sleeping in Whitman's suite. Judging by the twinsets and lilac powder, it was the two old ladies who first told us of 16G.

HERDS: The next cabin we searched was on the other side of the train. Luckily, we managed to get through the Bar Car before Joe and Meredith returned, with no one looking up. And so we were able to search the accommodations of the Frenchman, Napoleon Duplantier.

FLEX: Tell the people what we found, Herds.

HERDS: In the inside pocket of the dinner suit Napoleon Duplantier was wearing the first night on board, we found a police profile of a man called *Hugh* Booby.

FLEX: We know what you're thinking, listeners. Who the hell gives their child a name like Hugh Booby? Also, Duplantier is retired. What is he doing with a police profile? It's also clear that Duplantier is on board in pursuit of Hugh Booby. An old case, perhaps, or does Booby have something on him? Perhaps the mysterious Mr. Booby knows why Duplantier might be killing stewards. We could feel that we were onto something.

HERDS: And then things went a little crazy.

FLEX: Yes, we were, once again, caught in the act, as it were, but this time by Napoleon Duplantier.

HERDS: He was, to say the least, furious. I think he threatened us, but it was French, so it sounded like he was trying to seduce us…angrily.

FLEX: Either way, we made a run for it. Bear in mind, we were—are—wearing stewards' uniforms, and currently the dead men are both stewards. I must admit, Herds, that I was in genuine fear for our lives. Duplantier was on his own, and we are—and I say this without bragging, sturdy lads—capable of putting up a decent fight, and yet I knew we were in a world of trouble. Duplantier's manner was devoid of the civilized congeniality he displayed when we were first introduced. There was a calculated coldness about him even as he raged, the ruthlessness of a killer motivated by the ultimate oppression of the working class... It was truly chilling. To put it colloquially, I was packing it! Fortunately for us, Duplantier has a gammy leg and there was something going on in the carriages...some kind of commotion, stewards running everywhere. Otherwise, we might not have escaped to record this account! We are, dear listeners, recording this part of the show in the restroom of the sixth carriage in case Duplantier knows which cabin is ours.

HERDS: I must say, the acoustics in here are not bad.

FLEX: That much is true. Carry on, Herds. Who knows how long we'll have before some other passenger requires this room.

HERDS: So now, we have a theory of the crime or crimes. Stay with me, Flex. Hugh Booby, the passenger in 16G, is a criminal who, according to Duplantier's profile document, is wanted for multiple acts of fraud as well as one of assault causing bodily harm. Duplantier is pursuing him and seems to be at pains to hide the fact, which is of itself suspicious. He's no longer a policeman, so perhaps his intentions are not lawful either. We're forced to speculate a little here in the tradition of Holmes.

FLEX: I'm sure, given the circumstances, that Monsieur Poirot will forgive you, Herds.

HERDS: It seems this journey on the Orient Express is borrowing from noir. Napoleon Duplantier is clearly a crooked cop with possible links to organized crime! Hugh Booby might once have been a criminal associate of Duplantier's, but Booby double-crossed him. Now Duplantier wants to silence Booby and anyone else who might get in the way of said silencing. I'm willing to concede here that perhaps the fact that both victims are stewards may be a red herring and these are not class-based murders.

FLEX: Interesting. Certainly plausible. Duplantier has very artfully inserted himself into the investigation; some may say he's leading it. And he did overreact to finding us in his cabin…I think. We can't be sure what he actually said. But the question remains, Herds, where is Hugh Booby?

HERDS: I'm not sure, Flex. But it is worth noting that the people who should recognize him, haven't.

FLEX: And why do you think that is?

HERDS: Clearly, Duplantier does not want the Bar Council to find the passenger in 16G, the elusive Gregory Blackwell, who is Booby, because he intends to kill him. I expect murder would be more difficult to get away with if Booby were in custody. The two old ladies, with whom Booby lived as Gregory Harrington… maybe they don't actually want him to be caught. Perhaps they suspect Duplantier, or someone, is trying to kill Booby, and so, despite what he has stolen from them, they are trying to protect him from execution.

FLEX: Really?

HERDS: They're old ladies, Flex. If anyone is going to feel sorry for Booby, it's them.

FLEX: Yeah, you're right. But what about the stewards?

HERDS: One was guarding the door to 16G, standing between Duplantier and his quarry.

FLEX: But there was no one in 16G?

HERDS: Duplantier might not have been convinced of that. The other steward was fetching passports, and Duplantier did not want his fellow members of the Bar Council to know what Booby looked like, lest they capture him before Duplantier can kill him.

FLEX: That's quite a theory, Herds!

HERDS: Thank you, Flex. Sadly, it is still just theory. This is not a normal show…we're not talking about a book, and our critique is not enough. We will need evidence.

FLEX: So what do you propose, Herds?

HERDS: I think it's up to us. Duplantier seems to have everyone else snowed. Meredith Penvale is clearly in love, and I think even Joe is a bit smitten. French accent and all that.

FLEX: It is a very sexy accent.

HERDS: Despite the danger, indeed, because of it, we must continue our investigation.

FLEX: I do have some thoughts on that, Herds. The old ladies have moved to Whitman's suite, so their cabin is empty. And if your theory is right, they feel sorry for him and might be willing to hide him from Duplantier. Is it possible that they vacated their cabin to give Hugh Booby someplace to hide where no one would look?

HERDS: Sweet suffering Christie, Flex, that's bloody brilliant! And we remain in possession of a master key! We can be the ones to find him, to solve this.

FLEX: Stop a minute, Herds. Let's just think about this. What the hell are we doing? I mean, really. People are dying…not just those murdered but also the poor bastards who've been locked into the quarantined carriages… God knows how many of them are left. I'm not sure we can trust the management to tell us.

HERDS: What's the option, Flex? The missing passenger is the key to all this, and we have to do something before Duplantier has us arrested for breaking into his cabin. He has the ear of the Bar Council, and he could accuse us of killing the stewards. We have to expose him first.

FLEX: God, I wish we could trust Joe with this. It feels like we're going into this with no friends.

HERDS: Yeah—I guess it's every man for himself at the moment. But you know, mate, I don't think we're any safer sitting in our cabins…or the restrooms, for that matter.

FLEX: That's true. But honestly, Herds, we're a couple of crime fiction nerds with a podcast. I'm not sure that qualifies us to save the day.

HERDS: I'm bloody certain it doesn't, but again, what else can we do? We're in the middle of this story, and we can't hide out in the restroom forever.

FLEX: I beg to differ—

HERDS: *(laughs)* I don't like this any better than you, Flex, but I think we'll be all right if we watch each other's backs. If it makes you feel better, the genre has surely taught us that the reluctant hero invariably triumphs and, more importantly, survives.

FLEX: It seems our duty is clear, then. Our fate less so. Stay tuned, loyal listeners, for the final reveal, as *Death of the Reader* continues its dogged, possibly… definitely…foolhardy pursuit of justice and the truth about the mysterious passenger from 16G.

HERDS: All right, Flex. Let's go.

ACKNOWLEDGMENTS

The release of this book is the light at the end of a very long tunnel. The year in which it was written was one in which I had to fight for my life, but I did not do so alone. There were many people who traveled this route with me, who kept me on track and contributed to this book and its writer in so many ways.

My husband, Michael, the wall against which I lean and bounce ideas. There would be no books at all without you.

My boys, Edmund and Atticus, and my girl, Rhiannan, a constant reminder of how bright the future is.

My sister, Devini, who shared a cabin with me on the Orient Express and has traveled with me since.

Leith Henry, who laughed with me through the darkest moments. Who lent me her strength when mine failed.

All the brilliant doctors, specialists, surgeons, and medical professionals who have looked after me in the last couple of years, who have saved my life, time and again.

My publisher, Sourcebooks, who had my back every step

of the way. Who made sure the light at the end of the tunnel stayed lit for me.

My editors, Diane DiBiase and Anna Michels, who helped me turn a ragged manuscript into this story. Beth Deveny, who checked the minutiae for sense and form. The design team at Sourcebooks, who wrapped my words in this exquisite cover. Mandy Chahal, who has put the result into the hands of readers to whom it would speak. Dominique Raccah, whose belief in my work has made this all possible.

My wonderful agent, Jill Marr, and the amazing team at SDLA, who always make sure I get on at the right station.

My people, the community of writers, who have never wavered in their support and their solidarity. Who made sure I was not forgotten when illness kept me away. I cannot tell you how much your care and camaraderie have meant to me.

Robert Gott and L. M. Vincent, both dear friends and colleagues, who read the draft and gave me the vast benefit of their insights.

Felix Shannon and Benjamin Herder (Flex and Herds), who allowed me to place them and *Death of the Reader* into the midst of a murder mystery.

The incomparable staff and management of the Orient Express who gave me this experience without all the murders.

My friends and neighbors, who have knitted hats and brought meals, who have chauffeured me to appointments and tended my garden, who have looked after my laptop when I wasn't allowed to take it into treatment, and handed it back the moment I came out. Thank you.

ABOUT THE AUTHOR

 Published in English in Australia, New Zealand, the UK, and the U.S., and in translation in more than a dozen territories, Sulari Gentill is the author of the multi-award-winning Rowland Sinclair Mysteries, ten historical crime novels (thus far) chronicling the life and adventures of her 1930s Australian gentleman artist. The first book in this series was shortlisted for the Commonwealth Writers' Prize, and the second won the Davitt Award. The remaining books have been variously shortlisted for the Davitt Award, the Ned Kelly Award, and the Australian Book Industry Association Awards. *After She Wrote Him*, her metafiction thriller, won the Ned Kelly Award for Best Crime Novel in 2018. And her standalone mystery novel *The Woman in the Library* was a *USA Today* bestseller, won the UK CrimeFictionLover Award and was nominated for an Edgar.

Sulari's next novel, *The Mystery Writer*, was selected as one of Bookbub's Best Mysteries and Thrillers of 2024, was an Amazon Editor's Pick, a LibraryReads pick for March, and also nominated for the Mary Higgins Clark Award.

Sulari lives with her family, two donkeys, a miniature horse, four dogs, and a cat, on a small farm in the idyllic foothills of the Snowy Mountains, where she grows French black truffles and writes about murder and mayhem.